THE EYE
OF THE
NORTH

THE EYE OF THE NORTH

SINÉAD O'HART

ALFRED A. KNOPF
NEW YORK

THIS IS A BORZOI BOOK PUBLISHED BY ALFRED A. KNOPF

All rights reserved. Published in the United States by Alfred A. Knopf, an imprint of Random House Children's Books, a division of Penguin Random House LLC, New York.

Knopf, Borzoi Books, and the colophon are registered trademarks of Penguin Random House LLC.

Visit us on the Web! randomhousekids.com

Educators and librarians, for a variety of teaching tools, visit us at RHTeachersLibrarians.com

Library of Congress Cataloging-in-Publication Data
Names: O'Hart, Sinead, author.
Title: Eye of the North / Sinead O'Hart.
Description: First edition. | New York : Alfred A. Knopf, [2017]. | Summary: A boy called Thing works with a secret organization to rescue Emmeline from Dr. Siegfried Bauer, who wants her parents to awaken a powerful creature in the ice fields of Greenland.
Identifiers: LCCN 2016043830 (print) | LCCN 2017004324 (ebook) | ISBN 978-1-101-93503-3 (trade) | ISBN 978-1-101-93504-0 (lib. bdg.) | ISBN 978-1-101-93505-7 (ebook)
Subjects: | CYAC: Adventure and adventurers—Fiction. | Supernatural—Fiction. | Imaginary creatures—Fiction. | Kidnapping—Fiction. | Secret societies— Fiction. | Greenland—Fiction. | BISAC: JUVENILE FICTION / Action & Adventure / General. | JUVENILE FICTION / Fantasy & Magic. | JUVENILE FICTION / Social Issues / Friendship.
Classification: LCC PZ7.1.O42 Eye 2017 (print) | LCC PZ7.1.O42 (ebook) | DDC [Fic]—dc23

The text of this book is set in 11-point Village.

Printed in the United States of America
August 2017
10 9 8 7 6 5 4 3 2 1

First Edition

For Níamh Éowyn,

Emer Mary,

and Clodagh Réiltín,

star of my heart

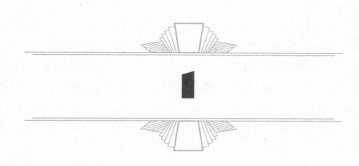

1

For as long as she could remember, Emmeline Widget had been *sure* her parents were trying to kill her.

Why else, she reasoned, would they choose to live in a creaky old house where, if she wasn't dodging random bits of collapsing masonry or avoiding the trick steps on the stairs, she had to be constantly on guard for booby-trapped floorboards or doors that liked to boom closed entirely by themselves? She'd lost count of the number of close calls she'd already clocked up, and so she never went anywhere inside her house—not even to the bathroom—without a flashlight, a ball of twine, and a short, stout stick, the latter to defend herself against whatever might come slithering up the drain. She'd started her fight for survival early. As a baby, she'd learned to walk mostly by avoiding the tentacles, tusks, and whiplike tongues of the various small, furry things in cages that would temporarily line the hallways after one of her parents' research trips. And she'd long ago grown used to shaking out her boots before she put them on in the morning—for, as Emmeline had learned, lots of quiet, dangerous, and very patient creatures liked to hide out in abandoned footwear.

Outside the house wasn't much better. The grounds were overgrown to the point that Widget Manor itself was invisible unless you managed to smack right into it, and that kind of lazy groundskeeping provided a haven for all sorts of things. The year Emmeline turned seven, for instance, her parents had come home from an expedition with a giant squirrel in tow, one with teeth as long as Emmeline's leg. It had wasted no time in getting loose and had spent three weeks destroying half the garden before finally being brought under control. Sometimes, particularly on windy nights, Emmeline wasn't entirely sure her parents were telling the truth when they said the squirrel had been sent back to its distant home. Even worse, a roaring river ran right at the end of their property, sweeping past with all the haughtiness of a diamond-encrusted duchess. Emmeline lived in fear of falling in, and so she never ventured outside without an inflatable life preserver (which, on its days off, doubled as a hot-water bottle) and a catapult (to fight off any unexpected nasties she might find living amid the trees—or even, perhaps, the trees themselves).

As a result of all this, Emmeline spent more time in her room reading than did most young ladies of her age. However, she'd long ago dispensed with fiction, having digested everything that lived on the lower shelves of her parents' library (for Emmeline most assuredly did *not* climb, no matter how sturdy the footholds seemed, and so the higher volumes had to lurk, unread, amid the dust). Along with these literary efforts, she'd also worked her way through several tomes about such things as biology and anatomy, subjects that entranced her mother and father. This was unsurprising, considering the elder Widgets were scientists of some sort who had, in their daughter's opinion, a frankly unhygienic obsession with strange animals, but Emmeline herself had found them tiresome. Now she mostly read the sorts of books that would likely keep her alive in an emergency, either because of the survival tips they contained or because they were large enough to serve as a makeshift tent. She was never without at least one, if not two, sturdy books, hardback by preference.

All of these necessities, of course, meant that she was never without her large and rather bulky satchel, either, but she didn't let that stand in her way.

And, as will probably have become clear by now, Emmeline didn't have very many—or, indeed, *any*—friends. There was the household staff, comprising Watt (the butler) and Mrs. Mitchell (who did everything else), but they didn't really count because they were always telling her what to do and where to go and *not* to put her dirty feet on that clean floor, thank you very much. Her parents were forever at work, or away, or off at conferences, or entertaining (which Emmeline hated because sometimes she'd be called upon to wear actual *ribbons* and smile and pretend to be something her mother called "lighthearted," which she could never see the point of). She spent a lot of time on her own, and this, if she were to be entirely truthful, suited her fine.

One day, then, when Emmeline came down to breakfast and found her parents absent, she didn't even blink. She just hauled her satchel up onto the chair next to her and rummaged through it for her book, glad to have a few moments of quiet reading time before she had to start ignoring the grown-ups in her life once again.

She was so engrossed in her book—*Knots and Their Uses*, by S. G. Twitchell—that at first she ignored Watt when he slipped into the room bearing in his neatly gloved hands a small silver platter, upon which sat a white envelope. He set it down in front of Emmeline without a word. She made sure to finish right to the end of the chapter (about the fascinating complexities of constrictor knots) before looking up and noticing that she had received a piece of Very Important Correspondence.

She fished around for her bookmark and slid it carefully into place. Then, ever so gently, she closed the book and eased it back into the satchel, where it glared up at her reproachfully.

"I promise I'll be back to finish you later," she reassured it. "Once I figure out who could *possibly* want to write to me." She frowned at the envelope, which was very clearly addressed to a MISS EMMELINE WIDGET. PRIVATE AND CONFIDENTIAL, it added.

Just because it happened to be addressed to her, though,

didn't mean she should be so silly as to actually *open* it. Not without taking the proper precautions, at least.

In the silence of the large, empty room, Emmeline flipped open her satchel again. From its depths she produced a tiny stoppered bottle, within which a viciously blue liquid was just about contained. She uncorked it as gently as possible, slowly tipping the bottle until one solitary drop hung on its lip, and then—very, *very* carefully— she let the drop fall onto the envelope.

"Hmm," she said after a moment or two, raising an eyebrow. "That's odd."

The liquid didn't smoke, or fizz, or explode in a cloud of sparkle, or indeed do anything at all. It just sat there, like a splodge of ink, partially obscuring her name.

"If you're not poisoned," murmured Emmeline, quickly putting away the bottle (for its fumes could cause dizziness in enclosed spaces, like breakfast rooms), "then *what* are you?"

In the side pocket of her satchel, Emmeline always carried a pair of thick gardening gloves. She put these on, and then she picked up—with some difficulty, it has to be pointed out—her butter knife. Suitably armed, she slowly slit the envelope open, keeping it at all times directed away from her face.

A thick sheet of creamy paper slid out onto the silver platter, followed by a stiff card. Emmeline, who'd been holding her breath in case the act of opening the envelope released some sort of brain-shredding gas, spluttered as the first line of the letter caught her eye. As quickly as she could, given that she was wearing gloves more suited to cutting down brambles than dealing with paperwork, she put aside the card and grabbed up the letter.

She stared at the words for ages, but they stayed exactly the same.

Dearest Emmeline, the letter began.

If you are reading this, then in all likelihood you are now an orphan.

2

"An *orphan*? How unfashionable!" Emmeline blinked and took two or three deep breaths, then read on.

If this note has found its way to you, then it is probable that your father and I [for it was her mother's handwriting, of course] *have been kidnapped. If so, then chances are, unfortunately, that we shall never see you again. The police are unlikely to find us, for reasons I cannot explain here, so it might be best if you don't waste time or money on that route. The house is yours, and Watt and Mrs. Mitchell are paid up in perpetuity, so you need have no worries on that score. However, your father and I have left instructions with Watt to see you to the boat (ticket enclosed) that you will take to Paris. You will—without fuss or commotion, and drawing no attention to yourself—*

make your way to the address below, and you will ask for Madame Blancheflour in your best French. You will live there with her until you are eighteen.

There is to be no resistance to this, Emmeline Mary. You will not plead with Watt, or Mrs. Mitchell, or anyone else, to allow you to stay; you will not barricade yourself in your room; you will not refuse. I hope I have made myself clear.

Yours with warmest wishes, and a fond farewell,
Mum

Emmeline read the letter three times before she put it back on its platter. *Paris*, she thought. She slipped her hands out of her gloves and picked up the ticket with fingers that quivered only slightly.

Admit One Passenger, Plus Valise and Luggage, it said in stylish gold lettering. **Inside Cabin, Shared WC, Starboard Side, Room 66B. No refunds or cash exchanges. Boat will not wait for tardy passengers. No money back in case of cancellation due to act of God or similar.**

Emmeline wasn't really sure what most of this meant, but her eye kept getting drawn back to the word at the top of the ticket: *Paris.*

A throat, politely cleared, made her blink and look up. Watt stood at the ready, stiff and upright in his crisp uniform.

"Miss?" he said, glancing meaningfully at the carriage

clock. "I've taken the liberty of packing a few bits and pieces for you. If we're to make the boat, we'd best leave in the next five minutes."

Emmeline stared at the ticket again, feeling faint. "Watt, my parents . . . are they dead?"

"Quite sure I couldn't say, miss." Watt was perfectly calm, his hands behind his back. "Let's hope not, eh?"

"But they're *mine,*" said Emmeline, tossing the ticket on the table. "It's not fair for someone else to just *take* them. *Is* it, Watt?"

"Life's a very unfair thing, miss," sniffed the butler. "Or, leastways, it is for some."

"Do you know this Madame"—Emmeline looked at her mother's letter again, just to be sure—"Blancheflour?"

Watt gave a small cough. "Can't say I do, miss, but I'm sure she's a right fine lady who'll take great care of you and keep you safe for Mrs. Mitchell and me."

"But she *could* be a horrible old hag!" Emmeline's nose was starting to feel like it was melting inside. Irritated, she swiped at it before wiping her hand on the tablecloth. She blinked up at Watt. "If I *have* to go, can I send you letters, at least? Just in case I'm being locked in a basement or something?"

"Not sure the postman'll pick up letters from a locked basement, miss." Watt turned to her and tried to smile, but it didn't really work. After the third attempt he gave up.

"But if they—if they come home, Mum and Dad, I mean, won't you let me know? So that I can come back?"

"Don't ask *silly* questions, miss," said Watt, drawing in

a deep breath and sticking out his chest. "You saw what your mother wrote, didn't you? So let's get a move on."

"But, Watt, I—"

"Now, miss. I know you was told not to plead or kick up a fuss or do anything like that. Come on. You've got your satchel?"

"But, Watt—"

"No buts! Chop-chop. We're running out of time. Good lass."

And that was that. Emmeline slid down off her chair, put the letter, envelope, and ticket safely in a satchel pocket, and followed Watt to the front door, her head spinning. As she walked down the tiled hallway, which seemed to be closing in around her, she became engulfed in a large and slightly sticky hug. It smelled rather cinnamony.

"Mrs. Mitchell," she gasped after a few moments. "I can't breathe!"

"Have a safe voyage, my pet," Mrs. Mitchell whispered, patting Emmeline's head with a floury hand. "And we'll wait for your first letter from Par-ee, so we will."

"Thank you," said Emmeline, overwhelmed by the thought of writing letters from anywhere that wasn't Widget Manor.

"Good girl. Now get trottin'. Watt'll have the car started for you." With warm, wet kisses drying on her cheeks, Emmeline fumbled her way down the rest of the hallway and staggered out into the day. Before she knew it, Watt had her tucked into the backseat of the car, bags of clothes and shoes and other useless stuff all around her, and they were driving off down the gravel laneway that led to the Rest of the World, the house and its ferocious garden fading into the background. Mrs. Mitchell stood on the front step, flapping and waving, until they turned out onto the road, and it was at that point that Emmeline's heart started to pound, just a little.

"Everythin' all right there, miss?" called Watt, peering at her through the mirror. "You're very quiet—eh! You billabong-nosed baboon!" he yelled, swerving out of the way of another driver and honking loudly. "Not you, miss," he clarified quickly, but Emmeline hardly heard him through the pounding of her heart in her ears. She grabbed the handle of the car door in sweaty-palmed panic as they drove on.

"Watt, will you keep my books safe? For when I get back?" she asked, breathing deeply through her nose and focusing her gaze on the horizon. She'd read somewhere that these were good measures against travel sickness. So far she wasn't finding them terribly effective.

"O'course. Either that or ship 'em off to you. Whichever," replied Watt. He paused to pound on the horn again, this time at a poor delivery boy who happened to step out at just the wrong second. "Take care, you pilchard brain! Honestly, some people shouldn't be allowed in public without supervision, I tell you. . . ."

As Watt muttered under his breath, Emmeline unstuck her fingers from the door handle, feeling her circulation return to normal. To distract herself from Watt's driving, she fished her parents' letter out of her satchel again. *You will make your way to the address below,* her mother had written, and printed at the bottom of the letter was the following information:

Madame Gramercy Blancheflour
224 Rue du Démiurge
99901 PARIS

How on earth was she ever going to find this place? She'd never been to Paris—she'd never been *anywhere*.

She read the beginning again, hearing her mother's voice in her head as her blurring eyes skipped over the lines.

If so, then chances are, unfortunately, that we shall never see you again. . . .

Emmeline noticed her fingers shaking a little as she replaced the letter, and she formed two fists on top of her satchel, her knuckles whitening. At the same time she told herself in no uncertain terms that she was to grow up and stop being such a nincompoop.

But that, of course, was easier said than done.

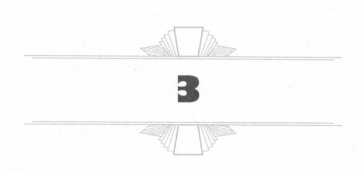

3

Watt drew the car to a juddering halt just in front of a long, low, white-painted building. Large double doors swung open and closed constantly as people passed through in both directions, most of them carrying luggage—or having it carried for them. Beyond the doors was a mystery, though from what Emmeline could tell, it involved light, and sparkling music, and lots of noise.

Just then a huge *MAAAAAAAARP* split the air into molecules. Emmeline jumped, dropping her satchel on the floor in the process.

"Only the ship's horn, miss," said Watt, covering Emmeline's embarrassment. "Nothing at all to be concerned about. Now let's get started, shall we?"

Emmeline couldn't find the words to ask Watt to let her stay. Instead, she gave a very tight squeak, like someone rubbing a finger on a wet windowpane. The next thing she knew, he'd flung open the car door and was bundling her out, making a rather unnecessary fuss about it. As soon as she'd found her feet, Watt whistled, and as if he'd been waiting for the summons, a boy ran over pushing a large, flat-based luggage cart. He had a wide face, covered in sweat, and a small hat tied to his head with string, and he almost bashed his cart into Emmeline's leg as he came to a stop. She was overcome with an urge to cower behind Watt for protection but glowered at the boy instead.

"Sir?" he said, ignoring her. "Cart, sir?"

"For Miss Widget's bags," said Watt in a rather grand and unfamiliar voice. "The young lady is sailing for Paris this morning, and so a bit of haste would be appreciated."

"O'course, sir," said the boy. "Very good, sir." Emmeline watched in amazement as the boy hauled every last box, bag, and case out of the car and placed them on the cart, all in the space of less than a minute.

"Miss?" he said, stretching out his hand to take her satchel. Emmeline clutched it to her chest, her nostrils flaring in indignation.

"The young lady prefers to keep that piece of luggage about her person at all times. If you don't mind," said Watt smoothly. The boy shrugged before turning away and taking off through the doors of the white building like a greyhound out of a trap.

"Best get a move on, then, miss," said Watt. His ordinary voice was back, sounding a little quieter than normal. "Don't want your worldly accoutrements sailing the high seas without you, eh?" Emmeline noticed him looking around, his scrawny neck and bulging eyes reminding her of a wary bird, as though he suspected predators everywhere. She felt her indignation drain away, replaced by a heavy coldness that settled around her heart.

"But, Watt. Why do I have to go right *now*?" she asked, feeling very small. Her eyes were hot. Something tickled her cheek, and she raised her hand to wipe it. Much to her surprise, her fingers came away wet. "Why is there such a rush?"

"Well, now, miss, I'm the wrong person to ask." Watt paused in his head-swinging and turned back to her, pulling at his collar. "I s'pose your parents wanted you to be safe, you know, and to get started off into a new life without having too much time to dwell on the past. The less you remember, the less it'll upset you." He gave her an uncertain grin, which ended up looking more like a grimace.

Emmeline narrowed her drying eyes at him. "Safe? Are you insane? With parents like mine, it's amazing I've even *lived* as long as I have."

"But you did, miss. Live, I mean," said Watt, glancing around again as if he were looking for something he'd lost. "That's the important thing."

"What are you *talking*—" Emmeline began, but she got no further than that.

"Yer luggage is loaded, miss!" shouted the cart boy from a few feet away. Watt snapped to attention, and Emmeline wanted to scream in frustration. "Boat's leavin' in twenty minutes," gasped the boy, right behind her. "I fair had a struggle gettin' all the bags on in time, and packed neatly, an' all. . . ." He let his words trail off into midair, where they hung, pleading. Watt nodded, reaching into his breast pocket, and Emmeline felt the boy tense up beside her as he stared intently at Watt's fumbling hand.

"Here you are," said Watt, drawing his fingers out of his pocket. Clutched between them was a crisp white card, which he presented to the boy. "Should you ever need admittance to the London Scientific and Zoological Institute, or any of its associated clubs, simply show this at the door and no questions will be asked. A very useful way for a young man like yourself to get ahead in the world, you know."

As Watt held out the small white rectangle, Emmeline recognized it as her father's business card, and a strange feeling washed over her, one that felt a little like missing your footing on the stairs. She noticed something she'd never seen before—letters, all in capitals, embossed above her father's name. Silently she read a single word, OSCAR, but she had no idea what it meant. Curious, she thought, and filed it away for future reference.

"Yeah," griped the boy, snatching the card from Watt's fingers. "Not goin' to buy me a new pair o' shoes, though, is it?" Grumbling, he swung his cart away, stuffing the card into his pocket as he went.

And with that, Emmeline's interest in OSCAR, whoever or whatever it was, burst like a soap bubble. Reality slid back into place all around her.

She turned to Watt, feeling a bit like she was drowning and he was a distant shore. "I don't want to get on this boat," she said hopelessly. "Please don't make me go."

"Miss, you read the letter," said Watt, putting his hand on her shoulder. "You know I've no choice. Your parents' wishes are my wishes, miss. They've had me by their side all these years, and I can't turn away from 'em now."

Emmeline's jaw dropped. "But don't *my* wishes count?"

"No," answered Watt after a second or two of contemplation. "I can't say they do, miss." He looked down at her, his eyes wet and red-rimmed. "I'm sorry, girl. I really am." He cleared his throat and straightened up, brushing Emmeline's shoulder like it was dusty. "Now, we'd best not waste any more time. This boat won't wait for the tardy, remember?"

4

Emmeline stood on the deck of the giant ship and watched the dark speck that was Watt, several hundred feet below. People all around her were yelling, shouting their farewells, pleading for telegrams and letters and visits and lots of other things, but Emmeline saved her breath. All she wanted from Watt was for him to come striding up the gangplank to take her home, and she knew that was completely pointless. Shouting and shrieking about it would make less than no difference, and so Emmeline stayed quiet and still, like a small, forlorn statue.

Eventually Watt was swallowed by the crowd, and no matter how hard or fast Emmeline blinked, she couldn't catch sight of him again.

She sighed and stepped back out of the crush, her

arms carefully wrapped around her satchel. As she walked across the boards toward the cabins, a sudden vibration under her feet almost knocked her flat. Her fingers instinctively flew to her satchel buckles, which leaped open beneath her practiced touch. She began searching for her life-preserving hot-water bottle, but then she heard a man nearby cry out with what sounded like joy.

"She's away!" he said, slapping his friend between the shoulder blades, making the other man cough. "Those'll be the engines firing up. We'll be at sea soon enough."

At sea, Emmeline thought as the guffawing, mustache-wearing gentlemen passed her by. *Also meaning "lost" or "confused," or both.*

"Apt," she said to nobody in particular,. grumpily refastening her satchel.

"Didja say somethin'?" replied a curiously metallic, hollow-sounding voice, seemingly out of nowhere. "Only, I *thought* you did, and I wouldn't want to be rude an' not make a suitably witty and interestin' retort."

Emmeline looked around. All she could see was a few carefully welded benches, a flotation device or two bolted to the wooden wall in front of her, and a seagull, peering at her sideways.

"I beg your pardon?" she ventured, clutching her satchel close, but the seagull said nothing.

"You talkin' to me?" The metallic voice sounded no closer nor any farther away, but every bit as odd as it had the first time.

"How very strange," she said, taking a step backward.

"I'm not strange," said the voice, now becoming a little less hollow-sounding. "I'm perfickly normal, thank you very much. And I'm over 'ere." Something moved to Emmeline's left, and her gaze was caught by a dusty head emerging from a grating in the wall. This head—the color of whose hair was impossible to determine—was swiftly followed by a grubby body dressed in overalls. The fingernails of this creature were clotted with dirt and oil, and its—his?—face was smeared with grease. As Emmeline watched, he slithered out of the hole he'd been hiding in, until all of him—and there wasn't much—was standing in front of Emmeline with a hand held out in greeting.

"Mornin'," he said. "M'name's Thing. Who're you?"

"I'm sorry?" said Emmeline, looking at his outstretched hand as if he'd offered her a used handkerchief.

"Yeah, me too," said the boy wearily.

Emmeline blinked. "Um. Pardon?"

"Sorry 'bout my name," he replied, taking back his hand and shoving it into a pocket, looking altogether unconcerned. "Wasn't that what we were talkin' about?"

"I'm quite sure we weren't talking about anything," replied Emmeline, adjusting her grip on her satchel and trying surreptitiously to look around.

"Need a hand with your bag?" The boy snuffled, like he had a heavy cold. "I'm good at that. Givin' hands with stuff."

"No," said Emmeline, aghast. "Thank you."

"Suit yerself," he replied, rocking on the balls of his feet. "So, are you goin' to tell me your name, or do I 'ave to guess it?"

"How on earth would you *guess* it?" said Emmeline, taking another step back.

"Bet I could," said Thing, grinning. His teeth were nearly as filthy as his face, and Emmeline's nose curled upward in disgust. Thing just grinned wider.

"Look, I have to go to my cabin now," she said. "So if you'll excuse me?"

"No," said Thing. "Is it Amy? Angela? Angelica? No— wait. Agnes. It's *Agnes*, ain't it?"

"What do you mean, no?" said Emmeline, wishing she had Burke's *A History of Tenting (Illustrated)* on hand. Thrown just right, it would have done considerable damage.

"Y'asked if I'd excuse you. So I said no. Agnes."

"My name is not Agnes," Emmeline muttered.

"Betty? Bettina? Bucephalus! Go on, say it's Bucephalus. Always wanted to meet one o' those."

"You're not even on the right *letter*." Emmeline's arm was starting to hurt from holding her satchel so tightly, and she really wanted to find her cabin and lie down.

"Right. Caroline. Carly. Christina. Chrysanthemum."

"Chrysanthemum is a *flower*. Don't be ridiculous."

"Lots of girls're named after flowers. Rose. Lily. Petunia. Gardenia. Viola. Violet. Daisy. Poppy. Lily."

"You said Lily already." Emmeline sighed, shifting her satchel to the other arm.

"So you *were* listenin'." Thing grinned.

"My name is Emmeline, all right? Now, can I please go?"

"*Emmmmmeliiiiiiine,*" said the strange boy, rolling her name around in his mouth like he was tasting it. "I like it. That'll do."

"Do for *what*?"

"Collect names, I do," Thing replied. "Someday I'll meet one I can't resist an' I'll keep it for meself."

Emmeline sighed. "Look, this is fascinating and all, but I really need to—look, I'm going now. All right?"

Thing shrugged, sucking on his front teeth. "Free country, innit?" he replied, yawning slightly, and pulled out a hand to scratch his head, fixing his gaze on something just beyond Emmeline's left shoulder. She struggled not to turn to see what it was. "Jus' don't come cryin' to me when you're on the point o' dyin' from boredom, yeah?"

"I'll try my *very* hardest," said Emmeline, squeezing past. Thing smelled like smoke and dirt and sweat, and as soon as she was clear, he swung himself back into the hole in the wall. Despite herself, Emmeline couldn't help but be curious about where it went.

"Well, cheerio, then," he said as he waved and disappeared from view. The grating clanged shut and Emmeline was by herself again. Even the seagull was long gone.

She was irritated to notice that she felt a lot more alone than before.

5

Her cabin, Emmeline soon discovered, was far less luxurious than she'd expected. For one thing, it was barely bigger than a wardrobe. For another, it was crammed full of her bags, which had been unceremoniously thrown in without any consideration for their shape, or their contents. She was fairly sure some of them had been deliberately kicked into place.

Sighing, she closed the door and turned to her left, where a tiny bed was folded flat against the wall. She pulled it down, its springs squealing loudly, and clicked it home. It was so close to the cabin door that you could probably open the door without lifting your head from the pillow. She grimaced. Clutching her satchel, she clambered up on the bed and stood on tiptoe to gaze out the porthole window set right above it. All she could see outside were planks and planks of empty deck leading to a railing and, beyond that, nothing but water, water everywhere.

Like a magician's rabbit pulled out of a hat, a head suddenly appeared outside the porthole, slightly distorted by the thick glass. Emmeline blinked, but it didn't go away.

Then the head grinned in at her, and Emmeline sighed again, this time from her toes. Her curiosity about Thing had dwindled on the way to her cabin, exhaustion sweeping in to take its place, and she really wasn't in the mood to have another conversation, particularly with him. But there he was, enthusiastically gesturing at her to open up. She pretended not to understand for a minute, but he just raised his eyebrows at her.

"All right, all right," she grumbled. After a few finger-rattling moments, when she had to strain against the tight seal, the porthole window finally unstuck itself with a loud pop.

"H'lo," said Thing. "Ice cream?"

"Sorry?" said Emmeline.

"Ice. Cream," repeated Thing. As he spoke, he thrust a small, battered cardboard carton through the window. His fingers were thick with dirt, and although the ice cream itself looked delicious, Emmeline couldn't imagine eating it without thinking of Thing, which was enough to put her off food entirely.

"Thank you," she said politely.

"Well, ain't you gonna eat it?" said Thing.

"Not really hungry just now, actually," said Emmeline, even though nothing could have been further from the truth. She realized that in the rush to leave she hadn't had breakfast, and despite the fact that looking at the ice cream was enough to make her weak, she refused to budge. She'd have to test it for contaminants and poisons, and check it thoroughly to make sure there were no traps embedded in it, and—

"Suit yerself," said Thing, leaning back and bringing the tiny carton with him. His grimy spoon was just about to sink into the clean white mound when Emmeline couldn't bear it anymore.

"No!" she cried. Thing paused, his spoon inches from the ice cream. "I mean, actually, I *could* force it down, I suppose."

"Thought as much," said Thing, grinning, and he handed the carton to her. He fished another spoon out of an unseen pocket and huffed a breath over it before polishing it vigorously on his sleeve. Then he presented it to Emmeline, handle-first.

"There y'are," he said, settling his elbows on the curved edge of the porthole.

Emmeline's stomach was rolling and growling and boiling inside her. She'd never eaten anything she hadn't tested, of course, as was only sensible living with parents like hers. *But,* she told herself, *it's going to melt away to nothing.* ... She stared at the silver belly of the spoon that Thing had given her, and tried not to see the millions of tiny germs that she felt quite sure were skating around on it, laughing up at her with their moldy teeth.

"Just get going, would ya?" murmured Thing. "I ain't got all day to 'ang around here, y'know." He paused thoughtfully before continuing. "Or, well, I 'ave, but I don't *want* to spend all day 'angin' around here. Better things to do."

Emmeline watched her fingers dig the filthy spoon into the pristine ice cream. As if her hand were being driven by someone else, it lifted itself to her mouth. Her lips opened, the spoon went in, and the next thing she knew, she was licking the carton clean.

"Weren't 'ungry, were ya?" Thing grinned.

"Sorry," said Emmeline, wiping her chin.

"Yeah," said Thing. "Now. Ready for yer adventure?" Emmeline, who felt she was already having the worst and most terrible adventure of her life, stared out at him.

"What adventure?" Thing didn't answer but instead spread his arms wide to the left and right, as though taking in the whole ship.

"Stand back," he said. When Emmeline didn't move immediately, he repeated himself, this time with a bit more force. "Stand *back*, yeah? I'm comin' through!" Before Emmeline could tell him she'd rather he didn't, actually, he'd stuck his head through the porthole. Like toothpaste being squeezed out of a tube, the rest of him followed, until—with a somersault—he was standing on her bed, grinning through his mop of filthy hair. Emmeline grabbed her satchel, using it like a shield, and snapped her mouth closed.

"D'you ever put that awkward-lookin' thing down?" said Thing, nodding at the satchel. He sniffed wetly. "Anyway. Are ya in or not?"

Emmeline thought about it for a few seconds.

"Well—what does it *involve*?" she asked, keeping a tight grip on her satchel.

Thing grinned again, and then, without giving Emmeline any chance to prepare herself, he jumped down from the bed, grabbed her hand, and started running for the door.

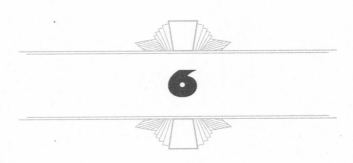

6

"So, what's in the bag, then?"

"It's not a *bag*. It's a satchel. My satchel."

"What's in the satchawatsit, then?"

"Stuff. I need. To keep me safe."

Thing snorted. "What about this, up here?" He tapped Emmeline on her forehead. "Or these?" He pulled at her sleeve, shaking her arm about. "Them's what keep a body safe, y'know. Not an overgrown handbag."

"*Satchel*. It's not a hard word."

"Yeah. Well," said Thing sagely. He sniffed and stared out to sea. "Hey, I wonder if we'll see any icebergs?" He sat up, straight and alert, on the lookout. They were lying in a quiet nook near the front of the ship, far from the first-class decks, sheltered by thick coils of rope and mostly hidden behind a large pipe. They'd spent hours exploring (or, rather, poking about where they didn't belong while dodging anyone in uniform). When they'd grown bored, they decided to camp out while they figured out what to do next. They hadn't come up with anything, and now dusk was closing in. It had been a long day, in every way imaginable.

Emmeline blinked. "I don't think they get this far down without breaking up, do they?" Thing just shrugged in reply, his shoulders slumping again. Emmeline sat up and gazed out across the expanse of water all around the ship, scouring it for any sight of the fabled ice mountains that were reputed to haunt the seas. Nobody (at least, nobody that had ever taken the time to explain it to her) seemed to understand why, but the frozen places of the world had been crumbling away for years, slowly sending white, freezing peaks into the oceans. They gradually melted as they went, raising the sea levels and, bit by bit, changing the weather into a cold, bad-tempered thing. It had started gradually, many years before, so nobody had bothered to do anything about it; now, Emmeline knew, it was happening so fast that it was changing the world for good, altering coastlines and destroying towns and cities, and it seemed hard to know where to start in putting things right. She didn't like to think about it much, but she knew her parents were worried, particularly since it had suddenly seemed to grow much worse over the past year or so. Or, she thought with a pang, it did worry them, before.

"In the old days, you know, the voyage to France was much shorter. Less water to cross. And Paris was a lot farther inland then," she said, trying to drown out her mind.

"Wouldn't know much about it," said Thing.

"Well, yeah. Me neither." Emmeline sighed. Several quiet moments passed, punctuated by nothing but the *skraaawk* of seagulls overhead.

"This ain't much of an adventure, is it?" Thing said, hopping up. Quick as anything, he wriggled between the bars of the ship's railing and swung out over the water, holding on by just his knees, his feet braced against the edge of the deck. "Whoo!" he yelled, bucking with the movement of the ship. "This is more like it!" He glanced back at Emmeline, who was too rigid with fear to notice the glint in his eye.

"Get in here, will you!" she shouted. "You'll fall!"

"Won't either," called Thing.

"You will! You could lose your balance, or *faint*, or anything!"

"Nah! I'm too clever for all that. Watch me!" Thing leaned farther out, his body like a bowsprit sticking out of the side of the ship. He laughed, his hair gluing to his face in thick, damp clumps.

Emmeline felt her heart knock against her collarbone. "Please! *Please!* Don't fall!"

"Or what? What do you care?" shouted Thing, his eyes bright.

"I don't *care*, I just—*hey!*" As Emmeline spoke, Thing's foot slipped—or seemed to. Before she knew what she was doing, she flung herself forward and grabbed his hand with both her own. She hauled him upright and then back through the railing where they lay together on the slick deck, panting and cold and tingling with exhilaration and terror. Thing looked at Emmeline and grinned, throwing her a wink. She just stared at him, breathing hard.

"Hey," he said. "You let go of yer satchel, finally." Emmeline was too busy trying to calm her heart to reply straightaway, but the realization that he was right jerked through her body.

"And you learned to say the word, finally," she muttered. She sat up and crawled over to where her satchel lay, then opened it to check that everything was as it should be.

"Yeah. Good with words, me," said Thing with a chuckle. Emmeline just sat there, dragging her satchel across her lap like it was a pet dog. She looked over at her strange companion and frowned, feeling somehow that she'd been outsmarted and not knowing why.

"So, why are you even on this ship? Where are your parents?" she asked, folding herself up small and trying to force her teeth not to chatter.

"Might ask you the same thing," said Thing. He settled himself, cross-legged, on the deck beside her, sweeping his hair out of his face with a wet hand.

"Well, I . . . ," Emmeline began. "It's sort of hard to explain." *Particularly when you don't understand it yourself,* she thought, picking absentmindedly at a loose thread on the buckle of her satchel.

"Fascinatin' story, that," said Thing after a minute. "My own tale, well, it's fairly similar. I'm here because I'm here, and I intend to stay here until someone realizes I'm not s'posed to be here and throws me overboard." He sniffed good-naturedly and flashed Emmeline his ever-present grin. Somehow it made her feel a little better.

"Well, I guess we're in the same boat, then," she said, glancing at him.

"Oh, an' a comedian, too," said Thing with a snort. "We'll need to work on yer joke tellin' if this here arrangement is goin' to get anywhere."

"Arrangement?" she echoed, looking back at him properly.

"You know. Me savin' you from terminal boredom."

"I think I'd rather be back at home," she said with a sigh.

"Ouch," said Thing, chuckling. "Not that bad, am I?"

Emmeline grinned through a deep yawn. "Can we pick this up tomorrow?" she asked. Her tiny cabin with its rickety bed seemed irresistibly inviting, suddenly.

"Don't see why not," he replied, getting to his feet in one smooth movement. He offered Emmeline his hand, but she and her satchel struggled up unaided. They set off in weary silence, and remained that way until they'd almost reached Emmeline's door. They'd just turned the final corner when, without warning, Thing stopped short. Emmeline walked into his back.

"Hey! Wait!" he whispered, dragging Emmeline out of sight.

"Not now, all right? I'm *wet*, and I'm *sleepy*, and I want to get out of these clothes—"

"Yeah, well, you're gonna be all those things and *dead* to boot if you don't shut it and stay hid!" said Thing between gritted teeth. "Just get over 'ere!" Emmeline rolled her eyes and slapped herself up against the wall beside Thing, clutching her satchel close.

"Y'see?" hissed Thing, nodding up toward her door. "Fellas movin'! Doin' stuff!"

Emmeline leaned out around him and looked. She could hear muffled thumping and raised voices coming from her cabin. A fluttering piece of fabric rustled out the door like a dying bird, and she saw with some embarrassment that it was her nightgown.

"Fancy," muttered Thing as it flapped sadly in the breeze before vanishing into the murky evening.

"Don't start," she replied.

"Are you, like, *rich*, or what?" he asked in a low voice.

"Not especially."

"Enough for those blokes to be rippin' your room to bits?"

Emmeline frowned. "Wouldn't have thought so."

"Right. Well, we've got to get out of here, ain't we?"

"What? Why? I can't leave all my *things* just—" At this, a large, bald-headed figure came striding out of Emmeline's cabin, a suitcase under each arm. He walked to the ship's railing and grabbed the handle of each bag. Then, without a second's hesitation, he shook them out like he was beating dust out of a carpet. Emmeline's belongings— her clothes, her shoes, her hairbrush, her favorite teddy bear for those nights when the darkness got a little bit *too* dark, her toothbrush, and at least five spare pairs of socks—tumbled out into the sea, lost forever in the churning water. The empty suitcases followed soon after.

Emmeline felt like someone had kicked her. *"Hey!"* she shouted before she could stop herself. The man jerked and turned, his meaty arms swinging.

"What are you—did you just—you *did*, didn't you?" spluttered Thing, pulling at Emmeline's sleeve. She didn't move.

"Oi!" yelled the man, shouting over his shoulder. "Out 'ere!" A crash, followed by a muffled scuffling, sounded from the cabin, and shadows skittered across the deck as people—*large* people—started moving toward the door. The bald man took two long strides in their direction, growling as he came.

"An' that's our cue to go. Go!" Emmeline felt Thing shove her out of their hiding place. His grip around her arm was like iron as he dragged her away.

"But we've got to—" she started to say, her eyes fixed on the light being thrown through her door. *Her* door, with *her* things inside!

"I ain't got to do nothin'," said Thing. "Come *on*, will ya?"

Emmeline turned, shaking off Thing's hand, and with that, they were gone.

7

"Come on!" yelled Thing, his voice barely audi-
ble. "This way!" They were running along a metal catwalk
suspended high in the air. Beneath their feet were massive turbines, slowly and hugely turning, and the whole
place was oppressively hot and smoky and steamy, and
the noise—well, the noise was unbearable. In the gloom it
was all Emmeline could do to follow Thing, keep herself
from falling over, and hang on to the satchel.

Eventually they reached a plain, boring-looking door
without markings or inscriptions and with a round window set into it. Thing barreled through it like a rugby
player making an illegal tackle. As soon as it swung closed
behind them, the noise was dampened enough for the
ringing in Emmeline's ears to settle into a faint buzz.

"You all right?" shouted Thing.

"I—yes!" she called back, her mind in a muddle. "Where are we?"

"Engine room," said Thing before letting out a wet, rattling cough. "C'mon—those blokes could be on us any minute." Following him down through a warren of passageways and staircases, Emmeline was sure they'd gone so deep into the ship that they were going to emerge on the other side of it.

"Nearly there!" he gasped after they'd been running for at least ten minutes, their feet clanking on the metal floor.

"How much farther?" Emmeline replied, barely able to speak. Her insides felt all jiggled about, like she was a doll in the hands of a particularly angry child.

"Just up here. C'mon. You can rest. Safe. Promise!" His words were coming in tight bursts. Emmeline forced her heavy legs to move, and within a minute they were inside another tiny room, dark and still, quiet except for a distant low rumble, and Thing was barricading the door with a mop handle.

"Jus' a minute," he said, his breath now sounding like great whoops. "I'll jus'—*whoop*—get the door—*whoop*—shut, and then we can light a—*whoop*—candle. Okay?"

"Are you all right?" she said, leaning in to help him with the mop. Together, they got it tight against the door. It wasn't nearly as good as a padlock, but it would have to do. "Your breathing sounds funny."

"Don' worry 'bout it," he croaked. "Be all right in a—*whoop*—minute." He tested the mop one last time, coughing as quietly as he could, before stepping away from the door. "Right. That's done it." Thing led her to a corner, and they flopped onto the floor. As Emmeline made sure her satchel was safe, Thing lit an old candle stub, and in the gentle glow of the flame Emmeline could finally look around.

They were in what looked like an old storeroom—all manner of bits and bobs and odds and ends had been thrown in it, higgledy-piggledy. She saw more mops and brushes and mirrors and bedsteads and crockery and kitchen appliances and old uniforms and mismatched shoes and, most unusually, a stuffed and mounted stag's head, which looked exceedingly old and in need of patching up. Thing tucked a blanket around her, and she accepted it gratefully. As it warmed her up, she realized that her legs were not only cold and damp but also cramped and sore and jittery from her long, unexpected run.

They spent several minutes alone with their thoughts in the candlelight. Thing's breathing returned to normal, and Emmeline's heart stopped galloping like an escaped rhinoceros.

"So, d'you want to tell me what's going on?" said Thing eventually.

"How am I supposed to know?" she replied, wrapping herself up as tightly as she could.

"You could at least thank me for savin' yer," he pointed out.

"I didn't . . ." Emmeline bit back what she wanted to say—which was something like *I didn't even ask you to get involved!*—because, firstly, it was a bit unfair and, secondly, she *was* grateful to Thing for spotting those men. Also, she thought, if he hadn't dragged her off on this so-called adventure, she'd have been there, in her cabin, when they burst in. A cold shiver ran up and down her spine.

"Thank you, Thing," she muttered.

"Yep," he said. She could hear that his grin was back. "So, what's the plan now? We won't be in Par-ee till the day after tomorrow, prob'ly. Can't go back to yer room, can yer?"

"I suppose not," said Emmeline grayly.

"Yer welcome to stay here, o'course," said Thing, gesturing around.

"Well—thanks." She glanced up, and the stuffed stag caught her eye again, making her look away fast. "So, is this where you live? Like, all the time?" She settled herself more comfortably on the floor and placed her satchel within reach.

"Nah, not *all* the time," replied Thing. "Jus' while I'm on board this partickler ship, but I've made, shall we say, sev'ral crossin's courtesy of this fine vessel. Best 'ome I've ever 'ad, but I don't want t'push me luck too far. When she docks this time, I'll be off into Par-ee to make me fortune. Jus' you watch!" He smiled, and in the candlelight Emmeline could pretend she couldn't see the fear in his eyes.

"Don't you *have* parents?" she said, swallowing a lump as she thought about her own.

"Must've done, once," answered Thing reasonably. "Why are we talkin' about me, anyway? Thought *you* were the one with the criminal record."

"I don't have a criminal record. I'm a *kid!*"

38

"No reason why you can't have a criminal record. Pretty sure I had one when I were your age."

Emmeline glared at him. "How old are you now?"

"Older'n you," he answered unhelpfully.

Emmeline huffed out a thwarted sigh. "So, how do you get food and things?" she asked, before yawning so widely that she felt sure her head was about to pop off.

"I liberate it, shall we say, from them as has a little bit more'n they need."

"You mean you steal it."

"In a manner of speakin'."

"You're sure we're safe here?" The candle was beginning to gutter and flicker. Emmeline shivered, pulling the blanket tighter around her. She thought of her poor teddy, drowned at the bottom of the ocean, and of her parents, wherever they were, and squeezed her eyes tight shut, wondering why they were suddenly starting to sting.

"Yeah," answered Thing after a few seconds. "I ain't never had no trouble down 'ere. Nobody ever comes down this far no more. Don't reckon those blokes as trashed your cabin could even *find* us. Maybe it's all a big misunderstandin' anyway."

"Do you think that's all it is?" She yawned. Gravity was sucking at her eyelids, and things were starting to get a little blurry around the edges. Her arms and legs felt heavy, and she was so cozy under the blanket that she was asleep before Thing answered her.

"No, little scrap," he said into the darkness. "I don't think it's no misunderstandin'."

After a few minutes he blew out the candle, checked that Emmeline's satchel was safe and secure, and settled himself down beside her. It took a while for thoughts like *Leave the kid here! Grab the bag an' sell what you can out of it! What're you doin', you turnip?* to stop whirling about inside his brain, but eventually they left him alone.

Then he slept, and the ship sailed on into the night.

8

Emmeline woke up alone. With a jolt she remem-
bered her satchel and flipped herself over so she could see
it—but it was there, all right, looking exactly the same as
it had the day before.

Check it, said a little voice in her head. *Check that everything's in it!* But she squished that thought away and busied
herself waiting for Thing to come back.

As it turned out, that took a bit longer than she'd an-
ticipated.

There was no real way to tell time in the storeroom.
The only clock was a large, broken thing lying on its
side in one corner; it read twenty-three minutes past two
and probably had for years. All Emmeline had to go on
was her stomach, which finally began to growl—and still,
Thing didn't appear.

Emmeline had finally decided she couldn't wait any longer, and had just about gathered up enough courage to leave the room by herself when Thing came barreling in as though Genghis Khan were on his heels. He slammed the door closed behind him, and with fumbling hands he replaced their security mop.

"Hey! Is everything—"

"Shhh! *Whoop!*" said Thing, putting a finger to his lips.

"But—"

"*Shhhh!*" He strode over to her and placed one hot and sweaty hand over her mouth. His eyes were huge, and Emmeline didn't think she was imagining the trembling she could feel in his fingers. He turned back toward the door, whooping quietly. After a few minutes of silence, he ushered Emmeline back toward their corner, where they huddled.

"Sorry I were gone so long. But the whole—*whoop*— ship is looking for you," he said. "Everyone. I 'ad a lot of dodgin' to do to get back 'ere."

"Looking for *me*? Why?" Emmeline couldn't imagine an entire shipful of people caring one way or the other about where she was.

"A missing kid? On a Northern Jewel cruise ship? *Whoop?* It's big news." Thing's eyes hopped about, and though his breaths were calming, they still sounded thick. "If that's all it is," he added quietly.

"Do you have asthma or something?" Emmeline asked, wondering if it was catching.

"Somethin'," replied Thing. "Forget me. What are we goin' to do about you?"

"What about me?" Emmeline leaned over her satchel absentmindedly, but it was just out of reach. Thing grabbed her wrist.

"Pay attention, Ems," he said. "This is important."

So is my satchel! Emmeline thought, the words lashing across her brain like a whip. "Should we go to the captain and tell him—"

"Are you *off* yer *head?*" whispered Thing, his voice sharpening to a squeak. "The captain? He'd announce it to the whole ship, and then d'you know what'd happen?"

"People—people would stop looking for me?"

Thing rolled his eyes. "Yeah, that. An' those two brutes who played hide-and-seek with us last night would know exac'ly where you were. Right? Not a lot of places to run on a ship."

"Oh," said Emmeline in her littlest voice.

"Yeah, oh. So we got to keep you hid, at least until we reach Par-ee. After that, well . . ." Thing rubbed at his face with a grubby hand. "After that, not even my brainpower knows what t'do."

"I have to meet someone in Paris," said Emmeline quickly. "I have an address to go to, and a person to ask for, a person who's going to . . ."

"Who's goin' to what?" Thing's eyes glittered in the dim light.

"Who's going to look after me, now that my parents . . . now that they're gone." A few seconds passed, silent but very full. Thing slid his fingers into Emmeline's hand, and she gripped them tightly, just for a moment. Somehow she knew he understood how it felt to have nobody.

"Right," he said. "Well, we gotta get you off the ship in Par-ee without anyone seein' ya, and without anyone shoutin' for a constable. We can do that." In the silence that followed, Emmeline's stomach rumbled as loudly as a round of applause in a packed theater.

"Gosh, excuse me," she said, clutching at her middle.

"Got just the thing for that," said Thing, reaching into one of his many pockets. When he withdrew his hand, it held two small croissants and several miniature chocolate rolls, which were doused with icing sugar. Emmeline's mouth watered instantly, and Thing let her have first choice.

"Where did you get these?" she asked through a mouthful of sweet dough.

"Found 'em, just lyin' around," replied Thing.

"Hmm," said Emmeline, but she didn't stop eating.

As soon as she'd swallowed the last crumb, Emmeline realized she had another problem that needed her immediate attention.

"So, uh, I need to go out," she said, hoping he'd understand what she meant.

"Go out?" he repeated, raising his eyebrows. "'Ave you 'eard a thing I've said?" He took a huge breath and whooshed it out through his nostrils. "The whole *ship* is *lookin'* for ya. So goin' out is not really somethin' you should be considerin', all told." He sat back a little, grumbling.

"But I have to . . . ," she began. "I have to—*you* know!"

"You have to what?" Thing's attention was already wandering. He slouched over to where Emmeline had

44

neatly folded the blanket and shook it out again, before settling himself on the floor and tucking it around his legs.

"I have to attend to something," said Emmeline through gritted teeth. "Something *private!*" Thing's frown gradually smoothed out, and Emmeline watched laughter tickle the corners of his mouth.

"Oh—*right!*" said Thing in an overloud voice. "That. Well—yeah. I hadn't considered that."

"What do you do when you want to—you know?"

"When I want to go to the toilet, you mean?" said Thing pleasantly. Emmeline felt her cheeks tingle and was glad of the semidarkness. "Well, I just pick a corner and have at it, me."

"Well, that's *not* going to work," said Emmeline in a voice as crisp as a freshly laundered sheet.

"I can go out an' liberate a chamber pot, if ya like."

"But I need to go *now.*"

"All right, all right," sighed Thing, flinging the blanket off and hopping to his feet. He paused and then looked at the blanket again, a small grin blooming.

"I've got an idea. O'course, it might be doomed to failure," he said carefully, "but so are most feats o' genius. Yeah?"

"Um," said Emmeline, getting up. She stumbled as she rose, and Thing reached out a hand to steady her.

"Whoa there! All right?"

Emmeline shot him a grateful look. "You just have better sea legs than me, I suppose."

"Somethin' like that," he said. "Now—you ready?"

Four minutes later the door to their hideaway creaked

open. A curious-looking creature stuck out its head and glanced up and down the corridor before finally creeping out on steady feet, heading for the stairs to the upper decks.

The creature was short and bent over, with what looked like a misshapen hunched back, and it was dressed in a strange tartan robe with a fringed edge. It clutched an old walking stick (pilfered from the storeroom) and wore a thoroughly odd top hat (also pilfered).

"What's the point of goin' out there in disguise," Thing had said, "unless we do it so over the top that nobody even *dares* to ask questions?" Emmeline had looked dubious at this but had said nothing. "Plus," Thing had continued, "if you walk with a cocky step an' yer head held high, and you give off this air that says, *I know* exac'ly *what I'm doin', mate,* you can pretty much do anythin' and go anywhere. Fact."

"If you say so," Emmeline had sighed before clambering up on his back and holding tight, her satchel snugly fastened to her front.

"Let the adventurin' begin," Thing had whispered with a grin.

9

Emmeline was finding it hard to keep her grip.
Her hands kept slipping from around Thing's neck, and
she was acutely aware that she couldn't move too much. If
she wasn't careful, anyone looking at Thing—who seemed,
to the unobservant, like a hunched-over old man with
strange taste in traveling cloaks—might wonder why his
back was wriggling. All it would take was one person to
shout, or point, and the whole game would be up.

Add this to the pressure in her bladder, and Emmeline
was in a very foul mood indeed.

Thing, however, whistled as he walked, even going so
far as to start swinging his cane in time to the tune. They
turned a corner and came upon some high-society ladies,
and Thing shuffled around them, turning his fumbling
steps into a short dance routine.

"Pardon me, me lovelies," he said in a raspy voice that was nothing like his own. "I'm awful sorry for even attemptin' to get in the way of such beauty."

"Perfectly all right, my good man," sniffed one of the women. Emmeline couldn't see her, but she imagined a tall, stout figure in a stiff, dark dress, her hair in a tight bun and her mouth puckered like an elasticized stocking. "Be on your way now."

Emmeline almost shrieked when she felt Thing topple forward—but he was just bowing. She used the opportunity to renew her grip on his neck, and she felt him twitch as she did so.

"Most gracious of you, milady," he said, sounding a bit choked.

"Quite," said the woman, and Emmeline heard the *tap-tap* of her heels as she walked away. Thing shambled on at a faster pace.

"Could ya quit yer attempts to strangulate me?" he whispered. Emmeline tutted and shifted her grip, but he kept grumbling under his breath anyway. To keep her mind off her bladder, Emmeline tried to peer out from under the blanket. She could just about make out people grimacing as Thing approached and quickly skipping out of his way. Someone, she was sure, was going to report him. *Did you see that strange old man with the crooked back? I wonder if he has anything to do with this missing child. . . .*

Terrified, she slammed her eyes shut and buried her face in the back of Thing's neck.

"Psst," Thing whispered after a few minutes. "This'll have to do." She heard the creak of wood giving way, like he'd forced open a cabin door, and before she could say or do anything, he'd stepped through and closed it behind them. Without waiting for him to tell her the coast was clear, she slithered down off his back, angrily blowing her hair out of her face.

"What are you *doing*? Where are we? Are we in . . ." Her words trailed off as something caught her eye. It was a long golden cloak made of the finest, lightest silk she'd ever seen, and there was a diamond-capped—*diamond-capped!*—ladies' walking stick right beside it. A feathered hat, magnificently plumed, was perched on the same hook as the cloak, and there were at least three other beautiful outfits hanging on either side of it.

"These folks can afford you the use of their pot," said Thing with a grin. "Just be quick about it, right?" Emmeline didn't need to be told twice, but she did pause long enough for a look around. This cabin was gigantic—at least five times the size of hers, and with its own bathroom. There was a massive bathtub, complete with gold taps, and the sink was big enough to take a swim in, and the toilet itself was polished to an eye-watering shine. Emmeline had never been so glad to see anything in all her life.

Just as she was washing her hands, Emmeline heard a thump, shortly followed by rapid muttering and the sound of Thing impatiently rattling the doorknob. She stretched to unlock the door.

"Outtamywayouttamy*way!*" he hissed, barreling through and almost knocking her down.

"What's wrong?" she asked as Thing threw a panicked

gaze around the room. There was something strange about the front of his overalls, but Emmeline couldn't put her finger on it.

Thing's whole body was taut, like a trapped animal. "There's *voices* out in the passageway, is what. Someone's comin', is what."

"But—no! What are we going to do?"

"Workin' on it," snapped Thing, still glancing around the room.

". . . but that's so *darling!*" came a woman's voice from the main cabin. "I mean, *really*, Clarence! Have you ever *seen* such a darling thing!"

"Quite certain I haven't, dear. Simply the darlingest thing in existence," replied a man. His bored-sounding drawl sent a shiver of horror right through Emmeline. She looked at Thing and he carefully placed a finger over his lips. Keeping his eyes on hers, he pointed to the bathtub. Emmeline didn't understand for a moment, and then it hit her—there was a porthole just above it, so if this room was anything like hers, the deck lay outside. *But the window looks so small. . . .*

"What time is dinner this evening, Clarence?" The lady sounded like she was close enough to touch. Emmeline imagined her removing another beautiful cloak and hanging it up along with all the others.

"Six, I believe, m'dear. Shall I have time for a sherry before we dine?"

The lady murmured a response, but Emmeline and Thing were concentrating so hard on staying quiet as they began their long, careful journey toward the tub that they didn't hear it.

"I say, Clarence. Clarence!" The lady's voice exploded across Emmeline's brain, making her jump. "Come here for a moment, would you?"

"Whatever's the matter?" A newspaper rattled.

"Clarence! Put down that blasted *Times* and come over here, this instant! One of my garments is missing." Thing turned to Emmeline, his eyes wide. *So that explains the lump under his overalls,* she thought. She glared at him before picking up the pace. Without making a sound, Thing climbed into the tub and reached up toward the porthole window. As carefully as she could, Emmeline climbed in after him, hoping the whole thing wouldn't tip over, or creak, or otherwise give away their location.

"Yes, dear," said the distant Clarence. "Are you quite sure you brought it?"

"Of course I'm sure! Clarence, honestly! I had Sara pack everything I thought I'd need for this trip, and that included my short sable!"

A harrumph was heard as the unseen Clarence presumably rose to his feet, followed by the sound of heavy footsteps as he crossed the cabin.

Emmeline looked up to see Thing struggling with the porthole. His face was red with effort.

"Well?" trilled the lady, her voice humming with impatience. Emmeline glanced back at the still-closed but unlocked bathroom door.

"Well what? How is one supposed to see what is no

longer there?" asked Clarence. Emmeline's ears pricked up as Thing let out a gasp of frustration. Silently she gestured to him to move.

"Well, is this or is this not *exactly* where I placed my short sable? Hmm?"

"I'm quite sure it is, dear, yes. If you say so."

"Clarence, you're *impossible*," sighed the lady. "I insist we summon the captain now. Someone has clearly been through our stateroom with sticky fingers." Right at that point Emmeline's own fingers were aching. The porthole window's seal was exactly the same as the one in her own cabin, but ever so slightly stiffer. Just a few . . . more . . . seconds . . .

"Now, now. You know there's a missing child, and the captain is understandably more concerned about that. Perhaps we should wait until we dock, and then—"

As soon as these words were uttered, the porthole window opened with a loud, sucking pop. For one long moment Emmeline and Thing stood gaping at each other, before Emmeline started unstrapping her satchel. She would barely fit out the window as she was, but with the satchel, too . . .

"Clarence, did you—did you *hear* something?" The lady's voice quivered, but it put a rod of steel down Emmeline's back. She threw the satchel out the window, and as fast as she could, she put her foot into Thing's cupped hands. He heaved her up, and she almost clanged her head on the porthole's metal frame.

"Perhaps—perhaps we should summon the captain after all," warbled Clarence. Emmeline's head was outside now, and she was struggling to fit her shoulders through. Desperation gave her strength, and she flailed around just enough to get loose. She fell out onto the deck with a plop and immediately got to her feet again, strapped on her satchel, and readied herself to help Thing.

"*Clarence!*" she heard faintly as Thing burst out of the porthole. He twisted in midair and landed on his feet, and before Emmeline even had time to draw a breath, he shouted:

"*Run!*"

There was no time to think, or speak, or pause for breath—Emmeline and Thing simply ran as hard as they could. The satchel jiggled up and down on Emmeline's back, and from the tinkling sound, she suspected something inside it had been broken. *Not the hydrogen sulfide,* she thought mournfully. She'd hate to lose that.

"This way!" Thing shouted every few steps, or "No! *This* way!" as they tried to dodge as many peering eyes as they could. They tore past a line of dozing people on deck chairs and bumped right into a heavily laden waiter with a tray of drinks as they raced around a corner without looking.

"Sorry!" yelled Emmeline.

"Shut it! *Whoop!*" shouted Thing. "No talkin'!"

"S-sorry!" she whispered. She risked a glance back

over her shoulder, but all she could see were some people helping the waiter up and picking his tray off the ground. Nobody was shouting their names or chasing them, and maybe, just maybe—

WAAAaaaaaaauuuaaaaAAAAAAauuuuuuuaaaaa-AAAAAaauuuuu…

"What on earth is *that*?" gasped Emmeline as they rounded another corner.

"Siren," answered Thing. "For—*whoop*—fire, or 'mergency, or whatever."

"There's a *fire*?" exclaimed Emmeline.

Thing shot her a look. "Just get in there, an' put a sock in it," he muttered, shoving her toward a canvas-covered lifeboat, which seemed, to Emmeline's eye, rather insecurely lashed to the side of the deck. A small corner of the canvas was loose, and it was short work to make the hole large enough for them both to clamber through.

"We're the emergency, aren't we?" she asked quietly once they were hidden.

"Bingo," whispered Thing. "Now button it." They crawled beneath a pile of coiled-up rope and spare canvas, and listened closely to what was going on outside. They heard whistles and shouting and lots of pounding, thundering feet.

"What the blazes is going on?" they heard. It sounded like Clarence. "My wife is in an *hysterical* condition! I demand …" His voice faded away as he lumbered past.

"I'm *sure* I saw them go this way!" shouted another voice. "Come on!" Emmeline shrank down as small as she could, barely daring to think in case she did it too loudly. Thing was having a horrible time trying to breathe quietly—his tiny, mournful whoops sounded so painful that Emmeline felt very sorry for him. She caught his eye and he nodded, giving her a thumbs-up, but she knew he was lying.

Eventually, the hullabaloo died down. Thing's lungs rattled, and his face was a strange color, even under the canvas, where everything looked odd.

"Think I might—*whoop*—think I might go an' have a look-see, right? You stay put." Thing moved, ever so slowly, toward the edge of the lifeboat, making straight for the loose flap of canvas.

"No—wait!" Emmeline could already feel her heart hammering in her throat.

"It's fine!" whispered Thing. "Jus' keep yer cool, okay?"

Emmeline watched as Thing gingerly peeled back the canvas covering their hiding place. He blinked a bit in the light, and carefully he poked his head up just enough to see over the side. He looked around in all directions, and finally he stuck his head right out. Then he ducked back inside the boat and held out his hand to Emmeline.

"C'mon! Coast's clear, for now. Get a wriggle on!" But before Emmeline could move, a large, dark shape blocked out the light behind Thing, and she shrank back into the corner of the boat, too scared to scream.

"Not so fast, young'un," came a low, rumbling voice. Thing jerked and ducked down out of the way of a pair of strong, thick-fingered hands that burst through the gap in the canvas, grabbing and grasping and searching for him.

"Aaargh!" Thing yelled. "Do somethin'!"

"Like *what?*" Emmeline shouted.

"*Anythin'!*" Thing kicked out at the searching hands, but Emmeline heard the man chuckle. He knew he had them trapped.

Emmeline's eyes fell on a heavy wooden oar lying in the bottom of the lifeboat. She grasped it with both hands and gave it to Thing, who immediately began using it to bash, rather inelegantly but quite effectively, at the man's hairy knuckles.

"Oi!" they heard him yell. "You little *brats!*"

"'At's right!" shouted Thing. "Take that, ya big lummox!"

Emmeline, meanwhile, was rifling through her satchel. Her fingers rattled their way between her bottles— gratefully she realized her hydrogen sulfide was safe and sound—until she reached the bottom compartment, where her emergency supplies were stored. She found what she was looking for and grabbed it.

"What the 'eck is *that?*" gasped Thing, turning just long enough to glance at a small, round object in Emmeline's hands. The man had recovered well and was almost inside the boat now. The whole thing was rocking on its mooring, in serious danger of plunging away from the side of the ship and crashing into the sea a hundred feet below.

"Hold your breath!" Emmeline whispered, her eyes on the man. She recognized him as the bald-headed creature who'd flung her belongings into the sea, and her resolve strengthened.

"What?" yelled Thing, but it was too late for Emmeline to repeat herself.

Quickly she squeezed the object in her hand. She felt the crunch when the inner pocket burst, mixing the chemicals together. It grew warm in her hand as she readied herself to throw it.

Now! This was her chance. The man leaned into the lifeboat again, roaring. His eyes were on Thing and the oar, so he didn't even see when Emmeline, quick as a flash, threw the object in her hand straight into his open mouth.

"Yurg!" he gurgled. *"Yaaaarg!"* A horrendous stench filled the air as the stink bomb started to fizz, making a yellow, disgusting foam gush all over the man's face. It filled up his mouth and started to bubble out of his nose, and within a second or two his whole head was covered. The man dragged himself back out of the lifeboat, and Emmeline saw him stagger down the deck a few feet, trying desperately to get the stink bomb out of his mouth.

"That is *foul!* What *is* that?" Thing looked like he was going to throw up. The smell was like old underwear and rotten cheese and bad breath, except a million times worse. Emmeline was quite proud of the final product, but she didn't have time to hang around admiring her handiwork.

"Come on! We've got to go, right now. He won't be long in getting rid of it."

Thing chucked the oar back into the bottom of the boat. Emmeline helped pull him up and out over the side, and soon they were back on deck again.

Out of the corner of her eye, Emmeline watched as Stink Bomb tried to shout, but it ended in a fit of coughing as the stench got caught in his throat. He took a few steps in their direction but soon fell to his knees, retching.

"Come on!" Emmeline took off, heading for the nearest staircase, and Thing was hot on her heels. They kept their ears wide open for any sign of pursuit as they went. Up and up they ran, dodging everyone they met, hiding when they could, and taking detours if they had to, neither of them with any idea where they were going. Eventually they began to realize that if Stink Bomb didn't catch up with them, exhaustion was bound to. They'd been running for what seemed like hours, and now they were running out of places to go.

"We can't go back to the storeroom, can we?" gasped Emmeline as they paused to catch their breath. Thing could only whoop sadly in reply as they set off once more. She took that as a no.

They were approaching what looked like a dead end. They'd taken a turn, and then another, blindly, and now they were running along a service gantry, where passengers weren't supposed to go. It led to a large piece of what looked like meteorological equipment, with a huge, round face and lots of levers, welded to a small balcony that was ringed by a low railing, and there was no way to get down from it unless you were a monkey or had wings.

"What are we going to do *now?*" wailed Emmeline, leaning out over the balcony. All she could see were layers and layers of ship and the crashing, freezing sea far below. She clambered up onto the railing, shaking off a horrible image of herself falling, like a broken doll, into the water, but it was impossible to reach the balcony beneath them.

She looked up, straining to see if there was anything—*anything*—that they could swing from or climb, but nothing was close enough. The next deck up looked miles away. Their only choice was to go back—or jump.

"You little *blighters!*" Emmeline and Thing whirled around to see Stink Bomb at the other end of the gantry, accompanied by another man, who was equally big and nasty-looking. There were hints of foam still lingering on his face, and as he spoke, a large yellow bubble sneaked out of his nose and popped, loudly and wetly. This seemed to make him even angrier, and he roared, flexing his arms as though getting ready to rip their heads off. Emmeline felt Thing's hand slip into hers, and he tried to get her to stand behind him. His breath was glooping through his lungs, whooping all the way, and his whole body shook with effort and exhaustion.

"Hey! *Up here!*" came a voice. Emmeline started, and Thing stared at her, confusion all over his face.

"What was—"

"Up *here!* Come on!"

Together, Emmeline and Thing took a few careful steps back, keeping their eyes on their pursuers. Stink Bomb started to pound his way down the gantry, growling, his every footstep like an earthquake.

Emmeline stopped walking when she felt the edge of the balcony at her back.

"About time!" came the voice again, this time from just above their heads.

Emmeline looked up. A young man, dressed in a white shirt and waistcoat, and wearing a sturdy-looking leather body harness, was hanging from a rope. He had curly black hair, dark eyes, an urgent smile, and a white flower stuck through his buttonhole—and his arms were outstretched to them.

Quick as a heartbeat, Thing threw Emmeline at the dangling man, who helped her—and her satchel—clamber onto his back. Just as the roar of their stink-bombed enemy got loud enough to set Emmeline's teeth on edge, Thing leaped from the balcony straight into the man's arms—and, with a sickening lurch, they started to rise through the air.

Emmeline clamped her eyes shut and prayed she wouldn't throw up.

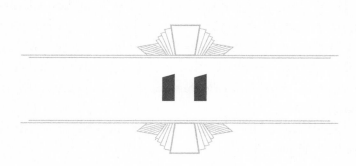

As it turned out, throwing up was the least of Emmeline's problems.

"Hang on!" cried the man. The rope they were clinging to was being hauled up *very* fast by something unseen. They swayed and swung in the wind, repeatedly bashing into the side of the ship. Each time, the jolt made Emmeline feel sure she was going to lose her grip. This, coupled with the freezing cold and the bone-rattling terror (which wasn't helped by the sound of what Emmeline felt sure was gunfire coming from their stink-bombed assailant below), was making Emmeline extremely unhappy, and she was growing less happy with every foot they climbed.

Then, with one final jerk, Emmeline, Thing, and the man toppled over a high balcony onto a cold metal floor, where they lay shivering. Emmeline ran a mental inventory of her faculties—she appeared to be thinking and breathing, and the rest could wait. Slowly, and with huge difficulty, she unstuck her fingers from their rescuer's collar.

"Edgar!" came a woman's voice. "Is everything all right? Who's the boy?" A deep, meaningful groan answered this, and Emmeline felt sure it had come from Thing. A throb of relief engulfed her.

"Let's just get them inside, Sasha." The man's words were hurried. "We owe this boy a great debt."

Before she could do any more thinking, Emmeline felt herself being gently but insistently lifted to her feet. Blinking, she saw a large winch, to which Edgar's harness was still attached. It was hissing in the damp air, like all its surfaces were hot.

"Come on, little one," said the other voice. *Sasha?* Emmeline thought. *Who on earth are these people?* "Let's get you warmed up, eh?" Emmeline tried to glimpse this new person, but all she could see was a slender arm, dressed in a billowing sleeve, that came to an end in a graceful, red-fingernailed hand. She slapped it away, even as her gaze was drawn by a soft, warm-looking light spilling from somewhere close by. She turned to face it. A huge, luxurious cabin lay to her right, and nothing separated her from it but a pane of glass.

"Ow." The voice belonged to Thing. *"Whoop,"* he added, just in case there was any doubt. Emmeline yanked herself out of Sasha's arms and flung herself down beside him. He was a funny color again, and his clothes were stuck to his skinny body. Emmeline hugged his narrow back as she tried to help him stand.

"Are you all right?" she gasped. Her teeth were chattering, which was rather annoying.

"Never better," moaned Thing, finding his feet and leaning gratefully into Emmeline as they rose. "What's happenin'?" Emmeline opened her mouth to answer, but nothing came of it.

"Warmth and food first," said Sasha in a firm but kind voice. "Explanations later."

Finally Emmeline looked around and got a chance to stare at her properly. She was tall and lovely, with dusky brown skin and dark eyes, and Emmeline was suspicious of her on sight.

"Who *are* you?" Emmeline asked, her teeth still clattering like a set of castanets.

"A friend." She extended her hand. Emmeline ignored this and simply imprinted the woman's image on her mind so she could recall it later and study it in more detail. For now, all Emmeline could see was that she wore a neat fitted waistcoat over a crisp white blouse and a pair of stylishly tailored pants, which looked so *practical* that Emmeline made a mental note to acquire some as soon as she had an opportunity. Pinned over Sasha's heart was a small, nodding flower, white, the tiniest of stitches around its petals giving away the fact that it was made of silk. In every other respect it looked freshly picked.

Sasha smiled and lowered her hand. Emmeline watched

as she turned away and stepped into the warm, dry-looking cabin.

"You can trust us, you know," said their rescuer from behind Emmeline. She whirled on the spot. "I'm Edgar, by the way." He was back on his feet, his hair soggy with spray and his clothes saturated. He finished shrugging off his harness before holding out his hand to her. Emmeline flexed her fists, willing herself to reach for him, but before she could work herself up to it, the man smiled, a bit wearily, and returned his hand to his side.

"Emm—" she began.

"I know who you are. Now, if you don't mind, *I* need to go indoors even if *you* don't. It would be wonderful if you and your friend would join me, of course." Edgar nodded decisively and maneuvered around her and Thing, who were left, bedraggled, on the balcony.

"Best go in, I s'pose," Thing said. He hugged himself, his breath hissing through his teeth. "You comin'?" he asked over his shoulder.

Emmeline rolled her eyes at Thing's back, but she followed him through the door.

Several things struck her at once when she stepped down into the brightly lit cabin. Firstly, it was *huge*. Secondly, it was every bit as plush and warm on the inside as it had looked from the outside. Thirdly, to her left stood a large table more suited to banqueting than—well, whatever was going on around it right now. It was covered in maps and charts large enough to drape over its edges, each of them crisscrossed with latitude and longitude lines, pencil-drawn trajectories, and lots of scribbled handwriting. Fourthly, Emmeline's tiredness begged her to curl up on the thick carpet for a snooze, but she forced herself to stay alert.

"Glad to see you've joined us." Emmeline's eyes fell on Sasha, who was standing in the center of the room like a lighthouse, isolated and gleaming. Emmeline immediately attempted to assume a dignified and detached air, standing up as straight as she could and wishing she weren't quite so half-drowned-looking.

"I think there's been some sort of error," she said. "I'm on my way to Paris, you see, to meet my—to meet my parents, and I can't have you delaying me." Her eyes stung a bit as she spoke, and she thought a tinge of sadness touched the woman's expression, like a drop of paint diffusing through a glass of water.

"Emmeline," Sasha said, taking a couple of steps in her direction. "As my colleague explained outside, we know who you are. That, indeed, is why we're here in the first place." Emmeline's heart thundered as she listened. *How on earth do they know who I am? Maybe Stink Bomb sent them! They've tricked us!* She looked around for Thing, but he was already sitting on an embroidered sofa, half-submerged in what looked like a cream-bedecked trifle, entirely unaware of her predicament.

Emmeline looked back at Sasha. "You'd better tell me who you are," she said, trying not to sound afraid, "or I'll—"

"Yes, of course." Sasha took three more steps toward Emmeline, who didn't move, despite wanting to reach into her satchel for the first caustic thing she could find. "My name is Natasha—or Sasha, to those who know me well. Edgar and I belong to an organization called the Order of the White Flower. We've been sent by someone you might have heard of already—Madame Gramercy Blancheflour."

Emmeline blinked, feeling like she was about to collapse on the spot from a mixture of shock, exhaustion, and sheer confusion, and forced herself to stare straight at Sasha.

"Likely story," she said, and yanked down hard on the straps of her satchel. Two tiny pops were heard, and Emmeline saw Sasha's eyes widen in surprise.

Seconds later the room was filled with thick, choking smoke.

12

"Blast it!" shouted Edgar. "What just happened?"

"Smoke bomb!" coughed Sasha. "Check the perimeters!"

Emmeline crouched beneath the table, hastily resetting the smoke canisters in the straps of her satchel with trembling fingers. Her eyes watered, and she took quick, shallow breaths. At ground level the smoke wasn't as thick, but even so, her shoulders rattled with silent coughs.

"Whoop!" Thing's chest sounded loud, and painful, and Emmeline shook away a momentary stab of guilt. *He'll be fine,* she told herself, trying to believe it. *They'll feed him full of trifle, and when the ship gets to Paris, he can fend for himself, like he said he would.* She felt then as though she'd swallowed something that was too big, that had stretched her throat and made it sore. *And I'll just have to do without him.*

"Emmeline!" called Sasha. "Please! We want to help

you!" *Yes, I'm sure you do,* thought Emmeline, peering through the smoke. *And to help yourselves to my family's money, no doubt, too—or whatever's left of it, at least.* Emmeline wondered if her parents' letter had been intercepted and how these people had managed to insert themselves into her life. Sent by Madame Blancheflour, indeed! Did they think she was a fool? How much ransom were they planning to ask for her, and could her parents be persuaded to put their work aside for long enough to get around to paying it?

"Emmeline, you don't understand!" This time it was Edgar, his voice stringy. "There are people out there who want to hurt you—who want to *use* you to do something very awful! Your parents entrusted you to—to . . ." His voice trailed off in a collection of splutters, and Emmeline ignored him, his words trickling down her back like droplets of cold water. *I've got to get out of here!*

An explosion shattered the rest of her thought.

The next thing Emmeline knew, her ears were ringing and she was lying flat on her back. Her first thought was for her satchel, of course, but she was lying on it and found that she couldn't really move very well, so she told herself she'd check it later. Vaguely, out of the corners of her eyes, she could see movement and flashes of light, and then—very gradually, like the sun rising on a dark winter's morning—sounds started to ooze back through her ears. Sounds like screaming, and yelling, and the *crack-ping* of bullets, and the roaring of a man in pain, or in extraordinary anger, or both.

There was a gigantic crash, and Emmeline instinctively rolled away from the sound, covering her face with her arms. Loud, heavy footsteps thudded onto the carpeted floor.

"Find the girl!" a deep voice shouted. "I don't care what you have to do!" Emmeline scrambled back beneath the table again, watching as several boot-clad pairs of feet poured through the now-shattered window. A freezing wind gushed through the jagged gap where the pane of glass had once been, doing an excellent job of clearing the room of the last few thready remnants of her smoke bomb.

"How *dare* you!" came a reply. Emmeline didn't need to see the speaker to know that it was Sasha. "How *dare* you break in here and *attack* us without just cause in *open* water—"

"Give it a rest. Who cares about open water? It'll *all* be open water soon! When it wakes—" Emmeline heard a sharp slap, followed by a scuffle and the man's growl of anger. "You'll regret that," he muttered, but Sasha didn't reply.

When what wakes? Emmeline thought, something in the words making her uneasy.

"We do not have the child, and even if we *did*, there's no way we'd hand her over to you!" This was Edgar, his words a little less strained than before. She squished back a memory of his face as he'd held out his arms to her, saving her from the balcony, and wondered for the briefest moment whether she'd misjudged this entire situation. "Get out of our cabin this minute! I've already called the ship's captain!"

"Now, now. D'you think we're fools, or what?" The deep voice had a layer of grease over it, like oil on water.

"Do you want an honest answer to that? Because—"

"Enough. We know you've got the kid—one of our fellas *saw* 'er bein' taken in 'ere. So forget the stupid tricks."

"We don't have time for this!" shouted another voice. "Just get the girl and come on!" Emmeline felt her breath drying in her throat, and an uncontrollable shiver started to rattle through her. Quickly she thought about her satchel again. If her fingers would stop trembling long enough to undo the straps, she could maybe grab her catapult. . . .

"*Ems!*" The hiss came from her left, and she snapped her head around to face it. Thing, crouched on the floor, met her eye. "This way!" He jerked his head toward a door behind him, which Emmeline felt sure must open to the ship's corridor and escape. It was within reach, if she sprinted. . . .

"Someone move this table right now!" barked the deep-voiced man.

That decided it. Like she'd received an electrical jolt to the spine, Emmeline jumped up and scurried toward Thing as quickly as she could.

"Nice one!" he said, and grinned.

"Oi! Captain!" came a yell right behind Emmeline. "You've got to see this!" Thing flicked his eyes toward something above Emmeline's head, and his expression changed. Emmeline didn't have to see what he was looking at; if Thing's fear-filled face hadn't been enough, she could feel her pursuer's hot, clammy breath down the back of her neck too. Like she was reaching for a distant star, she stretched out her hand to Thing, and he grabbed it firmly. A split second later she was on her feet and running, and Thing was dragging her toward the door.

"Get 'em! *Now!*" The deep-voiced man roared so loudly that it would have shattered the cabin's plate-glass window if it hadn't already been lying in a million sparkling pieces all over the carpet.

"Aye, aye!" came the reply from at least ten different mouths. Emmeline squeaked and picked up her feet.

"Go! Run, you two!" cried Edgar, appearing out of nowhere to unlock the door. Emmeline stared at his shirt-sleeves, ripped and bloodied, and the trickle of red tracing its way down his face. In his hands he held a gun, and in his eyes was the glint of determination. "We'll cover you. Just get out of here!" But as Thing bumped his way past, Edgar grabbed him by the upper arm. He leaned in close, muttering fast, never taking his eyes off the men. "Hide. In the highest place. Do you understand?" Thing, pale as a dead fish, nodded quickly before wrenching his arm out of Edgar's grip. Edgar flashed a grin, his face slick with sweat. "Good lad. We'll find you!" Then he flicked his eyes toward Emmeline and nodded at her before reaching behind himself to yank the door open wide. "Look after her, boy!" he shouted as Emmeline and Thing staggered out into the corridor, which seemed almost ridiculously neat and clean after the mayhem they'd left behind.

"Sir—yes, sir!" shouted Thing, struggling to keep from falling over.

Emmeline hurried after him, wondering what had happened to her ability to look after herself, as Edgar slammed the door shut behind them.

"What 'ave I got myself into?"Thing muttered as
they hurtled down the corridor. "See a young girl, all on
her lonesome, figure she'd be good comp'ny on the way
to Par-ee. Oh, what a great idea *that* turned out t'be."
Emmeline felt the bones in her hand crunching as Thing
tightened his grip on her fingers. He threw her a look, too,
his forehead like a landslide over two angry, piercing eyes.

"What are you staring at me like that for?" said Emmeline. "It's not like any of it is my fault!"

"No? Oh, right. Sorry. Maybe it was another kid they
were searchin' for back there, then. My mistake."

"Oh, leave me alone." Emmeline's feet hurt, and her
head was still ringing from the explosion, and Thing was
going just a little too fast for her liking. "Where are you
taking me, anyway?"

"Somewhere high, or didn't you hear what that feller Edgar said?" They were approaching a corner, and Thing flattened himself and Emmeline up against the wall before peeking out, very carefully, and checking in both directions. Satisfied, he yanked her forward and on they went.

"Yes, I heard," muttered Emmeline, trying to pull her fingers out of Thing's sweaty grip. "That doesn't mean I'm going to *do* it!" Thing whipped his head around to face Emmeline, and they ducked into a wide doorway.

"*What?*"

"Who says I have to explain myself to you? Let me go, will you!"

"No chance. Now tell me what your plan is, seein' as it's bound to be so much better than Edgar's."

"You met him ten seconds ago!" cried Emmeline. "How do you know we can even *trust* him?"

"Well, let's see. First, he saves our lives by draggin' us out of a threatenin' situation. Then he saves our lives by throwin' us out of a threatenin' situation. Then he promises to come an' help later, once the threatenin' situation, the one he saved us from already, is over and done with. Will that do?"

"Well, yes—but how did he even *know* I was on this boat?" said Emmeline, her voice an almost-hiss.

"Well, he . . . *obviously,* he . . ." Thing's words faltered before stopping altogether.

"Exactly. So maybe he's *in on it?*" Emmeline watched Thing's face as this thought settled. After a few seconds he frowned at her, like she was a jigsaw piece he couldn't find a place for.

"You have some serious trust issues, y'know that?"

"I don't see how there's any call for that," Emmeline sniffed, trying to straighten her dress and settle her satchel with her one free hand.

"Explains a lot, actually," mused Thing.

"What is *that* supposed to—"

"Never mind. So, what do we do, eh?"

Emmeline bit her lip as she thought. "I suppose we *could* go to that high place and wait for Edgar there. Be ready for him, if you know what I mean. Take him by surprise and then make him—I don't know. Confess or something."

"Right, yeah. And plan B?"

"We're on a *ship*, Thing," said Emmeline. "It's not like we've got a lot of choice about where to go."

"I wonder where y'learned that one." Thing's eyes grew alert again as he stuck his head out of their hiding place. "Highest place I know of on a ship is the crow's nest, right?"

"This is going to involve climbing, isn't it?" asked Emmeline as they started jogging down the corridor. She couldn't shake the feeling that someone was right behind her. She marveled at how strange her life had become—a couple of days ago she'd thought it was only her careless parents who were a threat to her continued existence. Now, it seemed, *everyone* was giving it their best shot.

"Right. Here y'go," said Thing as they stopped at a steep metal staircase that led, as far as Emmeline could see, up into shadows.

"What's this?" she asked as he shoved her onto the steps, his quick eyes keeping careful watch.

"It's a staircase, isn't it?" he said, only half listening.

"Yes, but where does it *go?*" snapped Emmeline, already three or four steps up, her feet making faint clangs on the treads.

"Jus' get a move on!" said Thing impatiently.

Emmeline reached the top, the sudden coolness of the air like an unexpected breeze. She found herself on the ship's uppermost deck, which was open to a sky filled with dark clouds and going faintly purple around the edges as evening began to set in. The deck appeared to spread out for miles. Gentle lights were spaced regularly along the waist-high railing, and muffled shapes in the growing darkness were probably benches. Most importantly, it looked deserted.

"This way. Come on!" Thing's whisper jerked her out of her thoughts. She turned to follow him, taking a few uncertain steps toward the center of the deck, where, as she'd feared, a very tall, spindly-looking structure was to be found, lashed to the boards by a multitude of wires. A light burned in the small cabin at the top of an extremely narrow ladder, and Emmeline swallowed hard as she stared up at it.

"Ain't got time to waste," muttered Thing, jumping onto the lower rungs. "You follow me, yeah? Or d'you wanna go first?"

Emmeline's stomach rolled over. "You go first," she said. Thing stopped climbing and leaned over the side of the ladder to peer down at her.

"You're not *scared*, are ya?" he asked, coming down a rung or two.

"I don't—I don't like heights, really," said Emmeline, coughing to cover up the tremor in her voice.

"No problem," said Thing cheerfully. "I mean, it's getting so dark up 'ere you can barely tell it's so high." With that, he scampered up the ladder, not even looking where he was putting his feet.

"I don't like the dark, either," muttered Emmeline, wrapping her fingers around the nearest rung and taking three deep breaths, in through her nose and out through her mouth. She nodded and grabbed another, higher rung. She found footholds and started to climb, telling herself that her knees weren't trembling—it was merely the movement of the ship. Slowly, slowly, she pulled herself up.

"Will you shake a blasted leg!" Thing's voice fell on her like a handful of iron filings dropped from a height, trickling all over her skin. She clung to the ladder and allowed the rattle of terror to skitter right through her before she trusted herself to answer.

"I'm coming!" she whispered back, her voice hoarse.

"Yeah, well—come quicker!"

As if his voice had summoned it, a huge, searing light switched on somewhere on the vast deck below. Emmeline froze.

"Ems!" she heard through the pounding of the blood in her ears. "Now, now, *now*! Get up here now!" Fear had made her hands and feet numb, but Emmeline moved.

"Hands, then feet," she muttered, trying to keep calm. "Hands, then feet." The light started to sweep over the deck in great arcs, like it was searching for something.

It *was* searching for something, she finally understood. *Her.*

"Please, Ems! Hurry up!" Thing's voice seemed closer, and she looked up to see him barely hanging off the top few rungs of the ladder like a flower on a long, narrow stem. She could see the anxiety on his face, but his outstretched fingers were just too far away for her to reach.

The light flicked in her direction and finally found her, making her eyes water as she struggled to focus. Thing was yelling at her, and she felt the ladder shudder as he started to descend. Her brain screamed as it tried to understand what was happening. Then something slapped Emmeline's face like a whip, and a weight dragged down her outstretched arm. Almost as if she'd been grabbed by a huge, rough hand, she felt herself being yanked off the ladder, and then, sickeningly, she was *falling* toward the deck far below.

14

"Gotcha!" came a voice, thick with smoke and halitosis. Emmeline landed among a forest of arms and hands, all of which grabbed and held her in a way that made one thing very clear—*there would be no running away.* Through her blurred and streaming eyes, Emmeline saw a net made of thick, coarse rope being lifted away from her and untangled from around her arms and legs. With a heavy thunk it was flung to the side once she was free of it.

"Yer won't need this where you're goin'," said a voice with a cruel laugh in it, and Emmeline felt two quick jerks as someone slashed her satchel away from her back, cutting its short straps without a second thought.

"No! You can't have that! Give it back this instant!" she yelled, trying to aim a kick. Her pulse pounded in her throat as she watched one of the men—she recognized some of them from the group that had attacked the cabin earlier, but most were total strangers—throw her satchel aside as if it were nothing. Distantly she heard something smash, and her heart broke.

"Now, now! A sprightly little thing!" a man laughed, somewhere close. "I'm sure that'll go down well, up north."

"Here! Shut it, Stanley. You know we're supposed to say nowt about that," said another voice, the owner of which currently had his hands around Emmeline's wrists. She felt something tight and very uncomfortable being used to bind them, and before she could cry out in protest, a foul-tasting gag was shoved into her mouth.

"Yes, well, *Harold,* you was told not to name names, yeah?" The man called Stanley was kneeling, very painfully indeed, on Emmeline's outstretched legs as he secured her ankles with another rope. Emmeline fought back a wave of panic as she realized she was totally powerless now—she couldn't run, she couldn't use her hands, and her satchel, which she'd never once in her whole life been without, was lying broken and discarded yards from her head. Her eyes burned.

"Where's the lad?" another voice said. Emmeline looked toward the voice and saw a short, squat man in a woolen hat squinting up into the darkening sky.

"Shall we search for 'im, sir?" A younger man, his foot already on the ladder, looked like he'd relish the chance to get climbing.

"Nah—small fry. We got what we came for. Right,

boys! We're away!" Emmeline saw the younger man re-move his foot from the ladder, looking thunderous, just before she was yanked up off the deck by many hands, none of which were gentle. Then her whole world went topsy-turvy, and she realized she'd been slung over some-one's shoulder.

"*Hmmmmmfff!*" she yelled through her gag as the per-son carrying her started to walk and then to jog away from the ladder, her satchel—and Thing. "*Plliiiffff!*"

"Oh, leave it out, do," snapped someone nearby. "Who d'you think's gonna hear yer? Save yer energy for the voy-age, I would."

The voyage? Where are we going? Red-hot tears started to bathe her eyes, and her nose began to soften. She wiped it on the back of the man carrying her, hoping it left a proper mess. She tried her best to kick at anyone and anything she could reach, but very quickly she felt a hand burrow into her hair, its fingernails scratching her scalp. The man carrying her slowed to a walk, and her head was jerked up, painfully. Emmeline saw another man in front of her, skinny, pale as moonlight, his eyes hidden in shadow over high, sharp cheekbones. He had a face that was full of folds and creases, and his strangely flabby lips looked overlicked.

"You will behave," the pale man said in a voice that made her feel like she'd swallowed a bucket of ice water. "You will behave like a lady, and not like a hooligan. Do you hear me? One more kick, Miss Widget, and we will fling you overboard, where the sharks can enjoy snacking on your flesh. Do you understand me?" Emmeline closed her eyes, a single scalding tear sneaking down her cheek. "Good," said the man, releasing her.

"Are we ready?" called the pale man, striding away from Emmeline.

"Aye, aye, sir!" came the reply. There were too many voices to keep track of.

Emmeline felt a strong, cold breeze blowing across her face. It smelled like salt, and it smelled of large, open spaces, and it smelled of all the fresh air in the world. The man carrying her slung her off his shoulder and thumped her onto the deck, where Emmeline saw she was right at the edge of the ship. Her head clanked off the metal railing as she stared straight down into the roaring sea below.

Into the roaring sea, where a brightly lit vessel sat waiting.

It was smaller than the passenger ship, of course, but that still made it the second-biggest boat Emmeline had ever seen. She squeezed her eyes shut again as she thought about what was likely to happen next.

What if they drop me, what if I fall, what if a rope breaks, what if the person carrying me has, I don't know, a heart attack or something?... She yelped when she felt hands going around her, securing her in some sort of harness, pulling straps taut and fixing buckles securely. She thought, for a panicked second, about Thing, wondering whether he'd been hurt. *What if that young, impatient sailor decided to disobey orders after all?*...

"Make 'er ready!" yelled a voice, and Emmeline felt herself lifted up and over the railing. She felt the world like a huge, dark vacuum all around her, star-speckled above and sea-foamed below. She screamed into the gag, but it made no difference whatsoever. Very few ears could hear her, and those that could didn't care.

"Heave!" yelled someone else, and Emmeline fell. It happened so quickly that she didn't have time to scream again. Before she'd even reached the bottom, the men had started their own descent, rappelling down the side of the ship using wires and ropes, as silently as ghosts. Within a couple of minutes they were all gone, and the top deck was completely deserted. The only things visible were a discarded net, a damaged satchel, and a lot of empty space.

"*Whoop*," said a small voice, loud in the silence.

With shaky hands and trembling knees, Thing emerged from the crow's nest. It took him a long time to make it all the way down the ladder, because he kept missing the rungs. His feet seemed numb and clumsy, and they didn't want to work properly. Eventually he stood over Emmeline's battered satchel, wondering whether there was anything inside it that could help her and if he even had permission to touch it.

After a few minutes he bent down, picked it up, and held it close to his chest. Then he wiped his nose on his grubby sleeve and, satchel and all, started running helter-skelter for the stairs, hoping he could remember the way back.

15

"**Whoop! It—whoop—was so fast I—whoop!—I** couldn't—"

"Yes, yes—that's fine. Just calm down, please, won't you?"

"But we can't—*whoop*—jus' calm down! They've *taken* 'er! Or don't you—*whoop*—understand what kidnappin' actually *means*?"

"Look, Thing—is Thing your name?—you're not going to be able to help Emmeline if you suffocate to death. All right? Now calm down. I mean it. Get your breath, and then tell us everything you remember." Thing nodded, trying to get his thoughts in order. He was still clutching Emmeline's satchel to himself and had refused to let it go. The severed straps, hanging like broken arms at either side of it, reminded him how important it was to get Emmeline back and return her most treasured possession, as soon as possible.

"Right. Well—*whoop*—we were climbin', right, up to the crow's nest, like you said, when some fellas—*whoop*—lots of 'em, just sort of *appeared,* yeah, and they turned this big *light* thing on, and they used it to—*whoop*—find us."

"A light? What sort of light?" Edgar's voice was calm, despite his obvious pain. He'd been slashed with a knife, and Sasha had done her best to patch him up, but there wasn't time for a proper job. He glanced over at his companion, whose every muscle was tense, listening to Thing.

"Dunno—a searchlight, I s'pose. Big round thing. Swiveled." Thing demonstrated swiveling with his free hand, just in case they hadn't gotten the picture.

"Okay, that's fine. So, then what happened? In your own time." Sasha's words were quiet and calm, but her eyes flashed and her lips were drawn thin.

"The blokes kept the light on Ems, yeah, and then they flung up some sort of—*whoop*—net or somethin', and they, like, *dragged* her off the ladder." Thing made a sucking sound with his mouth as he showed them, with a hand movement, exactly how Emmeline had fallen. "They caught her, and then they tied 'er up, and they took *this* away from 'er." He gestured toward the satchel. "Then they carried 'er to the edge and just chucked 'er off."

"Chuck—chucked her *off?*" repeated Sasha. "Are you sure?"

"Sure as I am that you're all a bunch of—*whoop*— blockheads who can't understand plain English," muttered Thing.

"Did she scream? Cry out? Anything?"

"Nah. Tough as nails, is Ems." Thing blinked hard, trying to focus on the battered leather satchel. A few loose threads were fraying around one of its corners, and he pulled at them until he was pretty sure his eyes weren't going to leak and he could look up again. "So—what's the story with all this?" He looked first at Edgar and then at Sasha. "I mean, why's everyone after Emmeline? What's she done? She's only a kid, ain't she?"

"It's not really something we can share, Thing," said Edgar in a low, dark voice. "She—or, rather, her *parents* are . . . well . . ." He paused, finding a new angle to begin from. "The men who took Emmeline have probably been paid to bring her somewhere." Edgar's words ended in a pained hiss. He clenched his teeth and grunted, his good hand flying up to the wound in his shoulder.

"You all right?" asked Thing.

"I'll live. Now, can you tell us anything you remember about the men? What they looked like, sounded like, how many there were?"

"Right." Thing closed his eyes and did his best to remember. A dim and indistinct picture started to form in his mind—men with bald heads, men with hats, stout and skinny men, all shouting. "There were a lot of 'em. I can't say how many. It was hard to see from where I were perched, you know? With the light, an' all?"

"Of course," soothed Sasha. "But please—you must try." Thing screwed his brain into a knot.

"There was one guy," he said, a memory coming to the surface like a rising bubble. "Tall, skinny fella, hair all slicked to one side, an' skin so pale he looked dead, y'know the sort. Either he was wearin' dark glasses or he had the oddest eyes I've ever seen."

"Were they sort of sunken, would you say?" Edgar asked.

"Yeah," Thing said. "Like they were sittin' in two carved-out holes in 'is head or somethin'." The memory made his head swim.

"No," whispered Sasha. Thing was vaguely aware of her putting her hands to her face. He stopped talking, his throat suddenly dry as his mind began to spiral. He realized his heart was thudding inside his chest, and the dirty, greasy smell that sometimes haunted his nightmares slithered over him. A raspy, long-forgotten voice began to scratch at the edges of his hearing, its cruel words seeping into him like poison, but he gritted his teeth and shoved it firmly away.

"What is it?" he asked, trying to clear his thoughts and pay attention to Edgar and Sasha.

"It's the worst we could've expected," said Edgar.

Emmeline had never been so cold, or so cramped, in her life. As well as that, her stomach was churning inside her, both with queasiness and a deep, bone-grinding hunger. She thought longingly of the ice cream that Thing had brought to her window. It seemed like ten million years since she'd seen him, but in reality it could only have been a few hours.

I hope you're all right, she told him inside her mind. *I hope you found help, and that you've gone to the captain and that he turned the ship around to follow me....* Hot tears bubbled up under her closed lids as she realized that whatever Thing had managed to do, it most certainly did not involve persuading the captain to pursue her. For a start, how would he know where to go? The ocean was vast, and the ship Emmeline was now being held captive in was tiny by comparison. It would be like looking for a teardrop in a lake.

"Well, well!" A voice burst into Emmeline's thoughts as a trapdoor into her tiny, frozen prison was lifted. Outside she could see cold, sparkling stars and windblown spray, and the sound of raucous laughter trickled in through the gap. "Everythin' all right in here with you, Your Ladyship?"

"I—please! I need . . ." But the man was already gone. The trapdoor clacked back into place, muffling his laughter as he replaced the padlock. They had been doing this at regular intervals, Emmeline realized—looking in to check whether she was alive, and conscious, but not actually giving her anything. She was desperately thirsty.

She tried to settle into a corner, doing her best to keep herself warm. *Think of fires, and sunshine, and hot soup,* she told herself. *Think yourself warm!* After a few minutes of this, however, she had to give up. Thinking about warm things was only making her feel colder—and she was starting to see her breath in the air like a tiny cloud, so she knew she wasn't imagining it. Inside her prison she was freezing.

She hoped they'd get wherever they were going before she'd never be warm again.

16

"You *ain't* leavin' me behind!" Thing's teeth were set, and his eyes glittered. He clutched Emmeline's satchel to his skinny chest like it was a lump of gold. "I ain't lettin' ya!"

"Look, Thing, we can't bring you with us. You have to understand." Sasha was busily folding up some sort of map, so big that it would have covered a wall. Thing couldn't read well enough to understand what was written on it, but a strange symbol near the top of the sheet caught his attention. It was like a large round eye with several wiggly lines that made him think of legs or tentacles coming out of it, and it was surrounded on all sides by a vast field of white. Something about it drew his gaze but made him want to look away at the same time.

"All I understand is that the only friend of the kid

you're tryin' to save isn't allowed to be part of rescuin' her," said Thing, dragging his eyes away from the map and renewing his grip on the satchel. "I can help, y'know! She trusts me!"

"She doesn't trust anyone, Thing," said Sasha, making one final fold in the map. She slid it off the table and into a large case, along with several others, then buckled the case closed. "She's been raised not to trust anyone, not even her own parents. They thought—for better or worse—that bringing her up like that would keep her safe." She shook her head and muttered something Thing couldn't hear.

"But she—she *saved* me, from that man. . . ."

Sasha turned to Thing, her eyes softening as she grasped him gently by the upper arms. "I'm not trying to hurt your feelings, you know. I'm sure Emmeline likes you well enough, but you're not her friend. So why don't you go home and forget about all this, and let us take care of it from here."

Thing grimaced at Sasha's words. "Well, if you can't bring me with you, will you at least tell me where you're goin'?"

"No. I can't," said Sasha, straightening up and releasing her grip on Thing's arms.

"Does it 'ave anythin' to do with that weird eye thing on the map?" said Thing, hazarding a guess.

"What do you know about that?" Sasha stood perfectly still, and Thing didn't think he was imagining the look of fear in her eyes.

"Oh, you know," Thing said, thinking as he spoke. "Only what Ems told me."

"Don't be ridiculous," said Sasha. "Emmeline is completely ignorant of anything to do with that map."

"Sure about that, are ya?"

"Yes," said Sasha, swallowing hard.

"Interestin'," said Thing. Just then Edgar came back into the room. Sasha had cleaned and rebandaged his shoulder. His color was back, and there was a sparkle in his eye.

"Are you ready?" he asked Sasha. "We'll be docking within the hour, and we won't have time to waste. We'll need to get to—oh. Hello," he said, finally noticing Thing. "What are you still doing here?" He smiled down at him, and only his restless fingers gave away his impatience.

"I were just tellin' Sasha 'ere about Emmeline and the wavy eye," he said, straightening his back. "Nothin' important."

"Emmeline and the *what*?" Edgar said, glancing up at Sasha.

"The sun is warm," said Sasha cryptically.

"But there is ice on the breeze," Edgar finished, blinking.

"Er—right," said Thing into the silence that followed this strange exchange. "Anyway. We was discussin' my role in the rescuin' of Emmeline, actually, just as you so rudely barged in."

"Your role?" said Sasha, shaking herself out of whatever dream she'd been in. "You don't *have* a role!"

"That's not what this says." Thing nodded down at the satchel in his hands.

"That's nothing! That's simply Emmeline's *bag*—her tricks, her gimmicks, her . . . her little means of making herself feel safe!" Sasha frowned, throwing her hands up in the air.

"Yeah, that," agreed Thing, remembering the vast sheet of white on the map. The odd words Sasha and Edgar had exchanged settled quietly into his brain too. "And also some very interestin' stuff about . . . ice." He felt his way into the next thought, very carefully. "Ice, and stuff what lives in it." Sasha's eyes opened wide, like someone had slapped her on the back.

"Are you—do you *even*—what are you talking about?"

"Guess you'll have to bring me along. It's far too much to explain here," said Thing with a sniff.

"But—what about your parents? Your family?" asked Edgar. "Won't they worry?"

Thing shrugged, shaking his head. "Shouldn't think anyone's worried about me for four, five years."

Edgar blinked. "How old *are* you?"

"Not sure, exacly. 'Bout twelve, or thereabouts." He saw Edgar and Sasha share a look.

"Well—all right. *If* we bring you—and it's only an if— will you tell us everything that Emmeline discussed with you?" Edgar's words had sharp edges.

"Yeah, yeah," said Thing, his heart beginning to race again. Despite this, he kept his voice low and bored, and even chanced a yawn. "Whatever. Just let me come, yeah? I'll be useful. Swear."

"Fine," said Sasha. "Come. But I'm not taking responsibility for you."

"Suits me," said Thing, who didn't know what it felt
like to have someone else take responsibility for him.
"Now. Finally. Will someone tell me where we're goin'?"

It seemed that hours were passing in Emmeline's prison,
but she had no way of knowing how many. All she knew
was that the cold was growing stronger, like a wild animal
getting more and more enraged. It had started nipping
at her a long time ago, taking bites of her warmth away,
devouring it until Emmeline was left with nothing but
her bare bones. Beside her lay an empty dish, which had
been half filled with warm, porridgy gruel a while back—
Emmeline had eaten it, but it hadn't helped to take away
the gnawing inside. She was in a constant state of half
sleep, never sure if what she was seeing or hearing was
real, or dredged up out of the depths of her mind.

Vaguely she heard a clatter and felt a gust of bitter cold
wind on her face.

"Girl! Look lively down there. The boss wants to
speak to ya." Emmeline didn't reply because the words
didn't seem to make any sense. She was feeling tired and
just wanted to sleep. If she could only sleep, everything
would be all right. . . .

"Woo-hoo! Girlie! Wakey, wakey!" Emmeline didn't
hear this, and so she didn't move. "Here—she's not doin'
anythin'. Give us a hand with this, will ya?" One of the

men dropped down into Emmeline's compartment, catching his breath at how cold it was. For a split second he gazed at Emmeline's small form—her bare legs beneath her grubby dress, her light jacket that didn't even fasten properly—and shivered inside his heavy winter coat.

"Get 'er up here!" called a voice from above, snapping the man out of his thoughts. Quickly he bent and picked Emmeline up, and within a few seconds she'd been handed out through the trapdoor. Her skin was ice-cold to the touch, and her eyes were firmly fixed shut. The bits of her skin that could be seen were a uniform gray, and her breathing was shallow.

"This is *your* fault, y'know," one of the men barked at another. "If you hadn't insisted on getting started with that card game, we'd never have forgotten to check on the kid."

"My fault? That's rich! Whose idea was it to put her in there in the first place? I believe—and correct me if I'm wrong—that it was *yours!*"

"Now look here—" began the other man, his face reddening, but he never got to finish his sentence.

"If one of you fools doesn't get that child covered up and warm this *instant,* you'll all be forcibly unshipped in Newfoundland without a stitch of clothing." Nobody moved. "And I will not be paying any of you so much as a red cent." Instantly someone grabbed a blanket and wrapped Emmeline snugly in it while someone else started warming up a pot of soup. A third dispatched himself to find warm clothing, and a fourth threw a few sticks into the furnace. Gradually the pink began to creep back into

Emmeline's face, and her eyes started to move, ever so slowly, behind her eyelids.

"Gentlemen. I want you all to feel for this child as though she were your own," announced the pale-faced man, looking around at his tattooed, gap-toothed crew. "On second thought, actually, I will say this: I'd like you all to feel for this child as though she were the treasured only daughter of your *employer*—for that's how precious she is to me, boys—and I want you all to know that whatever harm comes to her will be revisited upon your own persons, times ten. Am I clear?" The listening men stood to attention, each of them focused utterly on the weird, pale-skinned man who'd convinced them to come north. "At this time of year?" some of them had scoffed. "He must be mad!" But he'd shown them all the color of his money, and, one by one, they'd caved.

And now here they were.

"As ice, sir," said one. "Clear as ice."

"Wonderful," he replied. "Don't disturb me again until she wakes."

17

Emmeline wondered why someone was squeez-ing her head. It seemed like a pair of iron-strong hands were wrapped right around her skull, and whoever owned those hands was taking great delight in prodding her, repeatedly, in the temples. A tiny crack of light was just seeping in between her closed eyelids, and her mouth felt like she'd swallowed a pint of liquid nitrogen.

"Aaargh," she said.

"Quite," came the slippery reply. "Glad to see you're awake finally." Emmeline's tummy dropped down to her toes when she recognized the voice as that of the pale-faced man, and she concentrated on breathing, slowly and calmly, as her insides bobbed back up to their accustomed place.

"Where?" she croaked. "Who?"

"Excellent questions," he replied. "To which we shall return later. But first I need to know one or two small details. I'm sure you understand." Emmeline forced her eyes open, and a lancing pain howled through her head. She winced, and her eyes slid closed again as she tried not to cry out. "Don't move, or do anything strenuous, just yet," said the man. "You've been rather unwell for the last few hours, and I'm sure it will take your body some time to recover fully. All right?" Emmeline said nothing in reply. She was too busy trying to force her brain to stop hurting.

"Want to go home," she said, even though she didn't really. In books that was usually what people said when they were kidnapped, so she felt she should stick with protocol.

"Well, I'm afraid that won't be happening," replied the man. "Now. Before we begin, is there anything you need?"

"To go home!" croaked Emmeline.

"And they said you were such an *intelligent* girl," sighed Pale Face. "It appears to me as though you have a distinct difficulty in understanding what perfectly rational adults are saying to you."

"Water," said Emmeline eventually. She hated giving in, but her whole body was beginning to feel like she'd been placed in a tub of salt to dry out. Pale Face snapped his fingers, and Emmeline heard someone leaving the room.

"You will cooperate with me, young lady." The words sounded uncomfortably close. Emmeline jerked away from the sudden warmth of Pale Face's breath on her skin, her eyes flying open. She was finding it hard to focus still, but there he was, standing over her like a bad dream. She pulled the blanket she was wrapped in a little more tightly around herself. *What a horrible man,* she thought in a small, calm voice that came from deep inside her. *Maybe when I get a chance, I can get to my satchel and ...* But then she remembered, and despite her best efforts, a tear broke loose.

Just then a sailor entered the room with a metal tankard in one hand and a deep bowl with a wide brim in the other, both of which he thrust at Emmeline. She stared up at him—his face was mostly beard.

"If ye don't fancy self-service, I'll happily pour it over yer head," said the sailor after a second or two. Hastily Emmeline wriggled free of her blanket and took hold of the handle of the frigid tankard. She grabbed the lip of the bowl with her other hand and carefully settled it on the arm of her chair. The soup inside it was far too hot to eat; great gusts of steam rose from its surface. She gazed at the spoon that had been placed in it, marveling at how it was managing not to melt. The smell radiating from the bowl reminded her a little of wet wild boar, but anything was better than being too weak to run.

She took a sip of the contents of the tankard, squashing back a thought about how easy it was to hide certain poisons in water, and then poured the rest down her throat anyhow. She felt the water traveling to every inch of her body, filling her up. It was cold but good. For a few seconds she didn't even care about the pale-faced man, but he insisted on making his presence felt again.

"Now. Are you quite ready?"

Emmeline nodded. She placed the empty tankard down on the side of the chair, within easy reach. *There's a fishing rod on the wall over the door,* whispered her inner voice. *A storm lantern on the table. Possibly knives in the drawer, over there.* She wished she could turn and see what was behind her, but concentrated instead on looking small, tired, and cold.

"Wonderful. Now. First things first. How much have your parents told you about their most recent project?" The man settled himself into a chair right in front of Emmeline. His eerily white face, creased like melted candle wax hanging from his protruding cheekbones, wobbled as he leaned forward. He propped his elbows on his thighs, and his dark eyes, deep in their cavernous sockets, gazed at her. Emmeline just stared back at him. Parts of her body were starting to tingle painfully as she warmed up. Soon, she thought, she'd be able to move. Maybe she could find somewhere to barricade herself, even. She pressed herself back into her chair, trying to remember to keep breathing, calm and steady.

"My parents?" she said. "If you knew them at all, you'd know they have never, not once in my entire life, *ever* told me anything about what they do. Why would they?" Emmeline fought to keep her head from spinning and tried to tighten herself up even smaller.

"What do you take me for?"

"Well—" Emmeline began.

"Enough insolence," Pale Face muttered, cutting her off. "You will need to learn how to mind your manners if you're to survive long enough to be of use to me, young lady."

"Mind my manners?" said Emmeline, while her brain yelled, *Survive? What's he talking about, survive?*

"You're certainly not what I expected—no, not at all. But then, it hardly matters." Emmeline said nothing in response but just tried to soak up everything she could until—hopefully—it would start to make some sense. The man shifted slightly in his chair, leaning a little to his left, but his eyes stayed on her the whole time. "Now. Can you guess, my little Emmeline, where we are going?"

Frowning, Emmeline looked past Pale Face and noticed large windows at the cabin's far end that gave way to a view out over an icy sea. *It's cold. We're traveling very fast. There are icebergs on the horizon. The sky is a funny color.* She bit her lower lip. *We're going north, aren't we? But there's nothing up here but ice and emptiness.* Her thoughts lined up quietly, in an orderly if meaningless queue, and her frown deepened.

"We have much work to do, you and I," said the man in a voice that made Emmeline's whole body shrink. "Much work, and not much time."

18

"Y'know, I didn't volunteer to come along just so you could make me into a packhorse," grumbled Thing. He was bent almost double under a large map-carrying case balanced across his shoulders, and Emmeline's satchel, which was looped over his body by its single remaining shoulder strap, slapped against his side with every step.

"Everyone has to pull their weight," replied Edgar, his eyes on the milling crowd. It was a bright morning, and Paris gleamed before them. Edgar had changed into a clean suit, and Sasha had swapped her stained pants for a dark gown, gathered at the waist, beneath a perfectly respectable overcoat. Both of them still wore their white flowers.

"You appear remark'bly unencumbered, if I might say," muttered Thing. Edgar's wounded arm was now in a sling, and he looked a little better. *Strong enough to be carryin' somethin'*, Thing's thoughts said in a mutinous tone.

"I'm injured, remember? Now just pay attention. We have to try to get off this ship without causing too much of a commotion."

"Why . . ." Thing got a better grip on the map case, which was threatening to slip. He had an idea that if its contents spilled out all over the deck, Edgar would personally throw him overboard. "Why would there be a commotion?"

"Destroying a first-class suite can have that effect," said Edgar. "Particularly one you haven't paid for."

"You 'aven't paid? 'Ow did you even get on board, then?" asked Thing, impressed.

"I might have bamboozled the ticket seller with some rusty Russian and a story about being the czar's cousin, and how the bill would be settled in gemstones once we docked," murmured Sasha. "I don't think that story will work too well on the captain." Thing grinned, and Sasha couldn't help but return it.

The gangway wasn't far ahead of them now. They were hanging back as much as they could, but the motion of the crowd was gradually drawing them on, step by tiny step. Thing looked up to see people queuing politely, waiting their turn to step onto the swaying plank that would lead them from the ship to the quayside. At the other end was a gaily colored tent, complete with ribbons on flagpoles and a trumpeting brass band, where the passengers would go to retrieve their luggage, settle their bills, and personally shake hands with the ship's officers.

"We need to dodge that tent," muttered Edgar. Sasha, a few feet ahead of him, turned and nodded, a worried look in her eyes.

Thing was suddenly seized by an idea. "Here," he said, thrusting the map case at Sasha. "Hold this—just fer a minute."

"Thing—wait! What are you . . . ," Sasha called, but Thing was already gone.

We need to cause a diversion, Thing thought, his mind abuzz. *And what better way to do that than by threatenin' the safety an' well-bein' of some very expensive belongin's?*

Quick as a flash, Thing yanked the sable he'd stolen from the rich lady's cabin out from the front of his over-alls. It was a bit less glossy now than it had been when he first liberated it, but it still looked all right and—he took a quick sniff—smelled acceptable. Before anyone had time to react, he flung it over the head of a passing woman.

"What is it? Get it off me! *Getitoffme!*" she screamed at top volume. There were several shrieks as people turned to see what was causing the noise.

Thing cupped his hands around his mouth. "Thief!" he yelled in a voice that sounded nothing like his own and that was guaranteed to carry.

"Oh, my days! Didn't Lady Cunningham report a sable missing from her stateroom?" said a woman nearby, her words dripping with glee. "That *must* be it!"

"I believe it is! Oh, how thrilling!" said another, her bosom heaving with enough gems to make Thing's pulse start to quicken, though he squashed down his urges to relieve her of a few of her golden burdens. Their shouts of delight, and the resulting hullabaloo, made it easy for Thing to slip away unnoticed into the throng.

"Hello? Hello, I say! We've apprehended a villain!" The ladies grasped hold of Thing's poor victim, now shuddering beneath the sable. Several men, looking serious and official with their top hats and very impressive mustaches, stepped forward.

"That's quite all right, ladies—now if you would just release the miscreant—"

"I am not a miscreant!" came a muffled wail from underneath the fur. "This has all been an enormous mistake!"

"Are you calling me a *liar,* madam?" asked one of the accusing ladies, drawing back her head as though she'd been struck across the face. Two little red patches bloomed on either side of her nose.

"No! No, of course not! I'm merely saying—" But the lady's protests were drowned out by a shriek, of almost superhuman volume, from somewhere near the front of the crowd.

"Clarence!" it yelled. "My *sable!"*

Well, that did it. Hundreds of heads turned to see what was happening, and hundreds of feet started to move in the direction of the scandal—away from the side of the ship. Thing danced nimbly through the uproarious crowd, landing back in front of Edgar and Sasha with a huge grin plastered over his grubby face.

"Now'd be an excellent time to be makin' good our escape, don't ya think?"

Edgar closed his open mouth and shook his head.

"Come on, then," he said, thrusting the map case back at Thing. "We've no time to lose, right?"

"Right," muttered Thing, shouldering the case once again and setting off after Edgar and Sasha as fast as he could.

"My parents are *zoologists*," said Emmeline. She'd lost count of how often Pale Face had asked her the same question and she'd given him the same answer. "That's all! Scientists. I don't know anything else. They're always away, giving lectures or going to conferences or—I don't know. Discovering things or whatever."

"And did you ever meet any of their colleagues? Read any of their papers? Discuss any of their work over dinner, even?" The pale-faced man was no longer as pale as before—a light flush of color was just barely touching his cheeks.

"No. No. And no," she said. "Really. Honestly. I don't know anything. You've wasted all this time and energy kidnapping me—for nothing!" She flung herself back into her chair and stuck out her lower lip as far as it would go.

"Enough of that silly pouting," snapped the man. "It's tiresome."

"Well, aren't you going to let me go?" she said, knowing that it was hopeless.

"Don't be ridiculous. Even if I did, what good would it do you? Look around!" Emmeline didn't need to, but she did anyway. Nothing but icy rocks and a freezing sea lay outside the boat, and she shivered as she wondered where on earth they could be going.

"If I mentioned OSCAR to you, what would it mean?" said the man out of the blue. His voice was as smooth as melted chocolate. Emmeline, yanked out of her thoughts, didn't have a chance to stop herself from opening her eyes wide and taking in a small but very audible gasp.

"What? I—what? I've never heard of it. I don't know what you mean. Don't know what you're even talking about!" She bit her tongue, but she knew it was too late. The image of her father's business card, held in Watt's gloved fingers, bloomed painfully in her mind. OSCAR, she thought. *Dad would've known.*

"Well, well. Now, isn't that interesting," Pale Face crooned.

Emmeline took a deep breath and wondered how big a mistake she'd just made.

"Sorry!" said Thing again as he bumped the map case off someone's head. The grumbling all around him didn't stop, and everywhere he looked, eyes daggered into him. He'd found the map case almost impossible to manage while they were struggling through the slippery streets of Paris, and trying to keep it under control here, in a cramped Metro carriage, wasn't very much better.

"Just put it down, will you?" said Sasha, grabbing the case from Thing and propping it against a wall. "You're going to get us thrown off!"

"How much longer're we goin' to be?" Thing said, rolling his aching shoulders in relief.

Edgar frowned, looking up at the map above the carriage door. "Another five stops—so not long."

"Brilliant. And what's the plan then?"

"Well, Madame Blancheflour will instruct us further," said Edgar. "We'll probably have to gather whomever we can and equip ourselves for the journey, purchase appropriate clothes and gear, sort out our travel arrangements—" He stopped suddenly as Thing held up a still-grubby hand.

"Wait, wait, wait," he said, his eyes burning. "Are you tellin' me we're not goin' *straight* to where Emmeline is, right now? That we'll be faffin' around buyin' one another fancy underpants for the next—what? Week? Two weeks? I'm not havin' that, my friend. No way."

"But—Thing! You don't understand—"

"I don't understand? I'm the one who saw 'er bein' *taken!* I understand plenty!" Thing's voice rose with every word. The rest of the carriage's occupants began to tut and mutter under their breath again, and Thing felt their disapproval washing over him.

Thing squeezed his eyes shut. His thoughts filled with sharp whispers, the kind that often came threaded through his fear, and that he couldn't bear to listen to. They clawed at the inside of his skull, but he drove them back with the image of Emmeline's face. He opened his eyes again and glared at Edgar and Sasha in turn. "None of you *get* it, do yer? She's only a *kid,* out there on 'er own, and I ain't leavin' 'er!"

"*Mon Dieu,*" muttered a gentleman nearby, throwing a disgusted look at them. His companion, a lady wearing pince-nez, blinked slowly as she took them in from head to toe, looking at them as though they intended to set the carriage on fire, or worse.

"So much for keeping a low profile," muttered Sasha as the train clattered on.

✳

"Now. Let's have a little chat about OSCAR. All right, Emmeline?"

"I don't know what you're talking about!" *Where's that tankard gone? It had a good, sharp edge to it! Heavy, too! If I threw it just right—*

"Lying is pointless, my girl. A person cannot hide genuine shock, genuine horror. At least, not a person like *you.*" Emmeline wanted to scratch at the man's gloating face.

"Why should I tell you anything? I don't even know where I am, or who you are!"

"Who I am is probably the least interesting thing about me," Pale Face replied, extending his fingers and peering intently at his nails. "What is far more important is what I do. What *drives* me, perhaps."

"And what's that, then?" Emmeline shoved her hands into the blanket, in case the man saw them shaking. He looked at her, smiling knowingly.

"Why, *life,* girl. Eternal life, to be exact. Eternal life, complete power, and total control—three things that nestle together perfectly. I'm on a quest to find these things, you see. A *noble* quest, one might even say, if one were so inclined. I have been on this quest for many years, and I am close enough now to my prize that I can smell it."

Emmeline frowned as she listened. "That's ridiculous," she said after a few empty seconds. She felt she was standing quite firmly on the bedrock of science as she spoke. "Nothing lives forever. Besides in stories, I mean. It's impossible otherwise. You're wasting your time."

"Oh, you think so?" said Pale Face, turning his attention back to his fingernails. "How uninformed you are."

"I *beg* your pardon, but—"

Pale Face moved quickly, leaning forward once more. Emmeline forced herself to sit perfectly still. "If eternal life is so *scientifically* impossible, my dear girl, then why is your parents' research so closely tied up with it? Hmm? Care to explain that one, little Miss Know-It-All?"

"M-my parents' research?" said Emmeline. "What do you mean?"

"Your parents and their colleagues at OSCAR and indeed your precious Madame Blancheflour and her merry band of thugs, have worked *very* hard to keep me from my reward. But now that I have you? Well. That changes the game. That changes *everything*." He licked his lips quickly with an oddly dark tongue. Emmeline shuddered at how it left them glistening, like a slug had passed over them. *Another one who knows this Madame Blancheflour,* she thought. *How odd.*

"What *game*? I don't understand!"

"The race to the center of the ice, child," said Pale Face. "Where the power I seek lies sleeping, simply waiting to wake."

Emmeline jerked as the voice of the sailor who'd tried to kidnap her in Edgar and Sasha's cabin rang in her head again. *It'll all be open water soon,* he'd said. *When it wakes...*

She blinked and stared at Pale Face's hooded eyes, and he stared steadily back.

20

Thing's arms rattled with exhaustion.

"Why couldn't they 'ave built this blimmin' city somewhere a bit flatter, eh?" His voice was a strangled gasp.
They were trudging up yet another flight of stone steps.
Paris seemed full of them, and Edgar and Sasha appeared
to be making sure they paid a visit to every one.

"Here, give the case to me," said Sasha. "Or at least let
me carry the satchel. I won't offer again, you know."

"No way," wheezed Thing. He'd begun to take this
case-carrying lark as a personal challenge, and he wasn't
about to let it beat him now. And as for handing over
Emmeline's satchel? Laughable. "We mus' be nearly there,
yeah?"

"Not far now," said Edgar from up ahead. He carried
one smallish case with his good arm, and Sasha was laden

down with several valises of her own. Thing was beginning to wish he'd been stabbed too.

"I cannot wait for a hot bath," muttered Sasha. Her face was reddened with cold, and the hem of her gown was filthy.

"Will there be food and things? When we get there?" Thing asked. His stomach was painfully aware of how long it had been since his stolen breakfast of pastry, which he'd shared—his heart lurched—with Emmeline. As for the trifle he'd been about to dig into right before the attack in the suite . . . he'd managed to get only the merest taste before he'd had bigger things, like running for his life, to worry about.

"Let's hope so," replied Sasha as they turned another corner and entered yet another anonymous, cobbled, frost-flecked street.

"This is it," said Edgar, turning back to face them. "Rue du Démiurge. Excellent!"

"Hope it's not a long'un," said Thing, his feet pounding and raw inside his ill-fitting, thin-soled shoes. The wind was rummaging through his clothing like a pick-pocket looking for a payday.

"Well . . . ," said Edgar, looking up at the house numbers. A cloud passed over his face, and he started chewing on the inside of his mouth.

"You're about to tell me we're at the wrong end of the street, ain't ya," said Thing.

"Sorry," he said. "It's been a while since my last visit."

"Nothing for it," muttered Sasha.

On they trudged, the cold evening gathering around them.

"You're not going to get anything out of me!" said Emmeline, wondering why her teeth insisted on chattering. "I'm not going to tell you a *thing* about OSCAR."

"Really? I rather imagine that's because you don't *know* a thing about it," remarked Pale Face.

"You can imagine what you like," retorted Emmeline. "But you'll never find out the truth, will you? I could know *everything*, but I'm not going to say a word, no matter what you do." She took a chance then, feeling like she was throwing a stone down a well to hear how long it would take it to hit the bottom. "As soon as my parents discover what you've done, they'll come after you, anyway. You just wait." She squished back tears, hoping that the man didn't know—how *could* he know?—that her parents were . . . that they were . . .

"Your parents?" The man laughed, a hollow sound like a barrel being rolled down a rocky hill. "Your *parents,* my girl, are the reason you're here." Emmeline said nothing as this clanged around inside her, and the man shook his head slowly, like she was something to be pitied. "Why—you poor little thing! You didn't think they were actually *dead,* did you? Oh, no! How sad." He pulled his lips tight in what Emmeline supposed he meant to be a smile, but which instead made him look like an animal in pain. "No, you'll soon be with them again, never fear. I've kept them for you—not exactly *safe,* I'd say, but they're alive, all right. Or they were, the last I heard. They weren't terribly forthcoming with the information I required either. I see

114

now where you learned your helpful, obliging ways." Pale Face's deep black eyes twinkled, but not in a nice way.

"You're the one," said Emmeline, feeling like a gear was slowly turning inside her mind. "*You're* the one who kidnapped them."

"I certainly arranged it, yes," Pale Face replied, shrugging.

"But—where did you put them? Where are they?"

"Right where I need them, of course!" Pale Face sat back, flicking one leg over the other with a deft movement. "They're in the ice, my dear. *Deep* within it, if my orders have been followed. They've resisted helping me bring my plans to fruition up to now, but I think when they see you, they might change their minds. Not that it matters much, one way or the other," he continued with a soft sigh. "Once I have what I want, you'll all be together again." He turned his unsettling eyes back to Emmeline and gazed at her. "Forever."

Emmeline's whole body—every cell, every hair, every drop of blood—trembled as she stared back at him.

***

"Two twenty-two . . . twenty-three . . . We're here! Look! Two twenty-four rue du Démiurge. Finally." Edgar's voice was like that of a little boy opening his birthday presents. Thing's feet felt like they were bleeding. He'd been walking on willpower alone for the past ten minutes.

"It looks a bit—*dark*, doesn't it?" said Sasha, dropping her cases onto the bottom step. She grabbed handfuls of her skirts and hopped up, peering at the house. "Are you sure we're still using this building?"

"I haven't heard anything to the contrary," replied Edgar, gazing at the house with puzzled eyes.

"Gosh. Things must be bad for the Order if this is what Madame is reduced to."

"If you pair've dragged me up 'ere for nothin', I am *warnin'* ya—" But Thing's dire threat was interrupted by a curtain being twitched in one of the tall, unlit windows beside the large front door. Whether a face looked out through the glass, Thing could not have said. His entire focus was on the door, willing it to open, and for there to be food beyond it.

"Shhh! Thing. Show a bit of respect," Edgar whispered. "And get up here." Every muscle stiff and cracking, Thing clambered up two of the three steps and stuck fast, his feet unprepared to move another inch.

Before he could ask whether it would be all right, finally, to put the blasted map case down, the door shook as someone struggled to wrench it open from the inside.

"Just a moment!" called Edgar. Gritting his teeth, he set his good shoulder against the wood and pushed as hard as he could. Sasha hurried up to the door and leaned in beside him, heaving for all she was worth. Thing, for his part, closed his eyes, swayed on his feet, and focused on not falling over.

After a few moments, with a noise like a tree being torn in two, the door opened. A dark, narrow hallway was revealed, leading to rooms that looked cold and unused—but a powerful aroma of roasting chicken billowed forth, and Thing's stomach decided to take control of the situation. He took one faltering step toward the scent, and then another.

"Madame," said Edgar, bowing quickly, then straightening up and squaring his shoulders. "The—the sun is warm—"

"*Non, mon cher,*" a voice interrupted, its accent reminding Thing of polished shoes and well-padded stomachs, gold-topped canes and sparkling jewels. "You do not need to use passwords here, Edgar. Not with me." The voice warmed as it continued. "Natasha, *ma petite.* And your guest. *Bienvenue à tous.* Come."

"Ben ven who?" echoed Thing, peeling one eye open to see a tiny woman, barely bigger than he was, wearing a high-necked dress with a shawl around her shoulders—and, of course, a large white flower conspicuously placed over her heart.

"Welcome," she said with a small, tired smile. "I am Gramercy Blancheflour. *Enchantée.*"

"Chicken," muttered Thing before fainting at her feet.

Emmeline hardly heard Pale Face's explanation of what OSCAR was—an acronym for her parents' employer, the Office for the Sighting and Cataloging of the Anomalous and Rare, and not a name after all—because one thought kept drowning out everything else. *They're alive.*

Her parents were not dead. She felt like there were ants under her skin, so strong was the urge to be off, to find them, to tell them—

"Are you listening, young lady?" Pale Face's voice was like a needle jabbed into Emmeline's brain, and she nodded, her eyes squeezed tight. *How am I going to get Mum and Dad back?* burned across the inside of her mind in red-hot letters.

"Excellent. Well, since you apparently *know* so much, maybe you can tell me what your parents have explained to you about the Creature. How to rouse it, perhaps. Methods of extracting its blood, in order to harness its ability to live forever." Emmeline opened her stinging eyes to see Pale Face gazing at her, a mocking eyebrow raised. "No? Or maybe they've discussed the findings of their work looking into ways of controlling it once it's awoken. Ringing any bells?" None of this meant anything to Emmeline, but somehow, the way Pale Face said the word *Creature*, she knew it had to take a capital letter. Every muscle in her body tensed as she tried to ask a question that she felt, on the whole, she'd rather not know the answer to.

"What Creature?" she whispered.

"What Creature, indeed," replied Pale Face. "You know, I should just dispatch you now and find another means of bending your parents to my will. I'm sure I need only one of them to get the job done—your mother, I think. She always struck me as the brains of the operation." He cut a glance toward Emmeline, who was glued into her chair, her eyes steady. "Without her husband she might learn to focus. What do you think, my dear?"

"My mother would *kill* you if you hurt my dad," said Emmeline evenly. "Or me."

Pale Face chuckled. "I believe you. So I'd best keep her happy, eh? Bring her back her little girl, and all that sentimental nonsense."

"My mother's not *sentimental*. Have you actually *met* her?"

"That may be," said Pale Face. "But hearing the cries of a child in distress, particularly one's *own* child, is bound to have an effect, wouldn't you say?" He fixed his gaze on the silently staring Emmeline for several long moments before eventually blinking and looking away. "I should have learned my lesson with the Strachan business. Never work with children, or women," he muttered, apparently to himself. Certainly, the words meant nothing to Emmeline, and she ignored them, clenching her fists in the depths of her blanket instead.

"Why are you *doing* this to us? What have my parents ever done to you?"

Pale Face's cavernous eyes regarded her coldly, but Emmeline didn't let her stare drop for a second. "Your parents, with their unparalleled expertise, are the linchpin of OSCAR's efforts to find, conserve, and protect the beasts that live in the dark crevices of the world," he finally said, spitting out the words. "Those terrifying, nightmarish, *powerful* monsters that the rest of the world would like to believe are *myths* or bedtime stories. It is your parents' *job* to keep them hidden from people like me, people who have *vision*, who crave *progress*." He paused, licking his already wet-looking lips. "In fact, no—it is not simply their job. It is their *mission*. And you ask what they have *done* to me? They have done plenty."

Well, he's not going to use me for anything, Emmeline told herself. *Especially not anything that might hurt Mum and Dad. Let's see him try.*

Pale Face, as if he'd read her mind, simply smiled.

21

"Have you heard a word that anyone has said to you since you set foot in this room?" asked Edgar. He leaned back in his chair and gazed at Thing, whose grease-smeared face shone brightly in the light of Madame Blancheflour's kitchen.

"*Mmmff?*" replied Thing, raising his eyebrows as he chewed. He swallowed hurriedly, then slapped himself on the chest and released a burp so powerful that Sasha felt her eyes water and Madame Blancheflour had to excuse herself momentarily from the table. "What?" he said, wondering why all the adults were staring at him. "Did I do summink wrong?"

"Before you take another bite, young man," said Edgar, reaching over to stop Thing's hand from raising another lump of chicken to his mouth, "perhaps we'd better run through what we know. All right?" Madame Blancheflour settled herself in her chair once more, gazing with pointed eyebrows at Thing; this was disconcerting enough to make him stop eating and sit up straight.

"So," continued Edgar. "We know that Emmeline is more than likely being brought north. Judging by Thing's descriptions of the men who took her, we can safely assume that much."

"Alas, we were too slow," said Madame Blancheflour. Her eyes slid closed, and her head drooped into one elegant hand. "I should have known the *instant* I did not receive Eloise and Martin's telegram that their child was in danger. Instead, I waited. *It is delayed*, I thought. *They have forgotten.* But they would not forget."

"Don't blame yourself, Madame," soothed Sasha, placing her arm across the older woman's shoulders.

"Wait. What now? What telegram're we talkin' about?" Thing fought the urge to pick at a piece of stray chicken caught in his teeth, trying to suck at it inconspicuously instead.

"You really weren't listening, were you?" sighed Edgar. "The telegram that Emmeline's parents sent, every evening without fail, to Madame Blancheflour. It was coded so that she could be certain it was genuine, and it was supposed to let her know that they were safe."

"Oh—yeah," said Thing. "An' when the telegram didn't come, the whole emergency backup plan kicked off, yeah? With Emmeline bein' removed from home and sent packin' to France?"

"As you so pithily put it, yes," said Edgar. "But clearly

her captors were somehow monitoring Mr. and Mrs. Widget's communications with Madame Blancheflour too. They must have seen that the expected telegram never arrived, which meant something had gone wrong and Emmeline was vulnerable. So Sasha and I were alerted."

"That worked out well," said Sasha coldly.

"So, what do we do now?" asked Thing, looking from Edgar to Sasha and finally to Madame Blancheflour, who—not that he would've admitted it to anyone—scared him, just a little. "I mean, sittin' here jawin' about it ain't gettin' Ems back, is it? Who has the plan?"

"Well, we *think* we know where she's going," said Sasha carefully. "But really, we're not sure."

"That's a start, innit? Let's get on the road before any more time gets wasted, then. Come on!" The adults looked at one another blankly.

"You can't just rush into these things, Thing," said Edgar after a minute. "I understand how you feel, but—"

"You don't understand nothin'," snapped Thing. "I *owe* her, all right? I owe her. She's the first person in a long, long time who was nice to me, and that means somethin'. I ain't leavin' her to freeze up at the North Pole, or wherever it is she's gone."

"Greenland," said Sasha quietly, her eyes full of shadows. "Not the North Pole. We think it's Greenland they're going to, right into the center of what remains of the ice sheet."

"And how d'you know that, then?" He tried to pay close attention, despite something deep in his mind that suddenly sparked into sharp, cruel life. He closed his thoughts against it and focused hard on what was going on in this small kitchen, right now.

"Because—well, because we've finally worked out that's where the Creature is," Sasha said, her voice slipping into a whisper. Edgar's face fell, and Madame Blancheflour muttered something under her breath.

"What blimmin' Creature? The Abom'nable Snowman?" Thing tried to laugh, but nobody joined in.

"No. Something much older than that," replied Edgar tonelessly. "Something much older, and much more dangerous."

Thing's eyes flicked between the adults for a few seconds, willing one of them to crack a grin, but the kitchen was silent except for the faint ticking of Madame Blancheflour's clock.

"Who—who's taken 'er? I mean—jus' tell me. Who's taken Emmeline?" His voice was so quiet that, for a second or two, Thing wondered if he'd spoken at all. Then he glanced up at Sasha and saw her looking back at him sorrowfully, as if she were trying to think of some way to answer him, but her mouth refused to form the words. Thing watched as Sasha glanced over at Edgar, and then as they both gazed at Madame Blancheflour.

"Dr. Siegfried Bauer is his name," said Madame Blancheflour after a few long moments. "And he is a lunatic. But he is also, unfortunately, a genius, and even more unfortunately than that, he is extremely wealthy. Rich enough to bribe governments, rich enough to travel where he wants, rich enough to defy us for decades, rich enough to be asked no questions. None of this is enough for him, however. One more thing—the *biggest* thing, the one he wants most of all—still eludes him. And Emmeline and her parents, *les pauvres*, are the key to it."

"Yeah? And that is?" said Thing, hoping someone would give him a straight answer. Sasha's eyes were shut, and Madame Blancheflour was clearly unable to say any more.

"He wants to figure out how to cheat death," said Edgar eventually. At these words Thing felt his skin prickling all over, like it had been asleep all this time and was only now waking up. "He thinks he has found a way to make himself live forever, in perfect health and in possession of all his intelligence and his strength and his skills, and he wishes to use all this to rule the world. He believes, and he's probably right, that the Creature in the ice holds the key to this eternal life—that its blood makes a person immortal. That's not even counting its *other* powers, which are formidable enough. If he can harness it, he'll be an unstoppable force. He needs Emmeline's parents to wake the Creature up."

"And he needs Emmeline to *make* her parents do what he wants," added Sasha quietly. "All her life they've tried to keep her out of their work with OSCAR, make her self-reliant and tough just in case the worst happened, but she has no chance against him. Not really. If Bauer brings her up there, threatening to kill her unless they cooperate, the Widgets'll have no choice."

"Oh," muttered Thing.

"Yes. Oh," sighed Edgar. "The Order of the White Flower was set up a long time ago to thwart people like

Dr. Bauer at every turn, as far as it was possible, in conjunction with our allies at OSCAR. We've managed to keep him contained for many years, but this time—"

"We have not," Madame Blancheflour interrupted. "We have *not* managed to keep him contained! We have chased him, fruitlessly, from Antarctica to Siberia, from Alaska to the Northwest Passage, and he has laughed at us with every step. He has caused such damage in his attempts to find the Creature, such trails of destruction, and we have not stopped him. If we had contained him, then he would not be where he is!" Thing saw that the skin around her eyes was wet, and it shone in the gentle light. Her mouth was pursed tight and her whole body quivered, whether with cold or fear or anger, Thing didn't know. "There has never been enough time or money or people to keep him contained. We have tried. But we—but I—have failed."

"Madame, *you* have not failed," said Sasha quietly. "We have. We, the people you trained, the people you trusted to take over your work—we are the ones who have let you down."

"You, I, the boy—it is all the same," replied the older woman. "We are all the White Flower, and we will all suffer the same fate if he succeeds."

"What—what fate's that, then?" said Thing.

"He'll kill us, of course," said Edgar. "And he'll spare no time in doing it."

"Dr. Bauer! Sir!"

Emmeline's head snapped to face the door as footsteps began to clatter, loudly, outside it and voices started to shout.

"Idiots!" snarled Pale Face, rising to his feet. "I told you not to use names in front of the prisoner!" He yanked open the door. Crouched outside like so many scolded puppies were three huge sailors, each of them struggling not to be the one closest to the boss.

"S-s-sorry, sir!" stammered one man, his face a picture of terror. "It's just, sir, we're nearly there."

"That's it? That's what *three* of you had to barrel down here to tell me?"

"Sir, it's not just that, sir," squeaked another sailor. "It's just that there's *people* on shore, sir, Cap'n, sir, who shouldn't be there. We aren't expecting them, is what I mean."

"People?" said Dr. Bauer, straightening. Emmeline pricked up her ears and paid close attention, all the while pretending to be slumped in the chair, bored out of her mind.

"Sir—people, and they've got fires, and all sorts—"

"Fine! Enough! You and you, take Miss Widget and bind her securely, and have her brought up on deck. This instant!" As soon as these words had been spoken, Emmeline sat up, shrugging her upper body out of her blanket, and grabbed the handle of the empty—but still heavy—tankard. Then, as quickly as she could, she caught a handful of the blanket and casually draped it over her tankard-holding arm. Finally she rose to her feet, hoping nobody could see her quivering knees, and took a couple of long steps into the center of the room.

"Hey! Just a minute—" she shouted, but Dr. Bauer didn't give her any space to finish her sentence.

"You will do what you are told, young lady," he said in a low, dangerous tone, "or face what will be *severe* consequences." With that, he strode off down the corridor, one of the sailors hurrying along in front of him like dirt in front of an angry broom.

"Now, young miss," said the bigger of the two sailors that were left. "If you'll stand still for me, just for a minute, while I tie this lovely soft rope round your pretty little wrists, we can be off." Emmeline glared at him but said nothing as he smiled down at her like she was a simpering baby. It was a huge effort for her just to let him get closer, and closer, and *closer*, until—

"I don't think so," she muttered. In one very smooth movement she threw the blanket off her arm and took aim with the tankard, smashing it into the side of the sailor's head and knocking him out cold on the floor.

"Oi!" yelled the second sailor, a man barely as tall as Emmeline herself, but at least as wide again across his middle. Huffing out a breath, he dropped to his knees beside his fallen friend. "Ambrose! *Mate!*" He stared at the side of the fallen Ambrose's face, which was beginning to swell nicely. Quietly, and without any fuss, Emmeline picked up the soup bowl. Gently and silently she removed the spoon, weighing it carefully in her hand. *Good,* she thought.

"You little brat! Jus' wait till I show you . . . ," the second sailor growled, struggling to his feet. Before he'd quite managed it, Emmeline upturned the still-hot soup over his head, jammed the bowl down as hard as she could, and hit it with her fists. The steaming liquid poured around his ears and down his neck, and Emmeline was pretty sure she saw a hairy lump of meat slither down the back of his shirt. With a pop, the soup bowl finally slipped over the sailor's eyes, where it stuck fast.

"Ow!" he wailed.

"I'm sorry," said Emmeline truthfully. "But I can't let you keep me here."

"But you 'eard the boss." He grabbed hold of the rim of the soup bowl and tried to lever it off his head. "You've to go topside!" Thinking fast, Emmeline aimed the heavy silver spoon at the man's kneecap and threw it. Her aim was good, and the spoon clattered off with an almighty crack. The sailor tumbled to the ground again with a howl, grabbing his leg with both hands.

Emmeline quietly took the blanket and got a good, tight grip. Before she could talk herself out of it, she pulled it over the sailor's head, including his fetching soup-bowl hat, and down over his arms. Quickly she hopped over his flailing, uninjured leg and tied the blanket in the best approximation of Twitchell's constrictor knot that she could manage, hoping she'd remembered the diagram correctly. She placed her foot right in the center of his wide back and nudged him forward, as gently as she could without actually calling it a *kick*, until he lay on top of Ambrose's unconscious form. He was too round and too wide to pick himself up again easily, just as she'd hoped.

"Hello?" she called. "Can you breathe in there?"

Words Emmeline couldn't clearly hear but felt sure weren't complimentary burst out of the blanket in a thunderous muffle. She patted the sailor on the back and sprang to her feet again, looking around the room—properly this time. She finally got the chance to examine the wall that had been behind her while she'd been perched in the high-backed chair.

"Yes!" she whispered, grinning.

Avoiding the trussed sailor's still-thrashing legs, she made her way around to the back of the room. In one corner she saw a messy pile of coats, heavy-duty and designed for bad weather. The second she put her hand on them, a pungent smell of fish filled her nostrils, but she swallowed back her dislike and dug straight in. It didn't take her long to find a warm one with a belt, which she could tie around herself in such a way that the coat was both secure and also shortened enough not to trip her. As she strapped herself up, her stomach yowled, contracting like a closing fist, but Emmeline knew she didn't have time to stop and search for food.

She hurried to a tall cupboard that was propped against the wall near the pile of coats. One of its doors was slightly ajar, and she wriggled her fingers into the gap. As hard as she could, she pulled at the door, which *skreeeek*ed open slowly, and she peered inside. *Fishing rods . . . broken fishing rods . . . reels . . . snares . . .* On a shelf Emmeline found a tightly rolled coil of clear, flexible fishing line, which went straight into her pocket.

"Heeelp!" roared the sailor, the unexpected sound making Emmeline jump. She glanced over and saw that the knot was beginning to loosen. His arms would be free before too long. *Get out of here now!*

She scrambled over the arm of the chair again and swung herself down to the ground, landing neatly beside the still-unconscious Ambrose's splayed fingers. Automatically she bent to pick up the rope he'd been carrying, which, she realized with a shudder, should have been tied around her wrists and ankles by now. A second's work had it in her pocket. Then a flash of silver under the table caught her eye, and she bent quickly to grab the spoon. *You never know,* she thought, sliding it into her pocket beside the rope and the fishing line.

"Well, goodbye, then," she said, before turning and hurrying for the door.

23

Growing up in Widget Manor had bestowed upon Emmeline some remarkable talents, including the ability to walk as silently as a fly and hold her breath far longer than a respectable young lady should, as well as reflexes faster than a whipcrack. However, in an entirely different environment—for, in truth, no matter how challenging Widget Manor had been to live in, after a while none of its secret traps had retained their secrecy—she was discovering that things didn't come to her so easily. Another thing that wasn't helping was the furry hood of her unfamiliar coat, which, no matter how often she shoved it back where it should be, kept deciding to flop down over her head at just the wrong moment.

"Gah!" she whispered as the hood whopped down over her eyes yet again. Angrily she whipped it off and tried to peer around a corner. The boat was suspiciously quiet, she thought. Where *was* everyone? She crept down an empty corridor, keeping a close eye and ear out for anyone approaching.

Then she heard something. Something *huge*.

She tiptoed forward, her heart whooshing in her ears, her eyes open wide to catch every last droplet of light.

She came to a ladder, bolted to a wall, and an open hatch above it.

Carefully, slowly, and very, very quietly she began to climb.

"Disband! Go home!" she heard a voice shout from somewhere beyond the hatch. The sound of it made her freeze on the ladder. "Do you hear me? I say, go home and let us disembark!"

And then Emmeline heard the huge noise again and realized it was a crowd of people, all shouting at the same time. She couldn't pick out any voices, or even any words, but she had a feeling she knew what was being said: *Leave. We do not want you here.*

The air creeping down from the night outside was cold and crisp. Emmeline breathed deeply—it was like being cleaned out, she felt, like the air was scrubbing her out until she sparkled.

Whomp. Her hood decided this would be a good moment to flip down again. She raised an impatient hand and flipped it back before stretching herself to her full height and straining to see.

Up at the front of the boat, she could barely make out some shapes that had to be Dr. Bauer and most of the sailors. Beyond their heads all she could see was a dull orange glow, like that thrown off by a huge fire.

"Interesting," she muttered, and quickly pulled herself up the rest of the way. Keeping low, she cleared the hatch and scurried around to the side of the boat.

She found a secure-looking nook. Nestling herself between some discarded sacking and a pile of old packing crates, she finally got a chance to have a proper look at what was waiting for Dr. Bauer on the shoreline of this strange new country.

No wonder he wasn't happy, she thought.

A sound caught Thing's ear like a hook catching a fish.

"Oi," he said, his voice low. "Psst! You lot!"

"What?" said Edgar irritably.

"Cops!" Thing's eyes, wide and red-rimmed, flicked toward the front door of 224 rue du Démiurge. "We've gotta clear out of here!"

"I don't hear anything," mumbled Sasha, her face soft and puffy in the candlelight. Her hair was coming undone, and her cheek was covered in deep creases where she'd fallen asleep on her folded arms.

"I don't hear anythin' neither," muttered Thing. "I just *know* they're comin'."

"But how is that even—"

"Don't question it, mate. It's an instinct, right?"

"Madame?" asked Edgar. "What do you think?"

Madame Blancheflour turned to Thing and regarded

him quietly for a few seconds. "I do not think they are police," she said. "They are henchmen of the North—thugs in the pay of Bauer, would be my guess. But the boy is correct about one thing—they are coming."

"Well—yeah! Told yer! Get a move on, yeah?" Thing stood up from the table, scraping the chair legs against the stone floor. In a panic, he started trying to stuff Madame Blancheflour's plates and cutlery into his seemingly bottomless pockets while his eyes scanned the room, looking for escape routes.

"Thing! *Thing!*" Edgar called. "Calm down!"

"Calm down? Calm *down*? Are you jokin'? How are we goin' to help Ems if we're locked up?"

"Put back Madame's belongings, please," instructed Edgar in a quiet voice, keeping his eyes on Thing's. Thing looked down at his hands and seemed amazed to find them full of dirty silver cutlery, and he was even more shocked to realize he'd shoved a plate into the pocket on the left leg of his overalls, and several more into the one on the right.

"Sorry—sorry, Madame," he mumbled, placing everything back on the table as carefully as he could. "I'll—I can wash 'em for yer, if ya like." He tried to polish one of the knives with his sleeve but realized after a few seconds that he was only making things worse.

"*Non, mon cher,*" Madame Blancheflour said with a smile. "Not necessary. Now—are we going to listen to this wise child and get moving, or are we going to waste time talking nonsense, like adults? *Alors!*"

"But we can't just *go*—what about the plan? The others?"

Sasha had two spots of red high up on her cheeks, making her look like a doll in a shop window.

"There is, how do you say, a shortage of choices at the moment, *ma chérie,*" said Madame Blancheflour. As she spoke, Thing noticed her reach under her kitchen table, where, after a few seconds of searching, she seemed to find whatever she was looking for. A satisfied expression settled over her face.

"Now. Go! Take what you can—food, *mais oui.* But you must leave!"

"What about you?" asked Thing, already wrapping up a small loaf of bread and shoving it into a handy pocket. "Ain't you comin'?"

"At my age? *Non.* I have never been a fan of ice and snow. I will stay here, with the house, until your safe return—until *all* of you return safely."

"But we can't leave you here!" said Edgar, shrugging into his jacket. "Please, Madame. I offer you my personal—"

"*Ça suffit,* Edgar. You have a larger duty now. And besides—I am not without my own means of self-protection." With a jerk of her skinny frame, she pulled something free from beneath the kitchen table. When her hand reemerged, it was clutching a gun so large and so well polished that the sight of it knocked every single thought out of Thing's head.

"Madame!" breathed Sasha. "I thought you didn't approve of weapons!"

"There is a time for diplomacy," said Madame Blancheflour in a quiet and definite tone, "and there is a time for force. We passed the time for talking long ago."

Thing glanced at his friends as he looped Emmeline's satchel across his body. Sasha's eyes glittered with tears, which she blinked back as Thing watched, and Edgar's face was dull with something like sorrow.

Sasha shook her head, just once, and clapped her hands. "Right, then," she said, her voice tight and her eyes dry. "Let's get moving! Coats, food, whatever we can carry. Come on!"

Just as Sasha was tying the belt of her coat, and Edgar was filling an old food sack with some meat, a few apples, and a couple of half-finished loaves of bread, there was a noise—barely there, but a noise all the same.

This time they all heard it. Everyone's eyes slid to Thing, and he nodded slowly.

It was the sound of a heavy boot being placed carefully—but not, as it turned out, quite carefully *enough*—onto the top step, just outside the front door.

24

"You will leave! You will go!" Emmeline couldn't
see the speaker on the ice, but whoever it was felt strongly
enough to make the words heard over the crowd.

"Oh, please!" shouted Dr. Bauer. "You have no idea what
I'm even *here* for. When I'm successful, your country—
such as it is—will be the first to benefit!"

"No! We know exactly why you are here! What you're
doing is foolish. The Creature must not be woken!"

Emmeline strained her eyes, trying to make out in-
dividual faces. The boat wasn't quite in port yet—people
with long poles, tipped with balls of fire inside metal
cages, were standing guard over the harbor, refusing to
let it dock. A huge bonfire burned behind them, throwing smoke and strange shadows up into the oddly greenish air. Behind the crowd and the leaping fire, Emmeline

could see darkness, softly rolling, that seemed to go on forever.

"What Creature?" called Dr. Bauer. "I don't know what you're talking about. I'm here for the scenery!"

Another voice rang out. "Do you think you're the first to come up here and try to rouse it?" The speaker was a woman, and her voice was as clear as the stars overhead. "You're not, you understand? There have been fools before you, and no doubt there'll be several more after you're long turned to dust."

"That, my *dear* woman, will never happen," replied Dr. Bauer, his voice dripping with malice. "I have no intention of ever becoming dust, so let that put your mind at rest."

"Then you admit it? You admit you are here to rouse the Creature from its rightful resting place?" The woman turned to the crowd, raising her hand above her head. "He admits it!" They roared in response, shaking their flaming sticks and waving their fists at the boat and all its occupants.

"I admit nothing!" shouted Dr. Bauer, but his voice was drowned out by the cries of the people. Emmeline shrank back, afraid, into her hiding place. She wasn't sure what to do next, and she didn't like that feeling.

Make a plan, she told herself, thinking quickly. *Mum and Dad are in the ice, he said. I'm never going to find them if I stay here. I have to go and look. I need to get off this boat!*

The next thing Emmeline knew, something whizzed by her head and landed with a thud on the pile of sacking beside her, where it jerked once or twice before coming to rest. Emmeline studied it intently, trying to see through the gloom, holding her breath as recognition bloomed inside her head.

She figured out two things simultaneously: the first, that this strange object was a grappling hook, and the second, that she needed to move, right *now*. She started to get to her feet in a burst of electric energy.

But she was—just barely—too late.

Thing placed a finger on his lips and glared at Edgar and Sasha. Madame Blancheflour slowly and carefully pulled back the hammer on her gun. It made a tiny click, but that couldn't be helped.

"There is a back door," she whispered, her words more breath than sound. "Get to it, *mes chers*, and I will see to the rest." She aimed her gun directly at the front door, straight down the hallway, and Thing noticed there wasn't so much as a hint of trembling in Madame Blancheflour's hands.

"You've used a gun before, ain't ya," he whispered back, a grin in his voice. Madame Blancheflour didn't answer, but she didn't need to.

"Behind Edgar, there is a doorway," she said. "Go through it, and you will find a short corridor with a door at the end. It might stick a little, but it will open. When you are outside—run! You hear? Run, and do not separate yourself from the others."

"Bye, Madame," he said, laying his hand gently on the old lady's arm. "And thanks."

"*Au revoir, mon cher. Bon courage,*" she said with a wink. Thing turned to Edgar and Sasha, who were poised by the doorway, ready to fly. Sasha gestured to him while looking urgently at Edgar, whose gaze was trained on the front door. Thing had just started to move when a yell came from outside the house—a yell that sounded like "This is it!" Madame Blancheflour tightened her grip on her gun, and Thing dived for the doorway as Edgar tossed him the bag of food. Thing caught it, clutching it close to his chest.

"Go!" whispered Edgar, his voice hoarse. "Sasha knows where she's going. I'll meet you there as soon as I can."

"But—we can't leave you!" said Thing. "Madame said not to split up."

"Madame says a lot of things," muttered Edgar. "But one thing I won't have anyone say is that I left an old woman to defend herself, alone, against a bunch of mercenaries."

"Mercy-whats?" said Thing as Sasha dragged him toward the back door by the scruff of the neck.

"Go! Okay? I'll see you both soon!" He looked away from Thing and found Sasha's gaze instead. "Take care of yourself. I won't be long! I promise you." His eyes got bigger as he looked at her, almost like he wanted to see as much of her as he could.

"I believe you," she said, even though it sounded like she didn't.

A crash rang out in the front of the house—a crash

that sounded a lot like a front door being kicked in. Thing glanced into the hallway and saw at least three huge men come trampling down it, each of them armed.

Edgar rushed around the table and slammed the kitchen door closed, locking it with trembling fingers. His eyes were white all around, and his skin was pale.

"*Go!*" he yelled at Sasha and Thing. "Now!"

Sasha and Thing hurried down the corridor, and Sasha managed to get the back door open with three furious pulls. She and Thing burst through it into a crisp Parisian morning, so early that the sky was barely edged with light. Sasha took off down the narrow alley behind the house at a run, and as Thing did his best to catch up, a gunshot rang out, and then another.

"Faster!" shouted Sasha.

Thing didn't need to be told twice.

A strong hand grabbed Emmeline by the shoulder. Even through the thickness of her padded coat, she felt the fingers of this new abductor digging into her flesh. She stumbled backward, landing with a thump on her backside.

"Let me go!" she growled, yanking herself away, but the hand's grip didn't slip.

"What's this? A gnome?" said a voice, its accent unfamiliar.

"A *gnome?* Are you daft?" whispered Emmeline, still doing her best to wriggle out of the iron grip without wriggling herself all the way out of her coat.

"Well—let's see. Short, bad-tempered, deformed ... I mean, you've got everything a gnome's got. What makes you so different?"

Emmeline swung her head around, her eyes bulging with temper, but the person holding her kept dodging out of sight. "*Deformed*? I beg your pardon! Let go of me this minute!"

"Nah. Can't do that. You'll just have to come with me so we can examine you for gnominess and make sure you're not a threat."

"Oh, really? And then what?"

"Well—then I'd say we'll probably eat you. Do you taste good, by any chance?"

"Do I *taste* good? *What?*" said Emmeline. "Who *are* you?"

"Might ask you the same thing," replied the voice in a calmer and more serious tone. "What's a kid like you doing on a death ship like this?"

"So you've figured out I'm not a gnome, then?" Emmeline strained to see. All she could tell was that the person holding her was small and dark-haired and—probably, judging by the voice—male.

"Always knew you weren't a gnome, girl. Was just trying to be funny, you know. Ha, ha, here we are, it's the cavalry! No? Am I making sense?"

"Cavalry?" asked Emmeline, her mind filling with images of soldiers on horseback, their helmet plumes bobbing in the breeze.

"Not important. Look, are you coming with me or what?"

"Why would I do *that*?" Emmeline finally broke out

of the grip on her shoulder, but before she could do any-thing else, the strange person had grabbed her by the arm. Emmeline sighed and gave up the fight. She turned to face her captor.

"Greetings," came a voice from the shadows. The hand holding her was attached to a long arm encased in a seal-skin jacket, and the arm was attached to a short, stout body. Emmeline let her gaze travel downward a bit, and she looked as hard as she could, but she didn't see any legs. She glanced back up at the person's face and saw it was wide across the cheekbones, with narrow, dark eyes and a bright, gap-toothed grin.

"Who—who are you?" asked Emmeline.

"Name's Igimaq," he said. "Pleasure's mine."

25

"I've gotta—*whoop!*—stop. Jus' fer a minute. *Whoop.* Can't catch—*whoop!*—my breath."

Sasha slowed her pace and turned, looking back the way they'd come. Her lips were pulled thin. Thing could read her worry all over her face, and he knew she was aching to see Edgar hurrying along behind them, alive and unharmed—but the alley was deserted.

"We don't have time to rest, Thing," she said, but her sharp tone softened as soon as she glanced back at his face. She came to a halt and walked back toward him, frowning.

"Not restin'. I jus' can't. I—*whoop* . . ." Thing's feet stumbled, and slowed, and finally stopped. He leaned heavily against the wall beside them, desperately trying to get his lungs to behave and his heart to slow. He felt dizzy, and his shoulder ached under the weight of Emmeline's satchel. They'd already had to dump the bag of food—it had been slowing them down. "I jus'—I jus' need a minute. *Whoop.*"

Sasha lifted Thing's head gently and looked at him. "You sound like you're *drowning* or something. What's wrong?"

"It's jus'—jus'—runnin' and things like that. *Whoop.* When I'm afraid sometimes. Under pressure. Breathin' goes—*whoop*—funny. Always has done, I think."

Sasha sighed loudly through her nose and removed her hand from beneath Thing's chin. Her head swiveled, checking out their surroundings. Everything seemed quiet in the still-early morning, but Thing knew the sound of his heaving lungs would carry. His throat ached with effort and he closed his eyes, willing his chest to open up and work.

"Can you go on?" asked Sasha after a few minutes. Thing wondered for a second what she'd do if he said no. *Wring me worthless neck and chuck me over the nearest wall,* he told himself in a grim voice.

"Yeah, I reckon," he replied, coughing. Something inside him felt loose and rattly. "Let's go."

"You're sure?" She paced away from him, and he followed her with his gaze. Every nerve she had was on alert.

"Sure as I'm gonna get. *Whoop.*"

"Right." She hurried back to him and bent to peer intently into his eyes. He tried to pay attention. "If you're going to help me, you have to listen. We need to get to Monsieur Pichon, because he can get us to Greenland. Edgar and I were supposed to go together, but now . . ." She blinked and carried on. "That's not important. What's important is sticking with the plan. I've got an idea, but it's a long shot."

"Long shots are better'n nothin'," said Thing. "Who's this Pichon fella?" He tasted the new name in his mouth like a lemon sherbet, mentally adding it to his collection.

"A friend of the White Flower," Sasha replied. "Our only hope right now."

"Let's get movin', then," he said, pushing away from the wall. He adjusted the satchel, settling the strap more comfortably on his neck, rolled his shoulders, and nodded at Sasha. She shot him a quick grin, but her eyes remained dull. "How far is it to this only hope of ours?" he asked as they jogged away. He focused on keeping his breathing slow and even, timing it to his steps.

"Oh, not too far. About two hundred miles. Give or take."

Thing opened his mouth, closed it again, and kept running.

"Come on," whispered Igimaq. "I'm just down here." Emmeline looked out over the railing of Dr. Bauer's boat, and sure enough, a small vessel, pointed at both ends and lying high in the water, was moored alongside it. "It's not designed for passengers," he explained. "So you'll have to perch on the front. But don't worry. We're not off seal hunting or anything!" He grinned widely.

Emmeline glanced up at the front of Dr. Bauer's boat again. He still seemed distracted by the crowd, shouting and waving his arms about. *Go!* she told herself. *What are you waiting for?*

"A good diversion, aren't they?" murmured Igimaq, nodding at the yelling crowd. "Don't worry, girl. I'll get you away from here so quick and quiet you might not even notice it yourself."

"Diversion for what?" she asked.

"Wait and see," he replied. "Any other kids aboard?"

"No," said Emmeline. "Just me."

"That settles it, then," he said, grabbing the boat's railing and hauling himself up. He moved quickly, but Emmeline felt a jerk in her stomach as she realized she hadn't been seeing things in the dark earlier. Igimaq really had no legs. None at all.

"What—what happened to your legs? Can I ask that, or is it rude?" she said as Igimaq balanced himself on top of the railing and extended a hand to steady Emmeline as she climbed.

"Eaten by a rabid, savage narwhal on my first hunting trip," said Igimaq in a deep, sonorous voice as Emmeline neared the top of the railing. She stepped out over the side, wobbling a bit. "Steady there—one leg at a time. No rush," he said in his normal voice, which broke the spell of his story a little.

"Were they *really* eaten by a narwhal?" Emmeline asked

once she'd gotten her breath back and felt like she had a grip on the railing. Igimaq peered at her with a steely gaze for a few seconds before his grin broke out again.

"Nothing so interesting," he finally said. "Born this way. That's all. Boring old story, eh? But the truth."

"It's not boring," said Emmeline.

"You're terribly kind," said Igimaq. "Now, if we're quite ready, let's get ourselves off this sinking bucket and into a *proper* boat." Igimaq looped his grappling hook—which, Emmeline now saw, was made of bone—around the railing of the ship and lowered himself down to his little boat. He spent a few seconds making it steady before Emmeline heard his whisper from far below.

"Come on!"

So she clambered down the rope, trying not to think of losing her grip, and, before she knew it she felt the leather and wood of Igimaq's boat beneath her feet, and his strong hands on her arms, helping her to get comfortable. With a quick jerk on his rope, Igimaq's grappling hook came tumbling down from on high, and he wrapped it up with deft fingers.

"Just one more thing," he muttered before making ready to pull away. From somewhere in the body of his small boat, he drew out something that looked like a bundle of candles with very long wicks, all tied together. Next, from a pocket, he produced a lighter made of some sort of pale, pearly material, the carving on its front visible even in the strange half-light. He flicked it open, and a flame, bright and jaunty in the cold and darkness, illuminated his face.

Without really understanding what he was doing, she watched him light the wicks, but when she saw him brace himself to throw the lit candles, she realized—too late—what was happening.

"*Dynamite?* No!" she said in a strangled voice. "There are *loads* of people on that ship!"

"Wouldn't worry," said Igimaq, dipping his paddle into the water. "There's not enough to do any huge damage. They'll have plenty of time to get off, and they'll be safe, probably—just boatless." Before Emmeline had a chance to do anything else, their little craft was cutting through the water, leaving Dr. Bauer's ship in its wake.

"What's this place?" whispered Thing, doing his best to resist the urge to hide behind Sasha. It looked like an abandoned train station, with a ceiling high enough to fit a whole forest—not that Thing thought anything could grow there—and lots of windows, most of them broken, far above their heads. All around were piles of rubbish, discarded engines, car parts, pools of black oil, and spatterings of bird droppings.

"Shh. Don't worry. We have friends here."

"*Here?* You sure?"

Before Sasha could answer, a skinny man who seemed held together by hair oil and the clothes he was wearing shambled out from behind a wrecked vehicle a few feet from them.

"The sun is warm," said Sasha to the man very clearly.

"But there is ice on the breeze," he replied in the same strange, slow tone. They nodded at one another, satisfied. "This way," he said, raising a filthy hand and beckoning them forward. He turned and walked away, into the depths of the room.

"Look—are you certain about this, yeah?" said Thing, reaching out to steady Sasha as she stumbled across the trash-laden floor. Thing himself had no trouble—his feet naturally found the best and most secure route, as they always did.

"Just trust me. All right?" She grabbed his hand and threw him a grateful look as, together, they followed the strange man into the dark.

26

Emmeline was perched on the nose of Igimaq's boat, and her eyes were fixed on Dr. Bauer's ship, which had not—to her immense relief—exploded. Not so far, at least. She wasn't entirely sure yet whether Igimaq was telling the truth about the dynamite.

One thing had started to become clear, however.

"So, you didn't come just to rescue me," she said, already knowing the answer.

"How could I? Didn't even know you were on board. I saw you, though, as I made my way over. 'That's a kid, Igimaq,' I told myself. 'And kids have no business with any of this stuff.' So the plan had to change. Get you off, get you safe, *then* do the dynamite thing."

"How on earth did you *see* me?" asked Emmeline. "I was hiding!"

Igimaq grinned. "You grow up as a no-legged hunter in a place where the sun doesn't set properly for months at a time, and you get good at seeing things long, long before they can get close enough to hurt you," he said. "I have eyes that can see the wind before she blows, and that can tell where the seal's going to swim before he even makes the decision himself."

A distant yell drew Emmeline's attention back to Dr. Bauer's boat. A bright yellow flame had started to lick its way up the side of it, not far above the waterline.

"What's happening?" asked Igimaq, focusing on the water in front of them.

"The dynamite must have set something on fire," replied Emmeline, squinting as she tried to see. "The boat's burning."

"Good," said Igimaq, grinning wider.

Before Emmeline could answer, someone tossed the still-fizzling dynamite overboard, and it vanished into the dark water. At the same time there was a loud, metallic groan as the side of Dr. Bauer's ship began to open up. Something mechanical-sounding started to stir deep within it, something with a lot of gears and cogs and other moving parts. *Something that might have ground me up if I were still hiding on the deck,* she thought with a shudder of horror.

Then the water beside the ship erupted as a huge wheel, its spokes at least as long as five Emmelines placed end to end, emerged from inside the hull. All the way around the wheel's rim Emmeline saw metal teeth, pointed and curved, flashing cruelly in the light of the torches being held by the people on the shore. More mechanical groaning and gear shifting echoed across the surface of the water as the wheel settled itself into position, and finally, with a loud click sharp enough to make Emmeline jump, it started to rotate, slowly at first but rapidly picking up speed. The metallic teeth, Emmeline saw, were doing a great job at churning up the water. Then another gush of white sea foam from the ship's far side drew Emmeline's eye, and she realized a second wheel had begun to spin there, its speed slightly offset from that of the first.

"*That's* new," muttered Igimaq, bending to the task of paddling. "We're not far enough away for my liking. Hold on, little stowaway." Emmeline braced herself as the small kayak picked up speed. Dr. Bauer's boat was moving closer and closer to shore, powered by the wheels' spinning, and Emmeline could just barely hear the sound of people shouting and screaming. A distant, muffled boom told her the dynamite had finally exploded, deep underwater, and the shock wave spread across the surface of the sea.

Then, like a giant creature hauling itself up out of the deep, the boat rolled out of the waves. Its wheels bit into the ice as its shining hull, water running off it, crashed and rumbled its way up onto dry land. Emmeline saw that the front of the boat was covered in a metal plate that came to a sharp and horrible point near the prow, like a huge knife, and something inside her shrank away from the sight of it. The crowd scattered, dropping their flaming torches as they went. The engines driving the huge wheels groaned and squealed as the boat gained purchase and balance on the ground, and then it was off, rolling into the night like a monstrous insect, clanking as it went.

"So that's what silence sounds like," said Igimaq, making Emmeline turn back to face him. "Have you frozen solid, or are you still alive in there?"

"Did you see that?" she gasped, her mind still full and her eyes straining to follow the boat as it vanished into the distance.

"Didn't need to," sniffed Igimaq, paddling hard. "My nightmares're bad enough, thank you very much."

"Where's he going?" Emmeline pulled her collar up, but the cold got in anyway.

"Never you mind about that," said Igimaq, and it was like a screen had been pulled down over his eyes. The warmth faded from his voice. Emmeline tried to get him to catch her eye, but he refused.

"Where are you taking me?" she asked. Igimaq met her gaze for a split second and tried to grin, but it was a weak thing and didn't live long.

"I'll—um. I thought I'd bring you home to the wife. She usually knows what to do when things go a little bit belly-up. Get some grub into you at least. Just sit tight and everything'll be okay."

Emmeline took a deep breath and buried her face in her folded arms, and tried to pretend that everything around her was a dream. Just a dream, and nothing more.

"What do you need?" asked the man. Sasha and Thing had followed him between two towering piles of rubbish and down a short corridor into a surprisingly pleasant office, lit with a gas lamp and warmed by a roaring fire. Thing slipped away to stand beside it, feeling the marrow melting in his bones.

"Transport," answered Sasha. Her voice was just as clipped and official as the man's. "A colleague will be along after us, and he'll need the same." Thing looked at Sasha as she spoke, but her face betrayed nothing. *I hope Edgar's all right,* he thought. *And Madame, too.*

"What sort?" asked the man, licking his index finger and starting to flick through some paperwork on the desk in front of him. "I've got a flatbed, a reasonably good lorry—it's small, but—"

"The lorry—that should be fine. Thanks. Do you have the stuff to get us across the border?"

"Only got papers for one—the driver. The boy? He'll have to hide."

Sasha nodded, and the man reached into a desk drawer. He removed a sheaf of documents and slapped it into her outstretched hand.

"Safe travelin', young lady." He glanced over at Thing, who was still toasting himself. "And, you—stay out of sight. Right?" Thing could only nod in reply.

"Come on, Thing," muttered Sasha, tucking the documents into a pocket. "We don't have time to waste."

"Drive carefully," the man muttered as Sasha and Thing left the room. "If you're caught, you're on your own."

Igimaq nosed his small boat gently up into a sheltered cove. Snow lay on the ground all around, and the water was so clear—even in the poor light—that Emmeline could see straight down through it, as though it were highly polished glass.

"You can give me a hand with the boat," said Igimaq. "Get ready now." With a gentle thud they made landfall, and Emmeline hurried to her feet as the boat slid up over the rocky shoreline. She hopped off onto solid ground and grabbed the prow as firmly as she could.

"That's it! Hold it there," called Igimaq, hauling himself out of his boat and using one strong arm to pull himself up the shore and the other to drag the boat along behind him. Very soon, between the two of them, the boat was out of the water and stored, upside down, on a specially built rack along the side of a nearby boathouse, Igimaq's broad paddle placed carefully inside.

"Not far now," said Igimaq, propelling himself along the slippery ground, using his wide, flat hands like feet and his arms like legs. Emmeline had to hurry to keep up with him, her steps sliding on the icy rocks. The cold numbed the inside of her mouth and nose, and she could feel it creeping all the way down inside her, traveling into every corner of her lungs. Before too long a collection of low, colorful houses came into view, nestled together overlooking the small harbor.

"There it is! That blue one, in the middle. That's

mine," Igimaq called to Emmeline over his shoulder. "Let's hope Qila has some dinner ready."

Emmeline's stomach, which had wizened to the size of a small dried pea, perked up at the word *dinner*. Within a few seconds they'd reached the front door of Igimaq's house, and Emmeline already felt warmth starting to melt the layer of ice that had formed all over her skin, both inside and out. Her hands and feet ached.

"Qila? I'm home!" called Igimaq, making his way into the warmly lit living room. "I've got a guest, all right?"

Emmeline could hear noises coming from the kitchen, but she wasn't sure if they were sounds of delight or irritation.

Emmeline took a few steps into the living room, looking at the low, comfortable chairs dotted about and wanting to sink herself into one of them for at least a year. She put her frozen fingers into her pockets and felt for her fishing line, her spoon, and her rope, their weight reassuring and their shapes comforting. They couldn't replace her satchel, but they helped.

Then a small, dark-haired woman who, Emmeline presumed, had to be Qila stepped out of the kitchen. Emmeline prepared to smile and perform her best "Thank you ever so much" speech, but she never got a chance to say it. Qila, instead of welcoming her, threw her a look of such ferocity that Emmeline was frightened by it right down to the soles of her inadequate shoes.

27

"When we get near the crossing, you'll have to hide, like we practiced, okay?" Sasha's eyes were glued to the road.

"No problem," answered Thing. "Just gimme the nod in plenty of time, right?"

"Of course." Sasha smiled, flicking her eyes at Thing, just for a second. "So. Now that we have a chance to talk—are you going to tell me?"

"Tell you what?" muttered Thing. "Look out for that horse and cart there."

"I see it," said Sasha, smoothly maneuvering. She changed gear as she gained speed, the engine crunching and rattling as she urged it on. "Tell me about why you're called Thing. Tell me about yourself."

"Nothin' to tell," said Thing with a shrug. "I call meself

Thing because nobody ever bothered callin' me anythin' else. 'Hey, get that *thing* out of the way!' or 'Oi! Tell that *thing* to come down from there!' You know what I'm sayin', right?" He gazed out the window, away from Sasha, but she didn't get the hint.

"But where are your people? Your family?" The truck roared as Sasha missed a gear, and Thing was glad of the few seconds of silence it allowed him as she fought to get it to behave. The greasy stink that began to creep into his nostrils could be the engine, he supposed, but it could also be the other thing. The thing he didn't allow himself to think about, ever. He rubbed his nose with the heel of his hand and ignored it.

"I ain't got family," he said as soon as he was able. "I don't know my mother's name, or my father's. Don't remember, or *can't* remember, when I last seen 'em. Couldn't pick 'em out of a lineup, and I'm sure they've been in plenty o' those. Why d'you even want to know, anyway?"

"I'm just curious," she said, her voice light.

"Nosy, you mean."

"That, too, maybe."

"You want to know what sort o' person you have yourself trapped in a truck with, ain't that right? You want to check I'm not a murderin' type, or what have you."

"I'm already pretty sure you're not one of those," she said, glancing over at him again. "I'm just—I don't know. I'm interested, Thing. I want to know what's behind your eyes."

"M'brain, probably. Not that there's much of it to speak of."

Sasha sighed. "You're not doing yourself justice. Again," she said, adjusting her speed. Thing licked his lips and took a breath, and tried to find a place to start.

"Look, it's like this, eh," he said eventually. "There's things in my head that I don't want to remember. I know where I 'ave 'em locked up, all right; I can feel 'em. But I never look at 'em an' I never let 'em out, though they do their best to get loose every so often. All I know fer sure is, I been makin' my own way now since I were about six. Seven, maybe. Don't know how long." Thing let out a short, bitter laugh and wiped his face on his sleeve. "Don't matter anyhow."

"Of course it matters," said Sasha, keeping her eyes on the road. "Of course it does, Thing."

"Yeah. Well," he replied, and then he said no more.

Emmeline stood alone, feeling awkward, in Igimaq and Qila's living room, twisting the hem of her stolen coat in her shaking hands. From the kitchen came hissings and whisperings in a language she didn't speak and at a volume she couldn't really hear properly. Her mind was full of thoughts—*so* full, in fact, that she felt they were going to start spilling out. She felt like closing her eyes tight and sticking her fingers in her ears just to keep everything where it ought to be. She thought about Thing, wondering where he was, and she thought about Edgar and Sasha, even, and—more than anything else—she thought about her parents.

"He said you were 'in the ice'—but where's that?" she asked herself in a tiny voice. She thought about the landscape surrounding her and wondered if it meant they were close by. "But how do I even know it's true?" Emmeline had long ago concluded that most grown-ups lied, even when they weren't really doing it on purpose. She was personally convinced her parents had never told her the truth about anything, and she'd never understood why.

But she couldn't think of a good reason for Dr. Bauer to tell her that her parents were here, somewhere, and for it to be a lie.

Emmeline stood a little closer to Igimaq's fire, feeling properly warm for the first time in ages. *I have to try to find them before Bauer realizes I've escaped from the boat. I can't let him use me to get to them. And if he's hurt them ...* Something dropped into her brain like a fat, cold raindrop: *But he probably already knows I'm gone.*

Emmeline's thoughts were smashed to pieces by Igimaq, who came hurrying out of the kitchen again, his dark eyes wide.

"Um. Well. Qila says you're welcome to stay for dinner, but that once you've eaten, we need to get you to the village council." Igimaq licked his lips and tried to smile. "We can lend you some boots and mittens, and Qila's spare snowshoes, because you seem to have lost yours. When you've warmed up, we can get going." From the kitchen Emmeline heard a squawking cry, followed by another gush of words that meant nothing to her. She watched Igimaq's face as he listened. "Make sure you get the stuff back to us as soon as you can, if that's all right," he continued in a much louder tone of voice. "Boots and mittens cost time and money, and we can't be giving them away willy-nilly to whoever crosses our threshold." His eyes were apologetic as he moved closer and leaned in. "I'm sorry," he whispered. "But living here, in times like these? Nobody trusts strangers. Especially not my Qila, not since . . ." He bit off the rest of his sentence and shuffled backward, shaking his head.

Emmeline stared at Igimaq, and lots of things flicked across her mind like birds zooming through a wide, empty sky. *I don't know where I am!* was swiftly followed by *I don't know where I'm going!* and then *How will I find my parents?* She scrunched her hands up into tight fists, hidden inside her pockets, and took a deep breath.

"Thank you," she said in a voice that sounded a lot calmer coming out of her mouth than she'd expected it to.

"Great! That's great. I'm sure you'll be back home in no time," said Igimaq, guiltily avoiding Emmeline's eyes. Her insides felt like they were falling, very fast, from somewhere very high. "Now come on through to the kitchen. We're having my favorite—fish casserole! Qila makes it better than anyone else in Greenland, no doubt about it."

Emmeline felt empty inside but somehow couldn't bring herself to think about eating. She wondered about the village council, and what would happen to her there, as she followed Igimaq out of the room.

At least now I know where I am. She filed that thought away so she could think about it properly once she was on her own.

Because, she realized, she'd soon be alone again, and she had to be as well prepared as possible when the time came.

✺

BRUXELLES, said a sign by the side of the roadway, 25 KM.

"Right," said Sasha. "We're getting near the border with the RNB. You need to get hidden." Thing started unbuckling his seat belt as Sasha, checking her mirrors, drew the lorry to a halt in the scrubby grass that lined the edge of the asphalt.

"The border with what?" said Thing, feeling around for the catch that opened the secret compartment under the seats.

"RNB. République Neer-Belge," Sasha explained. "It used to be two separate countries once. Before the sea." Thing nodded. He didn't remember much from before the waters rose, of course, but he'd picked up enough, in bits and pieces, from other people to know that the world had looked completely different before the ocean had started to take bigger and hungrier gulps out of the land. Something was melting the ice around the frozen edges of the world, he'd heard somewhere, but Thing hadn't ever given it much thought. It was just one of those things that had nothing to do with him.

"We won't be long getting through the border, right?" He stuck one leg into the secret compartment and then the other. Wriggling, he curled his way around and out of sight, right down into the darkness. He refused to let himself be scared, though he did allow himself to wonder how much air was down in the hole, and how long it would take him to breathe it all up.

"No. Just a few minutes. Don't worry, okay? We'll be there soon. I'll drive as quickly as I can."

"Who's worried?" scoffed Thing, staring up at Sasha out of the dim hole beneath the seats, his eyes huge. "Not me, mate."

"Of course not." Sasha smiled and winked at Thing and snapped the secret compartment closed. Carefully checking her mirrors again, and hoping nobody had seen her pull over, nobody who might wonder what she was doing stopping her vehicle so close to the checkpoint, she pulled back out onto the road and kept driving. She didn't hurry, particularly, and she didn't go unusually slowly. She tried to clear her mind and relax her muscles. *Just out for a drive, doing a job across the border. Smile, Natasha, smile.* She checked, for the tenth time, that she had her documents in easy grabbing range. She looked at the fuel gauge and saw that she still had nearly a full tank.

Please, Monsieur Pichon, she heard herself begging. *Please, please be where you're supposed to be.*

Fighting hard to keep her hands from trembling, Sasha relaxed her grip on the steering wheel and drove straight for the border.

28

Despite her apparent lack of appetite, Emme- line's empty stomach welcomed Qila's casserole. It was hot, tasty, and full of barley and onions and potatoes, as well as more types of fish than Emmeline could recognize. A wide-bottomed glass of cool, frothy liquid sat by her plate.

"Told you it was good," said Igimaq. "I was right, eh?" Emmeline nodded, her smile fading as she caught Qila's eye. The woman was still staring at her with fearful suspicion. She muttered something to her husband in the language new to Emmeline's ears, and Igimaq's face fell as he listened.

He turned to Emmeline and tried to smile. "So, young lady. We'd better get you ready to head out. We'd have you stay the night, but it's probably best if we get you to the council. You must have parents somewhere worried about you, right?" Emmeline felt her stomach quiver, and her casserole started to taste sour in her throat. *If you hadn't taken me off that boat, I might be* with *my parents now!* Then she remembered the giant wheels and wondered whether, without Igimaq, she'd even be here at all.

"Yes. Of course," she murmured, placing her hands in her lap. She couldn't eat another bite. "Thank you. For the food, and the rescuing, and everything."

Qila made a small, spluttering noise and stalked out of the room. Igimaq turned back to Emmeline, who very carefully said nothing.

Igimaq placed his hands flat on the table. "Forgive Qila. It's just—well. It's just that she's afraid. Of you. Of anything to do with this whole thing. Mostly, she's afraid that if we keep you here, that man—that doctor, whoever he is—will set the Creature on us."

"The Creature?" repeated Emmeline, feeling like the words had spikes. The air in the once-warm kitchen became cold suddenly, like someone had flung a door open. Her mind flew to her parents and clung to them.

"I don't want to talk about it," said Igimaq quickly. "I mean, we shouldn't talk about it. Just in case."

"Why not?" probed Emmeline. Her voice dropped to a whisper. "Can it *hear* us?"

"No! What a silly question," Igimaq said with a grin, but it quickly faded. "Actually, you know, I'm not sure. The legends say a lot of stuff, and not all of it makes sense."

"*Legends?*"

Igimaq sighed, clenching his hands into fists. "You're only a kid. You shouldn't have anything to do with any of this."

"But I *do*," said Emmeline. "And I'm not a *kid*."

Igimaq folded his arms and sat back in his chair, looking across at her. "What were you doing on that boat, eh? How *did* you get mixed up in all of this?"

Emmeline felt a flood of frustration sweep through her, and it burst out of her mouth before she could stop it. "He has my *parents*! All right? He's taken them, and I don't know where. You have to help me." She gripped the edge of the table until her fingers stung, willing herself not to cry.

"He *what*? What does he want with you, then?" Igimaq unfolded his arms and sat forward, focusing on Emmeline.

"He wants to—to *use* me. To force my parents to do something he wants. Something—something bad. He mentioned this—this Creature too." She wiped her eyes with the backs of her hands. "So, don't you see? I have to know what he's doing. I have to know, so I can get my parents back."

Igimaq frowned gently. "It's not as easy as that, little one. We've been trying to figure him out for years, but he just never gives up trying. Every time we think we've foiled him, we turn around and there he is." He paused thoughtfully. "There've been reports for a while now of big, silent airships flying in under darkness, carrying equipment of some sort. Folks say he's building something: a bomb, maybe, or a drilling machine. Then there's the aurora—it's acting so strange lately. . . ." He rubbed at his tired face with one large hand. "We think he's actually breaking up the glacier, you know? It's been going on for years now, decades even, but lately it's been getting worse fast. Took us a while to realize what was going on, and then it took us longer still to decide what to do about it, and when we finally did . . ." He shook his head. "We've been doing our best to find him, but some who have gone haven't made it back, and the others have found nothing." He blinked sadly. "Qila's own brother went looking ten years ago, more maybe. Not much older than you. He never came home."

Emmeline swallowed. "That's awful. I'm sorry. For Qila, I mean."

"She's far from the only one who's lost somebody," said Igimaq.

"When you say he's breaking up the glacier—do you mean he's melting the ice?" said Emmeline after a moment. Her memory suddenly flooded with thoughts of Thing and their journey to France and the cold waves around the ship. "Is that why the sea's rising?"

"Could be," Igimaq said, and shrugged. "Can't be helping, at least."

"But what's so important that he'd do all this? Melting ice and stealing parents?"

"Raising the Kraken takes a lot of work, I guess," replied Igimaq, his face dark.

"The K—the *Kraken?*" Emmeline said. "But that's not *real*, is it?" Her head began to feel tight as it filled with thoughts. *What was that book Dad used to read to me?* Images piled up in her mind as she searched for a particular memory. *It had a mammoth on the cover, didn't it?* There had been a story in that book about the Kraken, she was sure. *But it was just a story,* she told herself. *A story to scare kids with.* A small voice in her head continued: *But it's a story about a beast that's stronger than anything imaginable—and with the power to live forever.* She swallowed hard. *The same power that Dr. Bauer wants.*

"I've said too much," muttered Igimaq, his eyes huge. "Look—just forget it. Forget it, right? I'll ask Qila again to let you settle for the night here, and we'll think about it in the morning. Okay?"

"But—"

"No buts! That's it, young lady. Once we've all had a rest, this whole thing will seem clearer."

Without meeting her eyes again, Igimaq swung himself out of his chair and hurried after Qila, leaving Emmeline alone with her racing mind.

Vos papiers, s'il vous plaît. Sasha smiled and reached over for the bundle of documents sitting on her dashboard. She handed them to the bored-looking border guard without a second glance, like they were nothing more than a stack of newspaper clippings. He grunted and began to examine them while Sasha fought the urge to drum her fingernails on the steering wheel.

"Your business in the republic?" the guard barked. Sasha smiled again, but his glower remained. *Losing your touch,* she thought.

"Pickup from the rue du Luxembourg, some sort of art consignment," she said. The guard huffed, flicking his eyes back to her documents.

"Passengers?"

"*Non.* Just what you see." The guard raised his eyebrow and looked at her, and Sasha tried not to shiver.

"Registration of the vehicle?"

"A-B-*sept-quatre-huit*-A-N," she rattled off, casually glancing at a sudden movement in her rearview mirror. Faster than she had time to process, she saw men running, waving one another on. Distant yelling reached her ears. One of the figures was carrying something that made Sasha's brain ignite—*a gun.* Realization sliced through her as she lifted her gaze to peer at the barrier before her. *Fool! You should've known this was a setup! Everything looks wrong. Even this guy's uniform is shoddy!*

She turned back to the guard. His eyes were fixed on her bodice, where her white silk flower was just barely peeking out beneath her open overcoat. He met her eyes and bared his teeth, his face twisting into a sneer.

"*Assistance!*" he yelled. "*Allez!*" He jumped up on her front tire and leaned in through the window in order to grab her keys—but Sasha was too fast. She started the engine and gunned it, flinging the fake border guard off as the lorry started moving. It roared as she headed straight for a gate, which wasn't open, praying she'd pick up enough speed to crash through. *I can make it,* she told herself. *I can make it!* A few hundred yards ahead someone stepped into her path, his gun raised to his shoulder. She ducked and pushed even harder on the accelerator, hearing a smash as his bullet pierced her windshield. *Who are these guys?* Whoever they were, they'd been strong enough to overpower the real border guards—and almost bring her mission to a halt before it had even properly begun. As she neared the gate, she realized there wouldn't be time to stop to release Thing from the secret hiding place or to look at her map— she'd have to hope she could find Monsieur Pichon's place from memory.

Another bullet hit her windshield, and the engine roared as it leaped forward, faster and faster and faster. Then, with a clattering, hissing bang, the lorry crashed through the metal gate. Sasha's head smacked into the ceiling of her cab as she bumped over the border and away, speeding as fast as she could through the streets of the republic, hoping that Thing would be all right for a while longer.

Far behind her she heard the sirens of her pursuers, and she gritted her teeth as she pressed the pedal to the floor.

* * *

Igimaq and Qila's muttered conversation from the kitchen was almost enough to send Emmeline to sleep. She'd been moved into the living room again as they discussed what to do with her, and she'd made the mistake of curling up in one of the soft chairs. Her head settled against a cushion, and she sighed as she gazed out the window. The sky was strangely light still, even though Emmeline knew that it was late, and to stave off the longing to close her eyes and drift away, she began to think about what to do next. If her parents truly were in the ice, then staying in this small, warm room would get her nowhere. The ice wasn't going to come to her, so she had to go to it, and she didn't want to sit about and wait for Igimaq to decide her fate—or, worse, her parents'. She didn't know much about the village council, either, besides how badly she wanted to avoid it. She imagined there'd be lots of discussion and worried mutterings and people sympathetically patting her on the head, which would accomplish nothing besides delaying her further.

She glanced toward the kitchen door. All was clear. *Now or never.*

Quickly and quietly she slid out of the chair and slipped into her warm outdoor gear, pulling on the boots and mittens that Igimaq had promised and that had been laid out by the fire for her. She picked up the snowshoes and stuck them under her arm, hoping she could work out how to put them on without too much trouble.

She tiptoed across the floor, checked her pockets one more time for her rope, her spoon, and her fishing line (discovering as she did so a small packet of food, which she wrapped her fingers around gratefully), and was gone through the front door like a gust of wind.

29

Emmeline's face tingled as the cold touched it.
Wrapped up tight in her stolen coat, borrowed boots, and
loaned mittens, she kept putting one foot in front of the
other. The straps of her snowshoes were too loose, but she
did the best she could with them and tried to force herself
to believe she was making good progress. The truth was,
she had no idea where she was going. She'd long ago left
Igimaq's tiny village behind, and now she was creeping
around a rocky shoreline, the sea gushing and hissing
to her left. Low on the horizon a pale sun burned, and
there was enough light to see for hundreds of yards in
every direction. The ground was barren. All that met Emmeline's gaze was a landscape so vast, and so flat, and so
unknown, that it made her bones rattle.

Walk with a cocky step and your head held high, she told

herself, Thing's jaunty voice playing in her mind, *and you can do anything.*

"Right," she muttered, swallowing hard.

As she walked, she dredged her memory again, and the book her father used to like to read to her floated to the surface. She could hardly believe she'd forgotten it, as reading with her father hadn't exactly been a regular occurrence, but then the cover burst clearly into her mind and the old fear she'd had of it washed over her. She shuddered as it filled her head—a drawing of a giant mammoth, its tusks huge and yellowed and its eyes red with rage, set above the words *Legendary Exploits!* in a garish font. It had been a collection of stories, each one gorier than the next, and she remembered her father's voice as he read, dark and booming at the gruesome bits and spookily whispery for the rest. She'd never let him know how much it had scared her. One story had definitely been about the Kraken, she felt surer with every moment, and she struggled to recall it in detail. As her mind orbited around thoughts of terrifying beasts that couldn't be killed, like a small moon around a planet, she began to wish she hadn't been such a scaredy-cat.

But they were just stories—weren't they? She wrapped her mittened hands around her coil of rope and her coil of fishing line. *Or were Mum and Dad trying to tell me ... trying to show me something ...* But her thoughts halted there, as if they had nowhere else to go.

Every step she took felt like she was walking farther and farther down into a dark tunnel with no light at the other end, but Emmeline's feet didn't slow.

In the belly of the lorry, Thing knew something was very wrong. He felt like he was inside a soccer ball during a very violent game, and there wasn't an inch of him that hadn't been battered or bruised by the journey so far. He could hear Sasha's muffled voice shouting something he couldn't make out, but her fear was plain.

I have to get out of here. He felt the whoop beginning to tie his chest in knots, but he forced himself to breathe slowly as he looked around, searching for the catch keeping the compartment closed. There was barely enough light to see, and so he used his fingers instead, running them around the inside of the box until he found it.

Crack-ping! The sound, sudden and far too close for comfort, made Thing want to fold himself up to the size of a postage stamp. His heart roared inside his chest.

"Come *on,* you great banana," he whispered, working at the catch, his hands shaking. Distantly he heard springs squeaking and brakes squealing and the deep growl of an engine under pressure, and he braced himself as the lorry's movement bashed him off the inside of the box again. He dug his nails in under the loosening catch and hauled for all he was worth.

Slowly but surely it started to give.

Emmeline rested long enough to eat the tiny packet of food. There was nothing to drink, but a small metal cup had been included with the food. After a few seconds' puzzling she realized all she had to do was dip this into some of the clear, cold meltwater all around her whenever she got thirsty. When she finished eating, she wrapped up the greased paper and placed it in her pocket beside the rest of her treasures, and she slid her small cup into the other pocket, glad to have something so useful so close to hand.

She'd only barely started to walk again when the sky above her head exploded with light and color, spreading in arcs from horizon to horizon. Her mouth fell open as she stood, transfixed, staring up at the dancing lights, her ears filling with a whispering, whishing buzz, like static electricity.

"What *are* they?" she breathed, feeling her entire body trembling. She wasn't talking about the lights in the sky, for Emmeline, of course, had read enough to understand that these were none other than the famed aurora borealis (she even knew the scientific reasons behind the phenomenon, not that she would have been able to remember them right at that moment). It was something else—something even *more* stupendous than the aurora itself—that had caught her eye.

They looked like creatures—*massive* creatures—in the sky. Bigger than bears stretched up to stand on their back legs, and taller than the tallest man. They were silhouetted against the northern lights, riding on them as Igimaq's tiny boat had ridden over the sea. As Emmeline watched, the creatures seemed to slide effortlessly over the lights, holding on to them like they were solid, sliding down them like they were made of some inexplicable fabric.

"It's impossible," Emmeline breathed, but her eyes refused to stop seeing it, so she kept looking. One of the creatures clung to a fold of the aurora as a chimpanzee would cling to a tree branch. It lifted one arm and pointed across the frozen landscape, right into the heart of the empty country. As it did this, it appeared to say something to the others. Its voice, which Emmeline now realized was the source of the low, bone-fizzing buzz that she'd heard a few moments before, made her already cold blood even colder, no matter that she couldn't understand the words.

Then the lights started to move again, but this time it was different. It looked as if something were dragging them down out of the sky, like a giant hand had grabbed hold of them and started pulling. With plaintive noises the creatures lifted their heads to the sky, and one by one they released their grip on the aurora and tumbled down, landing heavily on the ice. As soon as the last of them had fallen, the lights flickered and began to stretch out, finally vanishing into a glowing maelstrom that swirled slowly in the far distance.

Emmeline looked back at the creatures. They had gathered a few hundred yards from where she lay, and she immediately began to plan the best way to get across the bare, rocky ground without them seeing her.

For whatever they were doing, and wherever they were going, Emmeline wanted in.

Thing burst open the compartment in a flurry of kicks. He hauled himself out of the hole, pausing only to drag

Emmeline's satchel through after him, then found his seat again. Sasha's eyes were wide, flipping between the road ahead and her mirrors, but she managed to throw him a quick nod. Her knuckles were white on the steering wheel.

"You all right?" she called.

"Keep drivin'!" he shouted. "Don' worry about me." She just nodded again and went back to focusing on the road as Thing slipped the strap of Emmeline's satchel around his neck without a word.

"So," he said, glancing around at the bullet holes in the glass and noticing a large, official-looking vehicle speeding along behind them—its flashing lights in the mirror were unmistakable. "Did I miss anythin' interestin'?"

Sasha growled and put her foot down.

30

Emmeline ran as hard as she could. She kept catching her feet in gullies and crevices that were invisible until she was on top of them, and with every stumbling step the snow was deepening. The creatures were still too far away for her to make sense of their size and shape, but they looked a lot like the letter X, she thought: with no torso to speak of, their massively long and flexible arms and legs seemed to just meet in the middle. They were covered with long fur, and on the widest feet and hands she'd ever seen, they loped across the treacherous ground so quickly and smoothly that Emmeline knew she'd never keep up.

"Oh, please," she gasped. "Please wait!" She was *sure* these things, whatever they were, had to know how to find the Kraken—maybe they could even help her, if she asked them nicely. And even though part of her hated to admit it, Emmeline was desperate for a closer look simply because she'd never seen or heard of anything like them before. *Imagine!* she thought. *Will I be the youngest person ever to discover a new species?* Emmeline kept her brain warm by thinking about this as she ran. She had just decided on a name—the Widgetosaurus—when she realized that she'd started running slightly uphill.

Her heart hammering, and her mouth and throat dry, she clambered to the top of the snowdrift. Her exposed cheeks and nose were tingling. She blinked, trying to clear her eyes.

Before her lay some rocky, snowy ground, and beyond that something that looked like a huge black ribbon, and beyond that again a massive slab of ice stretching out in front of her like a giant's dining table. Distantly she could see the animals tumbling across it, getting farther and farther away with every heartbeat.

"Oh, no," she sighed, feeling her tiredness sneak up behind her and take her by the hand.

"Finally," Sasha gasped. The lorry rocked from side to side as they drove, slapping Thing's head against the window. They were headed right for something huge, stuck by itself in the middle of a field of mud. It was a tall metal tower with a large sphere perched on top like a grape on the end of a toothpick. Thick chains, attached somehow to the sphere, disappeared into the clouds overhead, which boiled and swirled in midair like they were trapped inside a glass jar. Pulses of powerful light flashed inside the clouds, and the closer they got, the more Thing could hear the rhythmic sound of metal clanking on metal. After a few seconds he worked out what it was—the chains straining to be released.

"What *is* that?" he said, gawping out through the battered windshield and trying to keep his grip on the door. Sasha didn't answer at first, her eyes glued to the rearview mirror. Thing looked too—their pursuers were closing in fast.

"We're not going to have time," Sasha muttered. Her eyes were wide, sweat rolled down the side of her face, and her hair was thick and ribboned, plastered to her head. "There's no way Monsieur Pichon can lower the ship now!"

"The—the ship?" Thing glanced around, but all he could see was this isolated field, flat and completely empty—except, of course, for the strange contraption that led up into nothing.

"The *Cloud Catcher*," muttered Sasha, lifting one finger from the steering wheel just long enough to point toward the tower.

"The what *what*?" Thing felt his mind start to get heavy and thick, like a sponge soaking up water. Sasha sucked her teeth and flicked her gaze toward the rearview mirror again. The lorry hopped and bucked over the ground. It seemed to Thing that their pursuers—or maybe it would be more accurate to call them *followers,* as they didn't appear to be in any huge hurry—were catching up to them. Then, suddenly, Sasha started fumbling on the ceiling of the cab, her fingers feeling blindly for something while her eyes flicked between the ground in front of them and the mirrors all around.

"What're ya lookin' for? I can help!"

"The horn!" she said. "We need to make some noise, get Monsieur Pichon out here."

"Right!" said Thing before realizing he had no idea what that meant. Eventually his scrambling, fumbling fingers found a cord, and because he couldn't think of anything better to do, he pulled it.

He almost fell back into his seat when a noise like a dying bull blared all around.

"Brilliant!" said Sasha, a smile breaking over her face. "Do it again! Longer this time!" Thing pulled it as hard as he could, and they battled on, roaring as they went.

A door opened near the base of the tower, and in the doorway a shape appeared. He—Thing presumed it was a he, maybe even Monsieur Pichon himself—stood in silhouette against the light of a tiny room.

In the same second a loud crack sounded from behind them, far too close for comfort. Sasha jerked, and Thing saw her face crumple. The lorry swerved but kept moving forward.

Thing let his fingers slip off the cord, and he flopped down into the seat beside her.

"Y'all right?" he asked her, even though he knew she wasn't. She couldn't be.

"Just peachy," she grunted. She turned to him and tried to smile, but her eyes were clouded. She clutched the steering wheel with her left hand and grabbed herself around the middle with her right, but when she brought her hand back around again, Thing saw bright red blood on her fingers and palm.

❄

Emmeline kept walking, following the tracks of the giant creatures whenever she could, but she knew that it was hopeless. There was no way she could cross the glacier, not alone. It went on for hundreds, maybe *thousands,* of miles, and there was no food or shelter anywhere. She felt the needling pain of the cold start to burrow its way into her skin, and not even touching her tools—her rope, her fishing line, her spoon, her piece of greased paper, and her dinged metal cup—could make her feel better.

"But I can't stop now. My *parents* might be out there," she said, squeezing her eyes tight. "And they're mine, and I want them back, and I've come all this way already—I can't give up now, can I? I *won't* leave them here." She opened her eyes again and wiped them dry, then peered out over the ice sheet, wondering if there was a way around it, or if she could *build* something that could take her over it, or if she should go back to Igimaq's village and beg for help, even from the council if she had to—and then something caught her eye.

"What on earth . . . ," she began, before her breath dried up inside her lungs.

Far out on the surface of the glacier, something was moving. In fact, Emmeline realized as she looked more closely, it was *several* somethings, all of them large and fast and inexplicable. She took a couple of nervous steps and then started to jog, her movements made awkward by her unfamiliar snowshoes.

Eventually she flopped down, belly-first, onto the hard ground, trying to make sense of what she was seeing.

"Horses!" she breathed, trembling from head to toe. They spilled up out of the crevasses on the face of the glacier in front of her, their flame-red tails and manes rippling as they moved. Their bodies shone white, and their hooves threw up sparks, like they were running on lightning. Even from Emmeline's perch several hundred yards away, she could hear their joyful, wild whinnying as they started to canter and then gallop, heading in the same direction as the vanished giants Emmeline had seen falling from the sky. *There has to be a reason they're following,* she told herself, her excitement building. *There's something important over there. I have to find out what it is!* As she watched, the horses leaped effortlessly over the ice, never missing a step, and a little voice in her head shouted: *Go after them!*

She hesitated, just for a second, before picking herself up off the ground.

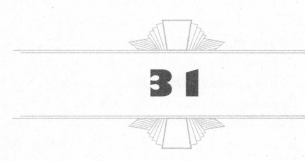

31

"Sasha! C'mon! Talk to me!" Thing felt his voice
snap and shatter inside him, and his words came out all
stretched. She put her bloodstained right hand back on the
steering wheel.

"Nearly there now," she gasped, yanking hard. The
truck turned, heading straight for the huge metal structure. Thing glanced up at the doorway, and he noticed
that the small figure was now scrambling down a ladder
to the ground. *Please have a first-aid kit,* he begged inside his
head. *Please be a doctor or somethin'!* He turned back to Sasha
and saw her gritting her teeth before finally bringing the
truck to a stop. She cut the engine and slumped in her
seat, her skin looking dull, its luster gone. Her hand found
her wound again, and she squeezed it tight.

"Go," she whispered. "You have to go. Get to Pichon

and tell him—tell him . . ." Her voice faded out as her eyes slid closed, and Thing grabbed Sasha's left hand, lying weakly in her lap. She grimaced as he did so, but her eyes flickered open again.

"Tell 'im what?" said Thing. "Come on! I need you, Sasha. Don't be doin' crazy things now, like dyin' or what have you. D'you hear me?"

As Sasha tried to reply, her eyes rolled back into her head and she fell silent. A grinding screech told Thing that someone—Monsieur Pichon, he hoped—had yanked open the door on Sasha's side, and a sudden gust of cold wind across his face confirmed it.

"What is going *on* here?" came a strange and unfamiliar voice. "*Parlez-vous français? Spreekt u Vlaams?*"

"Stop babblin' nonsense and see to her!" yelled Thing. Sasha's head lolled to one side. He squeezed her hand again, as hard as he dared, but she didn't stir this time.

"*Quoi?*" muttered Monsieur Pichon, scrambling into the lorry. "Natasha, what have you been up to, *hein?*" Quickly he checked Sasha's pulse. "She is still with us," he said, glancing at Thing with wide eyes. "But, I fear, not for long."

"Come on, then!" Thing clambered out of the lorry and raced, slipping in the muck, around to the driver's side. Together, they carried Sasha from the cab. Thing found it hard going, weighed down on one side by Emmeline's satchel and on the other by Sasha, but he didn't falter.

Distantly he was aware of crashing noises, loud beeping, and angry voices, but he didn't look behind him.

High above his head the unseen object attached only

187

by chains rattled and settled in the breeze, straining to be free of its moorings, but he didn't look up to see it, either.

All Thing could see, and all he cared about, was Sasha's rapidly graying face.

❄

The red-maned horses were still spilling out of the ice, and Emmeline's heart was thudding as she ran.

"Come on, come *on!*" she muttered to herself as her feet went sideways for the hundredth time. The ground was rockier now, and she realized the snowshoes were slowing her down. With a whispered apology to Qila, she unfastened and kicked them off as quickly as she could. She blinked the coldness out of her eyes and frowned as she gazed across the acres that stood between her and where she needed to be.

"No," she breathed. The flow of horses had slowed, and now only a few stragglers—smaller ones, younger ones maybe—were struggling out of the crevasses. In the distance, way off over the top of the glacier, the others were disappearing, their red tails like flashes of fire. *This is your last chance,* whispered her brain.

She crossed the rocks in the space of ten heartbeats, and the glacier loomed ever closer, big enough and terrible enough to fill up the whole world. The nearer she got, the better she could hear it groaning and shifting, cracking and booming as it moved, like a huge animal breathing.

A loud whinny made her look back toward the horses, and she realized one of them had lost its footing and was sliding sideways across the glacier. The horses near it were wild-eyed, clattering around their fallen friend for a few moments before tearing off after the rest of their herd. As the trapped horse flailed on the ice, Emmeline felt her already racing heart start to thunder even more loudly.

"Don't be injured, don't be injured, don't be injured," she chanted under her breath as she ran. Nimbly she hopped from rock to rock, crunching her way through undisturbed snow, her breath slicing its way down into her lungs. She glanced up again and saw the horse still struggling to get to its feet. Another horse, the smallest yet, burst its way out of the ice and galloped off without looking back, and after that there were no more. The last of the disappearing herd was a reddish blur on the horizon.

Emmeline dropped her eyes from the glacier just in time to watch her feet reach the end of the rocky plain. They skidded sickeningly on the ice-logged ground. Her toes poked out over a pitch-black chasm, her heels barely hanging on to the solid surface. Without thinking, she threw herself backward, ignoring the pain as her elbow got bashed on a hidden rock. After a couple of seconds she opened her eyes again and sat forward, just enough to look down—and *down*.

A dark gap between the earth and the glacier's edge yawned before her, an unknowable and never-ending drop—and it was a gap she had to cross.

If I fall, she thought, her mind sluggish, *they'll never even know I was here.*

"*Vite!* Quickly, boy!" gasped Monsieur Pichon. Thing heaved the heavy steel door closed, and it sealed with a loud, echoing clang. He'd barely done this when he heard an irritated "Come, come!" and he turned to see Monsieur Pichon, Sasha draped in his arms, standing in a small chamber with a thick glass door, which was open, ready for him. He hurried in, not waiting to be told to close the door behind him, and Monsieur Pichon slapped his hand down on a large button embedded in the metal wall. Thing felt his stomach lurch, very slightly, and the view outside the glass door went black. A few seconds later they came to a halt with a tiny jerk. The door unsealed with a *hss,* and next thing, they were clanging down a walkway suspended in midair, right across the heart of a giant, spherical room. Vaguely Thing realized they must be at the top of the tower he'd seen from outside, but his worry about Sasha kept him from nosing about or taking much in besides her barely conscious face. He focused his attention on helping Monsieur Pichon get her to a large platform in the middle of the room, where they laid her down with as much care as they could. They removed her coat, tossing it to one side, and the extent of her wound became clear.

"Ain't you got a bed? Or a couch, even?" said Thing. "She can't be left lyin' here!"

"This is a *research* station," muttered Monsieur Pichon. "And *underfunded,* at that. It was never designed to be a field hospital or a convalescent home." As he spoke, he got to his feet and crossed the platform to a desk standing in the far corner. Beneath it was a set of drawers, through which he began to rummage. Thing gaped helplessly at Sasha. Her eyes flickered behind her closed lids, and a small frown dimpled her forehead. He willed her to keep breathing.

"It's not perfect, but this will have to do," said Monsieur Pichon, lowering himself to his knees. He had a small box in his hand, which he placed on the ground beside Sasha's head before clicking it open. Thing could see a pair of scissors, a rolled-up bandage, a couple of glass bottles with stoppers in their necks, and several thick pads of cotton wool. As he watched, Monsieur Pichon reached into the box.

"Do you have steady fingers, boy?" he asked, holding out the scissors to Thing. "We need to cut away her clothing, expose the wound. Then, if we can, we must remove the bullet."

"What d'you mean, do I have steady fingers?" said Thing, his heart pounding. "I can't do it!"

"So I must do everything, *oui?*"

"But I—"

"Enough," Monsieur Pichon interrupted, slapping the scissors into Thing's hand. "Begin."

Thing stared down at them, wondering why it felt like the room was slowly spinning.

32

"Come on," Emmeline told herself. "You have to move."

She shuffled away from the chasm. A whinny from the fallen horse made her look to the glacier, her blood jumping. It hadn't quite found its feet yet, but it wouldn't be long about it. Once it did, Emmeline knew it would be off after its herd mates, and that would leave her here, trapped and alone, with no way of ever helping her parents, or finding out what was going on at the heart of this glacier.

Not happening.

Emmeline got a foot beneath herself and pushed up and away from the ground. She took a few steps back from the dark hole. Impatiently she rubbed at her eyes with a frosty mitten and blinked a couple of times. The horse was nearly on its feet, a sparkling white blur against the grayer, dirtier white of the glacier. Its bright red mane and tail were like splashes of blood on a handkerchief.

Emmeline stopped thinking and, with light and sure feet, started to run as fast as she could on the slippery earth.

Just before she reached the lip of the chasm, she leaped, high and hard, her eyes and every inch of her body focused on the glacier, and on landing safely, and on getting home.

She flew through the air so fast that she didn't even have time to cry out.

❄

Thing was sure his fingers were made of lead as, gently, carefully, he eased the blade of the scissors into the fabric of Sasha's dress. He tried hard not to listen to his thoughts, which were, just then, screaming things like *Careful! You're goin' to cut her!*

"Quiet," he growled through clenched teeth.

"*Pardon?*" asked Monsieur Pichon.

"Can't talk jus' at the minute," muttered Thing. "Busy."

"Pay attention, boy. We must hurry!" Thing stared at Monsieur Pichon, the scissors quivering between his fingers.

"If you'd like to take over, I'll be more'n happy to step aside," he said in a quiet voice. Monsieur Pichon just sat back, frowning, and studied Sasha. She lay completely still, and her breathing was slow and regular. Monsieur

Pichon had knocked her out with a few drops of sweet-smelling liquid from one of his stoppered bottles, and she seemed peaceful. Her blood had soaked through the fabric of her dress, and it was darker and more frightening than Thing had imagined anything could be.

As quickly as he could, he kept cutting.

"*Bon,*" said Monsieur Pichon as Sasha's wound grew clearer. "Now some pressure." He knocked the scissors, and Thing's hand, aside as he began to pack the wound with cotton, which soon grew red. "Can you sew?" he asked.

"Do I *look* like a seamstress to you?"

"Your attitude is not helping, young man," said Monsieur Pichon without looking up.

Thing stared at the top of Monsieur Pichon's head and felt his chest tighten. "This is *wrong!* Everythin's goin' wrong!" He threw the scissors to the ground, where they landed with a bang. "It's my fault, all of it! I got Emmeline kidnapped, and now I've got Sasha shot, an' it's all *wrong.*" He scrunched his eyes shut, and his nose started to run. In his ears a faint voice chuckled. *Typical,* it whispered, before Thing quenched it out.

"Emm-Emmeline?" said Monsieur Pichon, his tiny, frightened voice making Thing look back at him again. "Kidnapped? By whom?"

"Some bloke. Bauer or somethin'," replied Thing, sniffling. "Sasha was comin' to you—well, and Edgar, too, 'cept he stayed behind to help Madame Blancheflour fight the mercen'ries. Sasha said you could tell us what to do to get 'er back. Emmeline, I mean. She said you had a plan.

To get to Greenland." As Thing spoke, Monsieur Pichon's eyes grew round.

"You really should have told me this before," he said after a few seconds.

"I was sorta distracted, y'know?" said Thing, wiping his nose on his sleeve and nodding down at Sasha's sleeping form.

"Even so. If I had known—"

The words were interrupted by a large boom from outside. Thing's eyes met Monsieur Pichon's, and all he could see was his own terror reflected back at him.

Emmeline hit the glacier so hard that the breath was knocked right out of her lungs. She scraped across its surface, the ice scratching and biting at any exposed skin it could find. She rolled and slithered, slid and skidded, until gradually—and painfully—she came to a halt. She pushed herself over onto her back and, as quickly as she could, opened her eyes.

"Hello there," she said. Her voice sounded like a feather floating to earth.

"*Fmmffff*," replied the horse. It stood over her, gazing down with a curious expression in its huge, dark eyes. Up close Emmeline could see just how luminous its white coat was, and how vivid its tail and mane. It glowed like a pearl. Besides that, she had no idea what she was looking at. She'd never been a horsey type and had never regretted it—until now.

"You're a beautiful boy, aren't you?" she breathed, raising one hand to stroke the horse's nose, hoping she was being gentle enough. With the other she felt around inside her pocket until she was sure she had a good grip on her rope.

"Steady, little horse," she murmured, keeping a soothing hand on the animal's face as she slowly got to her feet. The horse, looking entirely calm and confident, was standing on the ice as easily as another, less extraordinary horse might lounge about in a meadow. "That's it. Good boy!" She ran her hand down the side of the horse's neck, and it started to prance about, throwing its gaze toward the horizon.

"Yes, yes—I know. You want to be off after your friends. That's fine. You just need to bring me with you. All right?" The horse tossed its head and gave a sort of scream, baring its teeth a little, and Emmeline took a step back. Her rope hung from her mittened fist.

"I don't want to hurt you," she said, reaching out her hand to the horse again. It nudged her with its nose, as if it understood. Emmeline slipped the rope around the horse's neck, and—hoping the rope wasn't digging in—she used it to pull herself up and over. This took a while, and Emmeline was sure it didn't look at all dignified. The horse, to its credit, stayed quite still and just let her get on with it.

"This is—wow. This is so high up," she said once she was settled. The ice beneath the horse's hooves looked like it was miles away, and she tried to ignore the thought of how much it would hurt to fall off.

She didn't have a chance to think another thing because, without warning, the horse reared. Emmeline grabbed her makeshift reins, and it took off over the ice like a flaming cannonball, its hooves barely touching the ground as it went.

Emmeline clung on, her eyes squeezed shut. She tried to imagine she was safely at home in bed, Watt outside her door with a steaming bowl of porridge heaped high with honey and cinnamon and raisins. However, she soon found that the burning cold air and the bouncing rhythm of the speeding horse made it impossible to imagine she was anywhere else.

Mile after mile of glacier spooled out behind them, crevasses crossed in single leaping bounds, and on they ran.

33

"We must get her away from here!" rasped Mon-sieur Pichon. "Quickly, boy. The cotton!" Thing leaned across Sasha and did as he'd seen Monsieur Pichon do, terrified that he was making things worse—but she didn't stir. With shaking, hurried fingers Monsieur Pichon fetched the bandage from his first-aid box and began to wrap it around her torso. Thing did his best to help, and somehow Monsieur Pichon managed to tie off the flimsy-seeming gauze. Just as he did so, another *booom* split the air. He struggled to his feet, looking exhausted. "They will be upon us soon. We must get to the ship," he told Thing.

"What are they *doin'*?" Thing rolled to his feet and leaned against a nearby handrail. He stared toward the door but couldn't see any movement.

"Trying to break into my workshop," said Monsieur Pichon sadly. "I knew the day would come eventually."

"Who?" said Thing, looking back at him. "The border fellas?" A grimace passed over Monsieur Pichon's face, but he said nothing as he bent to pick up Sasha's coat, which he threw over his arm. He dropped to his knees beside her and looked up at Thing.

"Please help me," he said. Grabbing handfuls of Sasha's dress, they lifted her as gently as they could. She was still unconscious, a dead weight in their arms.

"We must go to the right here," said Monsieur Pichon when they got to the end of the walkway, his voice sounding strained. "The craft is this way." Thing nodded, turning. The walkway continued all around the circumference of the room, its narrowness helped a little by the handrail that ran beside it. About a hundred yards away stood a sturdy-looking set of steps, and Thing guessed they were headed for it.

"So, what is this craft thing, anyway?" The words were barely out of his mouth before a third gigantic boom made him stumble.

"We are out of time!" yelled Monsieur Pichon, trying his best to drag Sasha along. "Help me!" Thing slipped his shoulder beneath her arm and gritted his teeth as he and Monsieur Pichon ran, stumbling, down the walkway, carrying her between them. After a few yards he felt the old, familiar clutching pain in his chest, and his breaths began to get thick.

"Stop!" roared a voice from right behind them, making

them clatter to a halt. "I am armed, and I will shoot!" Thing looked at Monsieur Pichon, whose eyes were bulging in red-rimmed terror.

"We shall see your friend receives the medical attention she needs," continued the voice. "But you must stop and give yourself up." Thing's heart thudded like someone had kicked it, and his knees began to wobble. *I didn't feel 'em comin'!* He looked over his shoulder, straining to see. All he could make out was a shadowy figure and the glint of a gun.

Beside him, Monsieur Pichon started whispering.

"Boy—you must run. Run fast! Take the ship and go north. That is where the girl will be brought, if you are right about Bauer. Go north!" Thing stared at him for a couple of seconds. He licked his lips as his brain started whirring, faster and faster. He glanced at Sasha, still out cold.

Then he blinked and met Monsieur Pichon's eyes again. He nodded, just once.

The wind was whipping the moisture from Emmeline's eyes before she had a chance to blink it away. She'd never traveled at this sort of speed before—not even in her dreams. There was no sign of the giant, loping creatures, nor even of the other horses in the herd she'd seen bursting from the ice, but still her steed ran on, sure and strong, as if it knew where it was going. It was hard to tell in the darkness and the vastness of the flat, empty place, but Emmeline felt that they'd left the sea at their backs and were headed inland.

Why didn't I just go back to Igimaq's village? she thought, every muscle in her body beginning to throb with a deep, rattling ache. *I should never have left in the first place!* She buried her face in the horse's red mane, realizing as she did so that it flowed over her skin like warm bathwater, soft and fragrant and comforting. She sank her nose into it and breathed deeply, her face tingling as it started to thaw.

Feeling calmer, she sat back a little and looked around. To either side there was nothing but emptiness. Miles above, in a thick greenish-purple stream like a river made of starlight, the aurora flowed. It strained and crackled as it tried to escape the pull of whatever was drawing it down toward the ground, tendrils of light peeling away as it struggled, but nothing seemed to have an effect. It looked so sickeningly *wrong* that Emmeline couldn't drag her eyes away from it. Her mouth fell open and her grip on the horse began to loosen.

"*Whiiinnnnnn!*" Emmeline snapped out of her trance at the sound of the horse's warning. Quickly she flattened herself against its neck once more and glued herself to its smooth back, as high above their heads, the lights blazed.

She was so focused on staying on the horse—and on keeping herself warm in its mane—that she didn't see what was lurking on the horizon like a huge black claw, and toward which they were galloping, full pelt, like there was a fire at their back.

Thing ran, his chest and throat burning, reminding him with every step: *You left her behind! You left her to die!* The crack of a gunshot, and voices that were raised but somehow unclear—like the words were being yelled through water—made his feet move faster, even though he hated himself for doing it.

His lungs felt like someone had tied his neck in a knot.

"Whoop," came a noise, unasked for, out of his mouth. *"Whoop."* He shook his head, angry with himself.

"Don't stop!" shouted Monsieur Pichon from behind him. "Get to the ship! You must—" The words were snipped off suddenly, but Thing knew he couldn't look back. *Please be all right, please be all right,* he begged.

Every muscle Thing had was focused on getting to the steps. They led upward, very steeply, into the curved ceiling of this strange spherical room. An open door, made of the same brightly polished metal as the stairway, stood at the top.

He reached the stairs and flung himself onto them. The rhythmic *clang-clang-clang* noise of a lot of heavy boots, all following him at once, made him race up the steps two at a time.

A tall, brown-skinned woman at the head of the gang of armed pursuers, some of whom were still wearing their fake border guard uniforms, raised a gloved hand, and the chase stopped dead. Her eyes followed his progress with amusement.

"Ma'am, I can take him," called a heavily muscled man, nudging his way past.

"Not yet," she replied, her voice calm.

"Ma'am." The soldier stood to attention, slamming the butt of his weapon against the metal floor with a loud bang. The tall woman glanced back up at Thing, whose terrified gaze met her cool, mocking eyes as he vanished through the open door. He remembered to swing it shut behind him, though his sweating hands almost lost their grip.

"Let the little fool think he's outsmarted us," murmured the woman, watching the closed door with what looked like glee. "Let him think he's escaped."

Beyond the door Thing was frozen in place. His eyes couldn't move fast enough to take in everything he needed to see, but even if they could have, his brain wouldn't have been able to think fast enough to understand.

34

"Okay," breathed Thing. "Okay." He gnawed on his lip, looking at the giant chain in front of him. A second chain, equally huge, rose from the far side of the platform Thing was standing on. They vanished into the sky, piercing the heaving belly of the gray clouds trapped above. The chain nearest Thing was attached by a complicated-looking series of locks and levers to a strut sticking out of the platform, which ran all the way around the sphere. Thing had a head for heights, but even he felt a bit ill as the wind sucked at him, threatening to toss him off the platform and down to the ground.

He glanced around one more time, but there was nothing else up there. No ladders, no stairways, no escape. The chain ground and wailed as it shifted in its moorings, moving so slowly and heavily that Thing knew the object being held captive, whatever it was, had to be huge. Monsieur Pichon's voice whispered in his mind: *Get to the ship!*

"But how'm I goin' to get up there?" he muttered. He peered out over the edge of the platform and saw the old lorry they had made their escape in parked in the mud miles below. In a ring around it were several more vehicles, large and black and shiny, like they were guarding it, or keeping it captive.

"No time for this," he muttered to himself. He stared at the chain for a second or two, and his brain began to tick over. Very carefully he caught hold of the lowest link. He ran his hand over the cool metal, seeing in it his slightly distorted reflection gazing back out at him as if wondering what he thought he was doing, but he ignored that.

"Watch yer fingers, yeah? One sudden move by this chain and yer goin' to be no good to anyone, least of all Ems." Lightly he hopped onto the chain and crouched low as he got a feel for its movement, sizing it up, keeping himself well away from all the pinch points.

He let his gaze travel up the length of the chain again. Each link was as thick as his torso and longer than he was tall. "Easy peasy," he whispered, half believing it. Then, taking a deep breath, he bounced elegantly to his feet. He swung Emmeline's satchel around to his front and took a firm hold of it with one hand. He catapulted himself toward the second link, and then the third, his feet finding their way as though he'd done this a thousand times before. He leaped from link to link never, ever looking down.

Within a few moments the gray clouds loomed right

above his head. Thing took another deep breath, ignoring the tight band of pain that wrapped itself around his lungs. Just as he prepared to make his final move, a flash of light burst from deep within the strange gray mist. His foot stumbled, and he lost his grip, and he began to fall.

✿

The green light overhead was growing thicker and brighter the farther Emmeline rode, and the whole sky was slowly swirling like a gathering storm. In the near distance Emmeline could make out some shadowy shapes moving in the strange glow from the sky, and she wondered if she'd finally caught up with the horse's lost herd—but then, just like that, they vanished again, as if the glacier had swallowed them up. Emmeline blinked in surprise.

"*Hmfff!*" snorted the horse, and Emmeline looked down. The ice was slick underfoot here, running with meltwater so deep it almost reached the tops of the horse's hooves. The sight of it made her uneasy. *The glacier is breaking,* she thought, remembering what Igimaq had told her in his kitchen. They came to a halt, and the horse whuffed as it lowered its head. It seemed as confused as she was.

"All right, boy," she whispered to it, rubbing its neck again. "It's all right." The horse calmed a little, and it shook out its mane, showering Emmeline with warm, fragrant air.

"If only I still had my *satchel,*" she muttered, blinking. She could have found something in there to help, she *knew* it.

Without any command from Emmeline, the horse began to move once again. It picked up its head, and its ears flicked this way and that, like it was listening to something Emmeline couldn't hear.

"Hey!" she said, wiping at her face with her mitten. "*Hey!* Where are we going?" She pulled a little on the rope, but it had no effect whatsoever. Emmeline realized that all this time she'd thought *she* was the one in charge—but now she knew better.

"*Fnnnnhmmm!*" said the horse, throwing back its head.

And then, all around them, horses burst out of the ice.

Emmeline had never seen so many horses in one place before. She clung to the back of her own mount as it skittered around like a newborn foal. All the fully grown horses seemed to be staring at her, rolling their great, shining eyes, as if wondering who or what on earth she was.

Then, with a cry, the horses reared as one, and like a white-and-red river, they turned and started to gallop— Emmeline's included. All she could do was hold on to its neck and try to breathe. The noise was deafening.

The flood of horses reached a crevasse. Its edges looked soft, and snowy meltwater trickled into it from many different streams, but it was still deep and dark and terrifying.

Before she could think, let alone do anything to stop it, her horse took its turn to leap straight into the chasm. Emmeline gripped it with all her might and screamed as loudly as she dared, waiting for the ice to swallow her up.

Thing's arms throbbed, but he didn't let go. He kept his focus firmly on the chain, not on the mud hundreds of feet below, and he locked his fingers together, hugging the massive link, barely able to feel what he was doing through the pain and numbness. Emmeline's satchel hung from him like a sack of rocks, its one unbroken strap digging into his neck, and he tried not to think about what would've happened if his fingers had missed when he'd grabbed the chain to stop his fall.

Come on, he muttered inside his head. His brain felt like it was bursting out of his skull.

Gritting his teeth, he swung his body in a desperate attempt to get a foothold. Every muscle screamed, but this time his left foot found the link.

35

Several seconds passed, and Emmeline was not dead. At least, she didn't *think* she was dead. She sat astride the horse with her eyes closed listening to trickling and gushing and cracking noises, some of them close by and others—sounding like distant thunder—far away. There was whinnying, and stamping, and harrumphing, and the clacking of hooves on ice.

"*Fnnnhh!*" objected her horse, startling Emmeline so much that she flung her eyes open. A split second later she shut them again, her mind reeling.

Hundreds of horses stood in the depths of an icy cavern. Standing beyond them, with their limbs extended, was a group of the huge, shaggy creatures Emmeline had seen falling from the sky. Dotted in among them were more . . . *things*—Emmeline didn't have a better word than that—which were short, ugly, and slightly moldy-looking and stared up at her with their lower lips sticking out and their foreheads wrinkled. She was pretty sure there were some big, four-legged shapes moving around, grumbling in dark voices, but she hadn't given herself long enough to look at them.

Emmeline took a few deep breaths, despite the strange and slightly pungent smell that clogged the air. *I can't sit here forever with my eyes shut,* she told herself, and so, slowly, she opened them. It looked more impossible than she remembered. She shrank against her horse, trying point-lessly to blend in.

One of the small, wrinkled creatures lifted its head and sniffed sharply at the air before turning in her direc-tion. It jerked, surprised, when its gaze met Emmeline's, then it started to shamble toward her, rolling its legs in a most peculiar way. It fixed her with a stare, mumbling un-der its breath. The horse whickered, taking a step or two backward, as the strange little figure approached, but the creature simply swatted its hand through the air as though waving away a fly, and soon it was standing, critically, in front of Emmeline. Raising one of its impressively tangled eyebrows, it spoke—but in a language she'd never heard before. It sounded like the noise a rock would make if it could talk, full of booms and creaks.

"S-sorry—" she began, but she didn't have a chance to continue.

"*Inglish?*" said the creature, its eyes opening wide. It cleared its throat and spat on the ice before looking back up at Emmeline. "You speak English?" it said, its words slightly clearer but its voice now sounding like a piece of metal being hit with a heavy hammer.

"Yes," ventured Emmeline.

"What are you doing astride the son of Hófvarpnir, you can tell me?"

"The son of what?"

The creature frowned. "Did you not wonder what manner of steed you had, child?"

"Well, yes, I—I mean—"

It waved its hand again irritably. "You ride the descendant of the Hoof-Thrower," it interrupted in a grand tone. Emmeline merely gaped at it as though it were speaking Greek. "An Æsirsmount?" it continued, slightly deflated.

Emmeline closed her mouth. "I have no idea what that is," she said.

Through the wispy clouds shrouding him, Thing could see the chain to which he clung disappearing into a hole in the hull of a huge vessel. Beyond the hole was nothing but darkness, but he knew one thing for sure: inside had to be better than where he was. He hurried to the opening and climbed in. Now he could clearly see a winch, securely bolted to a metal panel in the floor, and a narrow, dark doorway, which gave way to a narrow, dark hallway to his right.

"Fortune favors the brave, an' all that," he said, making for it. He found himself in a curved corridor lit at intervals by small, square windows cut into the left-hand wall.

Up ahead he saw a larger window, and outside that was something Thing couldn't explain. It looked like a circular chamber through which clouds and lightning and (if the creaking of the window was anything to go by) extremely high winds were being channeled. All of this was flowing down the center of the ship toward the metal sphere at the top of the tower far below.

"Unbe*liev*able," he muttered, pressing his nose to the glass.

A sudden bucking nearly knocked Thing off his feet. He slammed into the window just as a lightning bolt as thick as a tree trunk burst down the chamber. It struck the sphere with a deafening boom, crackling around it for a few seconds before fizzling out. The shock wave made the entire ship strain against its chains. A noise overhead drew Thing's gaze upward, and he saw a ball of pulsating light, like a trapped sun, gathering at the top of the chamber. His ears felt funny suddenly, and he realized—just in time—that the ball of light was about to explode into another lightning bolt. He flung himself backward, hitting the ground hard, and covered his eyes as the lightning let loose. It roared past the window, making every hair on Thing's body stand on end and his mouth taste like he'd swallowed a spoon.

Got to get this thing figured out quick, he told himself once his teeth had stopped tingling. *I hardly think whoever's after me is goin' to give up jus' because of a locked door an' a chain—an' that's if the ship don't tear itself in bits first.*

He clambered to his feet and carried on. He hadn't

gone far when a pair of large, important-looking doors met his eye. *Control room,* he thought. *Bound to be!*

He pushed the doors open and strode through, Emmeline's satchel at his side.

❄

"Look, I don't understand," Emmeline protested, her voice barely audible in the clamor of the ice cavern. "Please! You've got to help me. I'm here to—"

"She rides an *Æsirsmount* and thinks it of no importance?" interrupted the tiny, wrinkled thing in front of her. "What matter why *you* are here, human? We have larger things to occupy us than you."

"Like—like what?" asked Emmeline. "Does it have anything to do with the ice? M-melting, I mean?"

The creature frowned. "What concern is it of yours?"

"Nothing, only my parents—"

"Your parents are human too, hmm?"

"Well, of c-*course!*"

"Human like the white-faced man?" Suddenly the cavern seemed a lot more crowded than before.

Emmeline flailed for words. "I—no, he kidnapped me. He took my parents. He's not—"

"Silence!" said the creature. "This is not a matter for one so lowly as me. We are summoned to an audience— kobolds, Icewalkers, Æsirsmounts, all who dwell in or on the ice. Let the god-horse explain why it has seen fit to bring you here."

"*God*-horse?" echoed Emmeline. Quickly she unraveled her fingers from her horse's mane, wondering if she should slide off its back in case it was impolite to ride it like it was just any old horse, even though it hadn't seemed to mind up to now. "What's that?"

The creature stared. "You ask me to explain *Æsirsmount*, as though their fame and repute were not sung throughout the world?"

"Is it? I've never heard of them," said Emmeline. The creature blinked at her, incredulous. "Sorry," she added.

"The god-horses? Sons of the sons of the steeds who bore the old deities into battle and carried our greatest heroes unto death?" The creature paused, considering. "And unto other places besides death?"

Emmeline's face remained blank, and the creature's shoulders slumped a little. "Bred to pass between Above and Below with ease? To fly across the face of the ice faster than even the wind itself? Sworn to serve and protect the frozen lands with their very *lives*? The guardians of the glacier?" It looked pained. "No?"

"That bit sounds a bit more familiar, all right," said Emmeline, remembering the journey she'd taken to get here.

It sighed. "Dismount and follow me." It turned away, gesturing to the hordes of creatures all around. As one, they began to move.

"No—wait! Please!" Emmeline called, but her only answer was an impatient gesture from the creature and a soft whinny from the horse.

Wondering what "audience" the creature had been talking about, she swung her aching leg over the horse's back and slid, more heavily than she intended, to the ground. Her knees cracked. Step by creaking step, Emmeline followed the tiny figure deeper into the heart of the cavern, surrounded in every direction by things too inexplicable to look at. She kept her hand on the horse's warm flank, and—god-horse or not—it never left her side.

36

"Well, well, well," whispered Thing. **"What 'ave** we 'ere?"

The doors closed behind him, and he was standing in the exact center of a large room paneled in highly polished wood. The walls to either side were covered in floor-to-ceiling shelves stuffed with books, papers, and rolled-up scrolls. A chart was pinned to a stand in one corner. Three leather chairs stood on a raised dais directly in front of Thing, and they looked out through a window as long as two train carriages and easily as tall as a house. This window followed the curved sweep of the room and would have given a panoramic view to whoever sat in the seats—but at the moment it was entirely dark. In front of the window, facing the chairs, was a huge control desk filled with buttons and levers and switches and lights.

"Yeah," muttered Thing. "Anythin' else would've been *too* easy, o'course." He hurried to the chairs and settled himself into the one in the center, flinging Emmeline's satchel into the seat beside him. On the nearest control panel dials and gauges labeled with things he couldn't read met his gaze. Buttons with arrows on them, pointing every which way, sprouted from it. *Controllin' direction?* Thing asked himself, shrugging.

In the middle of the panel he saw a button with a lightning bolt on it and, beneath that, a button embossed with a soft-cornered rectangle. A rectangle that, come to think of it, looked a lot like the window in front of him.

Biting his lip, Thing pushed it and flung himself back in the chair as if the control panel had given him an electric shock.

Before his eyes a bright white line formed down the center of the window and widened as the shield that had been covering it slowly opened. Thing held his breath as he sat forward a little and peered curiously out. At first all he could see was the swirling gray mist of the clouds, and then his heart skipped a beat.

Over to his left a huge black aircraft appeared out of the clouds and hovered, its sleek lines the same as those of the vehicles that had pursued them here. It had four flat propellers and a round body with a tail sticking out the back. Thing squinted as he tried to see it clearly, but it was smooth and featureless, its windows dark, giving nothing away.

The next thing he knew, bright yellow flashes erupted from the front of the hovering black aircraft, and a soft pattering sounded as white splashes, like tiny explosions, began to bloom all over the window before him.

He gaped, confused, for a few seconds, and then it all became clear: this black aircraft, whoever was manning it, was firing at the *Cloud Catcher*.

Push the lightnin' button! screamed his brain, and without another thought Thing smacked it with his clenched fist. An almighty roar sounded from somewhere deep inside the ship, and a surge of power like nothing he had ever felt rocked the craft on its moorings, shaking it slowly from side to side. From all around he heard groaning and creaking and snapping noises, none of which sounded good.

Then, with a noise like a herd of elephants all trumpeting at once, the right-hand side of the *Cloud Catcher* started, quite suddenly, to rise. Thing lost his balance as the control cabin tipped alarmingly upward, flinging him—along with a rumbling tide of books and knickknacks—to the floor. He skidded along the highly polished surface, finally stopping his slide by bracing his feet against the base of the leftmost chair. Scrabbling to keep his grip, he used the chair like a ladder, climbing back into the center seat.

"Chains're still attached!" he muttered, quickly searching the control panel for anything that looked like it could release them. Sparks flashed outside the window as a fresh barrage of bullets hit the ship. At last Thing's eyes fell on a button that didn't look like too much of a risk, and he felt his pulse flicker as he pressed it.

The chains on the left-hand side released, and the ship righted itself so suddenly that Thing was flung across the room again, skidding along the floor and bashing, head-first, into the wall.

Emmeline followed the wrinkled creature's rolling gait down a tall, roughly carved tunnel. The ground was slick underfoot, but she seemed to be the only one having difficulty keeping her balance.

"Will you please tell me where we're going?" she asked.

"None of your concern," replied the creature without even bothering to turn around.

"It *is*, actually," Emmeline muttered before she could stop herself. The creature whirled on its heel and stared at her like she was something it'd found lodged in the drain.

Emmeline's horse let out a loud whinny, and it lifted its front leg. When it brought its hoof down again, the crash it made echoed around the icy passageway. The creature watched as the horse shook its mane, which started to glow just like flames licking their way up its proud, strong neck.

"We are—ah. We are approaching the halls of the Northwitch," the creature muttered, keeping its eyes fixed on Emmeline's horse. "She has summoned us to her presence, and your arrival here, at this time—well. That is a matter for her."

"Wait—who's the Northwitch?" *Maybe she can help!* thought Emmeline. *If she's summoning people here and there, maybe she's in charge?*

"You will see," the creature said before turning back

around. Emmeline wasn't sure, but she thought she saw a peculiar trembling in its step, and a doubt crept into her heart.

They walked on without speaking, the only noise the booming and cracking of the ice all around. Beside Emmeline the horse was warm and reassuring.

Then the corridor opened up into a chamber, the ceiling of which stretched away and was lost in the deep darkness overhead, and the floor was vast and covered with a fine, delicate layer of freshly fallen snow. Their feet whished and whispered as they walked, and their breath hung in the air like tiny clouds.

Their guide stopped walking and dropped to its knees in the snow. It turned to face Emmeline, its face an impatient, red-glowing mask.

"How *dare* you! No one stands in the presence of the Northwitch!" it said. "Kneel!" Emmeline's mouth fell open as she glanced around the empty-seeming cavern.

A frigid wind began to slice through the chamber, and the creature flung itself headlong onto the snowy floor, trembling from head to foot. As Emmeline watched, the air began to thicken and solidify, becoming a tall, thin column that swirled gently.

The whirling air started to crystallize, forming itself into shards as clear as diamonds. Before Emmeline's eyes they arranged themselves into an angular, refracted face with a long nose and eyes set so deep, and so darkly blue, that they seemed black; then came a slender neck and a narrow body and legs as thin as ribbons. From all sides more and more ice particles flew, organizing themselves into crystals of every imaginable shape and size, slotting themselves together like a giant puzzle, until finally a tall, cruelly beautiful woman stood before her.

She was made entirely of ice.

She was the Northwitch, and she was staring right at Emmeline.

37

"Ow," moaned Thing. He opened his eyes, but all he could see was blackness in every direction, and his head was splitting with the worst ache he'd ever had. It throbbed behind his eyes as he noticed that the ground beneath him seemed to be vibrating.

"This ain't happenin'," he muttered. "I've been asleep for the past four days, and this has all been a dream, every last rotten minute of it." Thing waited for several heart-thumping seconds, but nothing changed.

"Argh!" he finally yelled, sitting up. As he moved, he felt something slither off his face and hit his knees with a thump a second later. He blinked and looked down at his lap, where a large, brown-bound object gazed sheepishly up at him.

"Not the first time a book's got the better o' me," he said, laughter bubbling up inside him. He picked the book up and kissed it before chucking it on the floor, where it lay, along with most of its shelf mates, in a huddled heap.

Thing glanced up at the window and saw that it was *very* dark—the sort of dark you get on nights when there's no moon. A few far-off sparkles made him think of stars.

"Couldn't be," he murmured, confused. "It was broad daylight a few minutes ago. . . ." Slowly—because his head was still spinning—he pushed himself up off the floor, realizing as he did so that it seemed to be at an angle. Walking to the control desk was almost like walking uphill with a heavy weight tied around his waist, and Thing was breathless by the time he reached the chairs. He had barely settled into the middle one when something grabbed his attention.

A strange rattling, like the sound of hailstones battering a metal roof, filled his ears—and it was getting louder, and louder, and *louder*. He searched the control panel, but nothing made sense to him. The dials had lit up, he noticed, and in the largest one a thick red line, near the bottom of the screen, was dropping rapidly and tilting quite badly to the right. He didn't know what it meant. The screens were bright but full of nothing.

The rattling got so loud that it drowned out his thoughts. Finally his eyes went to the window.

"No!" he gasped, his mouth falling open. The entire pane was shaking in its frame, and small cracks were creeping out from the bullet holes like questing fingers, seeking one another out.

He raked his eyes over the control panel, searching for anything that looked like a stop button or a down button, because—as he was beginning to realize—it was dark outside, and it was growing harder to breathe, and the window was shaking itself to pieces because—

"We're too high," he said, battling for air. "Too high!" Gasping, he started bashing at buttons, but nothing seemed to work.

Then one of the instruments on the panel started beeping, which pierced through Thing's skull like red-hot pincers. The red line on the screen had pretty much disappeared, and a warning light beside it was flashing on and off.

"I know, I know!" he growled. The ship's vibration was so bad that Thing's teeth started to clatter, and he found it hard to move.

Just when he was on the point of blacking out, he saw something he hadn't noticed before. Right above the main screen, and covered with a clear plastic box, was a plain black switch. Beneath the switch, barely visible, was the symbol of a lightning bolt with a line through it.

With every muscle screaming, Thing raised himself on tiptoe, flipped up the box, and smashed his fingers down on the switch.

A split second later he smacked hard against the ceiling.

"Well, now. And who have we here?" The voice was light, like wind sighing through the branches of a snow-laden forest, and the words tinkled at the edges. Emmeline couldn't answer. She just stood gaping at the woman, too stunned to move, and watched as the Northwitch blinked with her ice eyelids. *Why does she bother? It's not like she can't see through them,* Emmeline thought, and fought hard not to shiver. The witch wore armor, of a sort, that was jointed at the elbows, shoulders, and knees, and carved with an intricate pattern across the chest. Both woman and armor seemed part of the same organism somehow, and the light bouncing off her multifaceted face and body was mesmerizing.

After a few moments of silence the Northwitch moved slightly, coming to stand a little closer to Emmeline. The ice crystals that made up her body clinked very softly as they slid and slithered over one another, and they were never still, not even for a second—they were constantly moving, over and under and around, melting and re-forming, shifting with as little effort as a human would use to move their muscles. The Northwitch smiled, putting her diamond-bright head to one side as she gazed at Emmeline, which made Emmeline feel, suddenly, as though she were walking along the edge of a very high cliff, with a hungry drop right beside her. Despite this, she couldn't tear her eyes away, and her brain kept trying to figure out what she was seeing, doing its best to find some sort of taxonomic or scientific classification for this new creature.

Without warning, the Northwitch took two rapid steps in Emmeline's direction, clicking and tinkling and scraping as she went. A flourish of icy air surrounded her like a miniature whirlwind, and when it settled, she had *changed,* transformed somehow into the shape of a small child, a little ice boy with a crystal-clear scarf and hat. He wore old-fashioned clothing and had a dimpled smile, but his eyes were the hollow blue of the Northwitch's, as dark as the deep sea. He was standing so close to Emmeline that they were practically nose to nose.

Stifling a small yelp, Emmeline staggered backward, smacking straight into her horse.

"I am not accustomed to those who do not kneel before me," said the Northwitch in a voice that sounded like a thousand whispering echoes, made even more terrifying by the fact that it was coming from a small boy's mouth. Even as Emmeline tried to work out what had just happened, the Northwitch's voice sucked at her like it wanted to strip Emmeline of all warmth and turn her into a solid thing, cold and dead.

"I—I'm sorry—" Emmeline began. The Northwitch held up one small finger and placed it on Emmeline's lips.

"I am also unaccustomed to being studied as though I were a curiosity," the Northwitch continued. The place where her finger was touching Emmeline's skin felt like it was burning, and a terrible, inescapable, horrifying cold flowed from the Northwitch's body like water. Emmeline felt it start to bite her ankles, and then her legs, and then her knees, where it stayed long enough to freeze them solid.

The ice boy who was the Northwitch smiled, shining dimples deepening.

Emmeline tried to speak but found her mouth was frozen shut, and her tongue was frozen solid, and her heart was like a bird trapped in a tiny crystal cage.

38

Thing's entire world was beeping, and lights were flashing from every corner of the control panel. The ship was falling far too fast. This wasn't helped by the fact that the chains were still dragging it down on the right side. Thing couldn't think of anything to do about that, so he shoved it into a corner of his brain. The screens were all lit now, and the largest one—the one with the thick red line, which Thing had worked out was supposed to be the horizon—was more or less stable. The others showed wavy lines, like coastlines on a map, and Thing felt pretty sure they were monitoring his position.

If only he knew where he was supposed to be going.

Wincing in sudden pain, he raised his hand to the bump on his skull caused by his tumble a few moments before. It didn't seem to be bleeding, but it hurt just enough to be a distraction.

"Gotta get 'er to stop fallin'," he muttered. He'd already pressed the lightning bolt button again, which had given the ship some upward momentum and slowed its descent for a while, but Thing knew he wasn't going to get very far if all he could do with the *Cloud Catcher* was to bounce it up and down through the atmosphere.

"There has to be a way to get her to *turn*," he said. His eyes fell on the buttons marked with directional arrows he'd seen before. *Left an' right,* he thought, his brain finally starting to tick over.

"Nothin' for it," he said as he scrambled across to the desk and hit the button marked with an arrow that faced slightly up and to the left. The second it was pressed, the ship jolted back and to the right. Thing yelped and pulled his hand off the button. The movement stopped, and the ship kept falling.

His fingers trembling, Thing slid his hand to the button beneath the one he'd just pressed, which was marked with an arrow pointing slightly down and to the left—but this time he braced himself. "Here goes nothin'," he said, taking a deep breath as he jabbed at it. The ship juddered forward and shot to the right, just as Thing had expected.

"Fantastic," he muttered, his heart quickening. He glanced at the other side of the control desk, which was too far out of his reach. "But you can't get nowhere, always goin' in the same direction."

Thing looked around the room, now topsy-turvy with

things on every conceivable surface, and searched for something he could use to help him navigate.

Finally his gaze fell on Emmeline's satchel, which lay like a beached whale on top of a pile of books, one of its buckles hopelessly dented and a large rip in its side seam.

"Jus' the ticket," he said with a grin.

"I require your name," breathed the ice boy. Emmeline simply stared into the sparkling face in front of her, trying to keep her logic train on its tracks. After a few seconds of silence, Emmeline saw the witch's upper lip curling— and she *heard* it too, a gentle rustling of ice particles as they resettled themselves. Her teeth, like shards of sharp diamond, drew Emmeline's gaze.

"Wh-what for?" Emmeline squished her sweating hands up into balls inside her furry pockets.

"What *for*? What for, indeed." The ice boy's soft, amused voice managed to sound like a bitter wind, the kind that strips leaves from trees. "Why, I simply want it, my girl, because it is my right to have it." Emmeline took a deep breath, feeling it claw into her lungs, and something popped into her mind like a sudden ray of sunshine.

"I'm—I mean, my name. It's Drusilla," said Emmeline, remembering a hideous porcelain doll her mother had forced her to own for a time when she was younger. Drusilla had been its name, and Emmeline had always thought it an entirely perfect match for the ugly thing.

"Drusilla *what*?" said the ice boy. "I'm given to understanding that your people bear two names. Terribly cumbersome, if you ask me."

Emmeline licked her dry, cold lips. "Nectarine," she said, spitting out the first word that came to her. Somehow the thought of a bright fruit was a comfort in this dark place. Beside Emmeline, the horse snickered, and Emmeline turned her head just enough to see it. There was a light in its eyes.

"How . . . unique," snarled the ice boy. "And do you come from a long and illustrious line of *Nectarines*, pray tell?"

"I—um . . ." As she tried to think, Emmeline felt a sharp pain in her chest, so sudden and throbbing it stole her breath. She coughed, and the pain grew worse.

"Never mind," snapped the ice boy. He turned on his heel and walked away from Emmeline, and as he did so, the whirling wind of ice enveloped him once more. When it cleared, the Northwitch was standing before the assembled crowd as a fully grown woman again. All trace of the small, scarf-wearing boy was gone. Now the Northwitch was dressed in a high-necked gown, its fabulous skirt flowing out around her like the petals of a flower. With a jerk Emmeline noticed a bright red tinge lingering on the hem of the Northwitch's dress—a red so bright it could only be blood. *Her* blood? Her heart thumped slowly, like it was confused and unsure of what to do.

Then she took a deep breath. The pain in her chest lessened, leaving a small, throbbing sensation behind, like a bruise. She placed one mittened hand over the sore spot, but it did no good.

"Kobold!" snapped the Northwitch in a voice like a shower of spiky, icy rain. "On your feet." Like a rat scrabbling through a sewer, the wrinkled creature on the floor flailed for a moment, eventually managing to stand. Brushing the snow off its clothes, it trembled before the Northwitch.

"My lady," it whispered.

"You have done well, bringing me this human child," she said, her neck clinking faintly as she leaned her head to one side.

"Th-thank you—"

"But you did not think to question her?" The Northwitch's words were like an avalanche just before it falls.

"Not—well, my lady, I felt—that is, *we* felt it would be best to leave that up to you." Emmeline saw its fingers flickering as it spoke, like it was trying to restore circulation to them. "In your immense wisdom, of course—"

"Peace, creature," said the Northwitch, her voice deep and dark, echoing around the cavern. Showers of ice, the slivers smaller than dust motes, started to hiss down from the ceiling. A thrumming quiver filled the air as the columns holding up the roof began to vibrate. In a whirl of frozen wind, the Northwitch vanished, then rematerialized in front of the quaking kobold. "I will deal with you later," she told it.

"Th-th-thank you—" it began, but the Northwitch reached out her sparkling arm and grasped it around the neck. The kobold's words faded into splutters as it struggled to breathe.

"Save your thanks for one who cares to hear them,"

she growled. Flinging the gasping kobold from her, the Northwitch straightened up.

"Icewalkers," she called. "Bring this human child to the dungeon."

"*Dungeon?* Just a minute!" called Emmeline, but her voice was lost amid the clamor in the cavern. She twined her fingers into the horse's mane once again as the giant silver-gray creatures, the ones she'd seen sliding out of the sky, stood to their full height. Their upper limbs disappeared into the gloom of the cavern's high ceiling. Beside her, the horse whinnied loudly, kicking up its hind legs in protest, but the Icewalkers ignored it.

Before she could do anything, Emmeline had been picked up—not ungently, but in a way that made it clear that fighting would be pointless—by a hand with soft fingers longer than her entire body. The Icewalker tucked Emmeline into the crook of its elbow before setting off, its balance seemingly unaffected by its wriggling burden.

Within seconds they were gone.

"Nice one." Thing grinned, his breath coming in gasps. "Nice one, Ems! I knew that ol' satchel o' yours would come to good." He smacked his hand on the forward propulsion button on the control panel's left-hand side and used the object he'd found in Emmeline's satchel to whack the corresponding button on its right-hand side. The object was a long, wooden, brass-bound thing that shone beautifully in the light of the *Cloud Catcher*'s control room, and that looked quite at home with the fittings and the topsy-turvy books. It was also serving Thing very well as an arm extender at the moment, although that was far from what it had been designed for.

"Now all's I need is an enemy ship, an' I can stand on the deck and peer out at 'em. When I'm not bashin' buttons, that is," he said, raising the telescope (for that, of course, is what he'd found) to his eye. All he could see were wisps of distant clouds and the bright blue of a jewel-like sky, so he snapped the telescope shut and tucked it into his pocket with a satisfied tap.

For now, the ship was holding steady.

Almost twenty miles away, and far out of the reach of Thing's telescope, the large black aircraft—the one that had, a short while ago, opened fire on the *Cloud Catcher* before Thing had managed to shoot it halfway to the moon—was zooming through the bright, clear sky. Its pilot, the dark-skinned woman, smiled as she watched a small red dot bobbing on her screen, a small red dot that she'd been tracking as it shot up into the stratosphere and then fell back down again. When it had reappeared, buttons had been pressed and switches had been flicked, and within a couple of seconds the black aircraft's trajectory had been trained to intercept.

The commandeered *Cloud Catcher*, its pilot oblivious to the danger it was now in, lurched on, complete with the unknown, unseen enemy Thing had so carelessly wished for.

As Emmeline looked around her tiny, shimmering prison, barely bigger than Mrs. Mitchell's scullery back at Widget Manor, she found herself in a dream. A freshly baked scone, dripping with jam and butter, was being plonked in front of her, along with a cup of tea large enough to dunk her entire head into; she heard a merry tune being whistled by the floury-armed cook as she bustled about her work.

A droplet of cold meltwater splashed off the end of Emmeline's nose, and her eyes popped open. There was no more Mrs. Mitchell and no more scone. The tea vanished like a puff of steam.

Sighing, Emmeline slid across the floor to a low bed, carved out of the ice along one wall, and huddled on it. Some ratty-looking furs had been left out for her, but she shoved them away in disgust and wrapped herself up in her coat instead. Despite its rich thickness, she still wasn't properly warm—there was a hollow, sad, and echoing space right at the core of her, where it felt like something important had been taken away. She rubbed at the sore spot just above her heart again, absentmindedly, and looked around. Her cell was completely bare. There was no food, no real furniture, nothing to read, and every single thing was made of ice. Not pretty or delicate or light-filled ice either, but thick and ancient and hard as iron. She might as well have been locked in a concrete box.

So she tucked herself up tighter and did an inventory of the things at her disposal.

"One length of fishing line," she whispered. "One length of rope. One piece of greased paper. One tin cup. One silver spoon. One thick coat. And this." She opened her hand to reveal a strange clump of shimmering strands that she'd managed to pull from the pelt of the Icewalker— *Widgetosaurus*, she corrected herself sternly—who'd brought her here. It glowed like a tiny torch.

She had only just tucked the clump of Icewalker fur into the pocket of her coat when a wind started to howl through the bars of her cell door, picking up speed as it came, spitefully hurling pieces of ice at her exposed skin. She buried her face in her collar and tried to tuck herself up into a knot, but the wind kept coming, stronger and stronger. Just as she was sure she couldn't take any more, the wind whirled one last time and was still, settling into the tall, solid shape of the Northwitch. She stood before Emmeline like a nightmare made of starlight, faintly tinkling as she moved.

"So, Miss Nectarine." The Northwitch smiled, and it looked like someone pulling out a knife. "Now that you and I have a chance to be alone, you can tell me what you're doing here."

"What does it matter to you why I'm here?" Emmeline asked, trusting her voice to remain steady. The Northwitch's slushy eyes widened.

"What does it matter?" she asked. "You're in my territory, child—in my *country*. On my glacier. I want to know why you're here, and if you don't feel like behaving—well, I hope you like starvation, because that's what will be in store for you. I don't eat, myself. No need. It's so easy to forget that others do." The Northwitch paused, glaring down at Emmeline with those frighteningly endless eyes. Almost like it was waiting for its cue, Emmeline's stomach gurgled, and the Northwitch smirked. *Do not trust her,* whispered a little voice in the back of Emmeline's mind. *As if I would!* she whispered back.

"I'm just lost," Emmeline said out loud. "That's all.

The horse found me and he brought me here." *Thanks a lot, horse,* she muttered inside her head. *So much for my plan to find the Kraken.*

"Do you take me for a fool, little girl?" asked the Northwitch, tapping her chin with one long finger. The *chink-chink-chink* of it made Emmeline's teeth hurt. "Do you expect me to believe you simply wandered away from the warm, wet world"—she shuddered at these words with a noise like a crystal chandelier being shaken—"and walked here?" Emmeline kept quiet, and kept watch.

"Nothing happens on my ice without my knowledge," the Northwitch continued. "I know, for instance, that your arrival coincided with the return of the man I have been monitoring. I felt your footsteps across my surface, small as they were. I also know you mounted the god-horse, and it *allowed* you to. Yes, you're an interesting creature." Pausing in her chin tapping, the Northwitch bent at the waist—causing some rapid clashing and crushing of her icy body—and stared at Emmeline as if she were a stain on a carpet. "Aren't you afraid of me, little human girl?" Her voice made Emmeline think of wolves howling in the distance. Biting winds and long, dark skies. Absolute loneliness. Being lost and nobody knowing. She took a deep breath.

"No," she lied.

"Remarkable."

"When are you letting me out of here? You can't keep me here forever."

"Oh, can't I?" The Northwitch smiled. "And why is that?"

"Because I have *parents*," said Emmeline, raising her eye-brows. "Who are *expecting* me, and they'll come looking."

"They might, at that," said the Northwitch, straightening up once more. The ice groaned and complained as it clicked into place. "No matter how hard they look, however, they will not find you here."

Emmeline felt a painful tightening in her throat. "This isn't fair! I haven't done anything to you," she said.

"You haven't done anything to me—*yet*," said the North-witch. "But you will."

"What? I don't know what you're talking about!" Emmeline's heart pattered as she tried to think. *Do I have enough fishing line to tie her up? Would she just be able to slide her way around it? If only I had something to make a fire!*

"You're here because of the Kraken, are you not?" said the Northwitch, her entire body flashing golden, like she'd been caught in a sudden sunbeam. "Well, little human girl, that makes you valuable to me."

Emmeline held her breath and stared into the North-witch's frozen face, trying hard not to move a single muscle.

Thing didn't like thinking overmuch. However, there were times when it became not only necessary, but unavoidable.

"Come on, come on, come *on*," he muttered. "Turn on yer brain!" He remembered arriving at Madame Blanche-flour's house, and he remembered the chicken—oh, boy, did he remember the roast chicken—and he remembered talking to the others about Ems, and what was going to happen to her.

But what he couldn't remember was where Sasha had told him Emmeline was being taken. *Go north!* Monsieur Pichon had said. But *where?*

"The North Pole?" he whispered as the name of every place he'd ever heard of started to click through his mind. "Was it the North Pole? Come on, you plank!" But something inside him didn't seem convinced.

Then there was movement in the corner of his eye. He spun on the spot, his fists held up in a fighting stance—but all he saw was a large wooden globe, broken away from its handsomely carved stand, rolling across the floor. He let his breath out and hurried over to it, dropping his fists as he went. It was beautiful, he saw, covered in drawings of countries that no longer existed and depicting an entirely different landscape from any that Thing had ever seen. *The world before the water started risin'*, he thought. He ran his hands over the smooth, carefully worked surface, watching the light shimmer on the gold lettering, examining the delicately colored seas, the greenish brown of the land, and the pure white of the ice fields.

The ice fields . . .

Thing's eye fell on a large, vaguely triangular country that, on this old globe, appeared to be mainly ice with a little bit of land around the edges. Across it a beautifully drawn word was written. Thing had never had much use for reading beyond a few essential words, like *shillings, pounds, police,* and *prison,* but something about this globe, this delicately painted word, grabbed his attention. This white island near the top of the world drew his eye and wouldn't let go.

Then something wriggled into his brain like a worm, the memory of a scratchy old voice that haunted the corners of his mind, always waiting for its chance to break through. It had found a crack now, and like water hissing through a broken dam, it began to fill him up and overwhelm him.

... Get the face paint now, this minute! It's the green stuff. Can't you read? G-r-e-e-n!

Thing's nostrils filled with the greasy smell of the paint, the heat of the big tent, the stink of the animals, and his body thrilled with the feeling of the high wire. . . . His fingers shook as he gripped the old wooden globe.

Face paint . . . g-r-e-e-n—*that* word—it was on this globe. He blinked as he looked at it, but there was no doubt.

And finally, he remembered.

40

"What?" Emmeline's pulse throbbed in her ears.
"What about the Kraken?"

"I am powerful, my girl," the Northwitch replied. "Powerful beyond your imagining, I have no doubt." Emmeline, who had a wide-ranging and well-fed imagination, didn't bother to correct her. "But the Kraken? It is an ancient thing, old as the ice itself, and powerful even beyond my *own* imagining. What I could do with power like that!" The Northwitch paused, her hands clenching into sparkling fists. "But it has long been out of my reach. I have tried, believe me, to wake it, but it lies buried deep in the glacier's heart, where none may go—or so it seemed." Her eyes grew darker blue, narrowing as she stared Emmeline down. "Until a *human* came, with machines and men, and began to succeed where I had failed . . ." She paused, a look of angry disgust tinkling over her face. "A human will not take my place!"

Emmeline threw her hands up as another whirling, bitter wind began to rip around her cell, taking her breath with it. Every drop of moisture in the air froze, becoming a multitude of tiny, sharp darts that flew to join with the body of the Northwitch. Something—Emmeline couldn't see what—was happening to the ice woman. She was growing darker and more solid.

Sudden cold soaked through Emmeline, creeping into her skin, and the dull ache in her chest exploded in a bright bloom of pain.

"The Kraken is a creature of the glacier—it *belongs to me!* And its power belongs to the North, not to the world of flesh and blood," shouted the Northwitch. "No mortal will steal it away from me by force, through cogs and wheels and metal, things that have no place here." Her voice made Emmeline's bones quake. "Its power shall be mine, and I shall use it to turn the world to ice!" The sound of the Northwitch's roaring words was like a river out of control—it burst over every bank and levee, running rampant.

"But—my parents!" said Emmeline, her eyes watering. "He's going to kill them!"

"I have no concern for that," boomed the Northwitch. She stood before Emmeline, no longer sparkling. Shards of darkness made up her body now, gleaming like oil. She reached out a hand, and the pain in Emmeline's chest grew stronger. Horrifyingly, it felt to Emmeline like something *inside* her was responding to the Northwitch. Like iron being drawn to a magnet, her body was being dragged up off the icy bed, toward the witch's dark, beckoning fingers.

"What are you doing?" Emmeline fought the pull as hard as she could, but the pain was too much. It spread around her heart like a crushing bruise. "Stop! You're hurting me!"

"A sad but necessary side effect," said the Northwitch. "The less you struggle, the less pain you will feel."

Emmeline looked down at herself, and what she saw made her brain spin. She was *vanishing*, like someone had taken a giant eraser to her chest. Tiny shards of her were flying toward the Northwitch, becoming part of her, making her more solid, less like ice and more like flesh and blood.

Emmeline looked back up at the Northwitch. To her horror, the face she saw gazing back at her was her own, right down to the eyelashes.

Didn't you hear me, you ignorant lump? Get up there now, or feel the back of my hand!

"But, Dad," gasped Thing. "I can't—"

You can't? More like you won't! What's the use of 'avin' an 'igh-wire boy who can't even catch 'is breath, eh? I should sell you, I should! You're not worth the food I pay for!

"I'm sorry! I—*whoop!*—I'm sorry, Dad! I'm doin' me best!"

Yer best ain't good enough! Yer nothin' but a clod! Yer mother'd die all over again, this time out o' shame, if she could see you now!

"Mum . . . ," whispered Thing.

I should sell yer—I think I will, an' all! I think I will, an' all. . . .

"No," sobbed Thing. "I can do it, Dad! I can! I can!"

His heart *thunk-thunk-thunked*. His breaths boiled. He dug his fingernails into wood. "Don't sell me, Dad. I'll try 'arder, I swear." Then he blinked and looked around, and realized he wasn't in the big top and his dad was gone and the stink of greasepaint in his nostrils wasn't actually real. Not anymore.

He dropped the globe and rubbed gently at his chest, feeling a hollowed-out sort of pain.

"Don't sell me, Dad," he whispered to himself. He closed his eyes again, and an image of the farmer who'd paid his dad ten shillings for him washed over his memory like a wave of dirty water. He saw himself, a sniveling child of six, watching the gaily colored circus caravan, the only home he'd ever known, rolling and rocking its way down the muddy lane as it left him behind. He'd shouted for his dad, but all he'd gotten was a clip around the ear and a snarled reminder that he had no dad now and would do well not to forget it. He remembered the fists, and the barn he'd had to sleep in, and the cold. . . .

G-R-E-E-N! Can't you even read a simple word?

"Quiet, Dad," said Thing, wiping his nose with the back of his hand. He rolled expertly to his feet, half hearing applause in his ears. The heavy, clinging weight in his lungs shifted, and he took a deep breath, and then another.

One more fumble, an' I promise you—

"I said *quiet!*" yelled Thing. He stumbled toward the control panel, blinking the memories away. The screen with the red horizon line showed the ship listing at an angle, and something was flashing like a warning. The screens with the wavy coastlines—which were gradually becoming clearer to Thing's eye—showed him he was drifting too far to the east, the archipelago of Ireland and Britain far behind him. Dead ahead lay open water and emptiness.

And to the northwest Thing saw his destination light up like a beacon, drawing him on. That word—g-r-e-e-n—yelled up at him in his long-gone father's voice. He adjusted the ship's course, watching as the screens settled and the warning lights all went out. *The ship knew where to go,* he thought. *Good ol' Monsieur Pichon. If it hadn't been for me flingin' it about the place, we'd prob'ly be there already.*

"I'm comin', Ems," he whispered, leaning on the lightning bolt button once again.

He was too distracted to notice that the ship didn't leap forward as much as, all things considered, it really should have.

***

"What are you doing?" screamed Emmeline. Already her mouth felt strange, like it was numb and not entirely under her control. "Leave me alone!"

"I'm afraid not," came the Northwitch's reply, her voice a shimmering copy of Emmeline's own. "I can feel the ice stirring. It won't be long now until the Kraken wakes, and

I intend to be there to greet it." The Northwitch stretched her new body. From the chest up it looked human, if a little dusted with frost. The rest of her was still cold and sparkling, but traces of Emmeline were making their way down into the ice shards with every heartbeat. "I'm sure the meddling man with the clever machines will be so glad to have you returned to him; he must have missed you terribly. Won't he get a surprise when *you* turn out to be *me*! By the time he figures it out, of course, it will all be too late."

"Who?" whispered Emmeline. She wondered who'd turned the lights out, and why the room was tilting to one side. "Figures out what?"

"Why, the white-faced man who thinks he can steal away the power of the Kraken from under my nose, of course," replied the Northwitch. "But don't you worry about that."

The Northwitch smiled with Emmeline's face—red-cheeked and dark-haired—but her eyes remained her own, a cold and slushy blue, like two holes cut into an iced-over lake.

The pain in Emmeline's chest gave another feeble throb as the Northwitch drew more of her strength. "No! Leave me *alone!*" she groaned through gritted teeth.

"You don't like making things easy for yourself, do you?" said the Northwitch. "Believe me, it will be so much easier if you don't fight."

Before Emmeline could summon up the strength to reply, she noticed a reddish glow flickering in the corner of her vision. The Northwitch hissed, her head whipping around to face it, just as the wall of the cell exploded inward. The thick, ancient ice shattered into freezing powder, and the shock wave knocked Emmeline to the floor. She felt a tingling warmth, like pins and needles, fizzing right through her. Flipping herself onto her back, she watched in amazement as the Northwitch—still Emmeline-shaped, but now made of crystal-clear ice again—splintered neatly into billions of tiny shards, like a cloud of priceless diamond dust. They hovered in the air for a second or two before tumbling to the ground, gathering in piles like a small snowdrift.

Emmeline didn't even have time to catch her breath before her horse, magnificent in the gloom, its mane glowing like a forest fire, was standing over her. With a single whuff of breath from its nostrils, the icy powder that had been the Northwitch went skittering out between the bars of the cell door and off down the ice corridor outside, screaming all the way.

"Critical fuel failure," said a pleasant-sounding voice from somewhere close by. Thing hadn't minded the first time the announcement had come on, or even the second or third. But this disembodied warning had begun to grate on his nerves after its twentieth repetition. *"Cloud cover needed,"* the voice added.

"All right, all right, all *right!*" Thing muttered, slapping buttons here and flicking switches there, trying to keep the *Cloud Catcher* steady and upright. The ship needed clouds in order to draw the wind and lightning out of them, Thing had figured out, just a little too late; he'd been flying through clear skies for ages, and he'd used up so much power in messing about that it was no wonder things were getting desperate now.

He was over the sea. There were no clouds to be seen anywhere, besides some wispy ones high up. He didn't have enough power to reach them, he felt sure.

Something appeared on the central screen of the control panel, flipping in and out of view as the power dimmed and flared.

"'Greenland,'" he read, knowing he was right. The jagged coastline of the massive country—the massive country where Emmeline had been taken, and where goodness knew what had happened to her—was looming just a couple of inches away from the bleeping red dot that was his ailing ship. "Come on! Jus' a few more miles, and we'll be there. Come *on!*"

"*Critical fuel failure,*" the ship informed him again. "*Please maneuver to intercept cloud cover. Engine can no longer fire. Cloud cover needed. Please refuel. Critical fuel failure.*"

Thing watched the horizon finder. For every foot the ship traveled, it dropped three; it would be coming down hard, and there was nothing he could do about it. His stomach felt like it was being held in an iron clamp, and he clutched the edge of the control panel, his knuckle-bones sticking up. He bit his lip, hung on for dear life, and hoped that somehow the ship would glide far enough to crash-land on the ground.

If not—he gulped at the thought—not only would

he fail to save Emmeline, but he'd go to a freezing (if mercifully quick) death beneath the frosty waves of the far north.

❄

"Hyup!" came a cry. In their harnesses the dogsled team yipped and howled, delighted to be out on the trail. The sled they pulled was light, even though it was laden with furs and clothes and drinks kept hot in insulated flasks and as much food as could be tied on, and the snow was smooth and crisp underfoot. The going was good.

A sudden crashing, thundering noise from the sky made the driver of the sled turn in his seat and crane his neck. A massive object was careening through the air, trailing flames, its engines screaming as it went. As the driver watched, part of the strange ship exploded with a bright orange light, the boom that followed it a second later making his dogs thrash and howl. His breath caught in his throat as he watched the object come rocketing toward the frozen ground. The driver waited, knowing what he had to do but not liking it very much.

Then, with a whistle, Igimaq steered his team toward the stricken vessel, hoping Emmeline would forgive him for the delay.

"I won't be long, little girl," he muttered as his sled team picked up speed. "I let you down once, and I don't intend to do it again."

41

Emmeline clutched the horse's mane, trying to catch her breath. Her heart was thumping so hard her whole body was shaking, almost like it was making up for all the beats it had lost while the Northwitch had been busy turning it to ice. The pain in her chest was easing, but a thought floated across her mind: *If she steals your life, even a bit of it, are you hers forever?* These words rolled around inside her as the horse flew over the ground, its hooves barely making an impression in the snow. Emmeline told herself she didn't care where they were going, as long as it was away from that tiny cell far beneath the ice.

Somewhere in the distance, faint as a match flare in a cave, Emmeline saw a bright orange light. They were headed right for it. *A fire? On a glacier?* she thought, squinting at it, before realizing that it was one of the *least* unlikely things she'd seen lately. *I'm on the back of a horse that just walked through a wall of solid ice like it was water,* she told herself, feeling dizzy. *And I'm trying to save my parents from a Kraken that's been sleeping in the center of this glacier for who knows how long. How much odder can things get?*

Thinking of her parents made her mind start to settle, and the reality of her situation weighed on her again like a heavy cloak. She blinked away from the flames of the far-off fire and looked to the sky, where the iridescent glow of the northern lights was bathing everything around her in eerie green—yet it still seemed they were being pulled by an unknown force. Her gaze followed the lights to her left. It looked like something was forcing them downward, and they struggled like an animal caught in a trap. *Almost,* Emmeline thought, *like they're being sucked into the middle of the glacier.* As she watched the swirling aurora, she felt, in a corner of her heart, the sharp, pinching words of Dr. Bauer: *I've kept them for you—not exactly safe.... They're in the ice, my dear.*

"Hey, boy," she called, her voice cracking slightly. "Hey. Whoa there." She pulled, as gently as she could, on the horse's mane, and after a few head tosses and splutters, it came to a halt. It tottered about on the spot as she patted its neck, its breaths deep and rasping, its chest heaving. "We can't keep running forever, you know," she whispered, leaning against its trembling neck. She squeezed her eyes tight and took three deep breaths, then tilted her head back and stared at the sky again. The light of the aurora filled her mind, and she remembered how Igimaq had also said that something was wrong with the lights; his people had seen it. *There must be a connection to Dr. Bauer,* Emmeline told herself. *I need to find out.*

Gently Emmeline nudged the horse around until they were facing the place where the lights appeared to meet the ground. The horse stamped in displeasure, but Emmeline urged it on with a click of her tongue. They left the distant fire behind them, and before long the horse was up to top speed again, flying across the ice.

As they ran, cold tendrils like icy fingers traced up and down Emmeline's spine and licked around the inside of her collar. She shrank into her coat, but it didn't help, and Emmeline felt her heartbeat slow and struggle as the pain in her chest flared again.

The thin wind carried the laughter of the Northwitch to her ears, and with every hoofbeat the inescapable fact drew closer.

The Northwitch was coming to get her, and there was nowhere to hide.

"Balto! Hey!" Igimaq urged his trusted lead dog on, and the sled began to pick up pace. Already Igimaq could hear the hissing of the flames. Whatever this thing had been, it sure was *big.* Debris was strewn in huge pieces across the face of the ice, and pools of melted snow were dotted all around it. Igimaq's keen eyes picked out shards of glass and bits of splintered wood, which he was careful to guide the dogs around—but old Balto and his team were clever enough to do that by themselves. Sometimes Igimaq wondered whether he'd trained them *too* well.

"Hello!" he called. *"Aluu!"* There was no reply. Igimaq peered into the wreckage as the dogs cantered past, doubting that anyone could have walked away from such a mess, but knowing he had to be sure. "Hello!" he shouted again. "Anyone in there needing help?" The only answer he got was a distant explosion as something—a gas tank, an oxygen canister?—succumbed to the flames.

"What's this?" he muttered, pulling the sled to a halt. A gigantic chain lay in the snow like an iron snake. A huge piece of wrenched-off metal was attached to it at one end. Igimaq followed the chain with his eyes to where it went into the side of the mangled hull through an aperture, half expecting to see someone come staggering through. Close by, another shattering boom rang out over the ice, and the noise of millions of shards of glass trickling to earth was heard. A fresh flare of leaping flames cracked out, whiplike.

"Aluu!" Igimaq called again, rapidly losing hope of hearing a reply.

Then Kiista—the dog he trusted most behind Balto—started to keen and cry, rattling her harness. Soon her restlessness spread to the whole team, and the others took up her complaint, yapping and howling, throwing glances back at Igimaq.

"Something's got your nose, eh, Kiista girl? Eh?" called Igimaq, and the dog whirled around as far as she could, meeting his eyes with a pained gaze. That decided Igimaq. His dogs had a scent, and that was good enough for him.

"Hup!" he called, settling his grip on the sled. "Ho!"

With that, the dogs were off. To Igimaq's surprise, they veered to the right, Balto leading the team away from the stricken ship. The snow all around the crash site was slushy and kicked up, but after a hundred feet or so Igimaq began to see footprints—*small* footprints—trailing away into the empty wilderness. *A child has been here,* he thought with a jolt.

"Hup!" he called again, urging the dogs on—not that they really needed it. Their noses were full of the trail, and they raced in silence, intent on following their quarry. The jingling of the harnesses and the dogs' ragged, excited breathing were the only noises for miles around.

And then Igimaq saw something lying in the snow up ahead.

Within moments the dogs drew up alongside the huddled shape, and Igimaq brought the sled to a jerky halt. Igimaq hauled himself off the sled and quickly made his way, hand over hand, to the small figure lying on the bitter ground.

"Hey! Hey, hey!" he said, leaning close. "Hey in there! Can you hear me?" The person—a young boy, Igimaq saw—made no reply. His face was white and pinched, his hair studded with ice. His arms were clenched tightly around something that looked like a saddlebag, made of old, bashed-up leather.

With one large hand Igimaq grabbed hold of the child's

collar and slowly but carefully dragged him toward the sled. Soon the boy was bundled up in a nest of warm, dry furs, as far out of the wind as Igimaq could get him, the worn leather bag tucked right in beside him.

With a whistle from Igimaq, the sled was off, flying over the snow as though its newly acquired cargo weighed no more than a feather.

In the depths of the gloomy sky overhead, the black craft flew. Unseen, unheard, it followed the trail left by the crashed *Cloud Catcher*. Nothing but burning wreckage remained of the White Flower's finest ship, its fastest and best.

"Such shoddy workmanship," tutted the woman in the pilot's seat. "But that's what comes of employing a renegade to build a skycraft." She glanced over her shoulder at her passengers—if they could be called that—who were sitting, tied hand and foot, in the seats behind. Two pairs of flashing, angry eyes glared back, and two muzzled mouths worked around their gags, doing their best to loosen them. "Worse than a renegade, one might even say," she continued, staring straight into Sasha's face. "A *charlatan*, maybe."

Rage filled Sasha, and she strained forward in her seat, forgetting about her injury—and about the thick strap keeping her tied down. Pain flared up her left side and she fell back, moaning. Beside her, Monsieur Pichon trembled, his eyes wide as he stared at her. She turned to him and tried to pretend she was all right, but he wasn't fooled.

"Well, we'll see whether we can find a use for you two when we get down there, eh? I'm pretty sure I can think of just the thing." The pilot settled herself at the controls again, and Sasha's eyes spat fire at the back of her head.

In the darkness, unseen, Sasha leaned her head against Monsieur Pichon's. Together they wept for Thing, never dreaming that he could have survived the disaster spread out before them on the face of the glacier.

42

"Hmff?" Thing snorted awake, wondering why he felt like he was on fire. For a horrible moment he thought he hadn't made it out of the ship, and his mind filled up with crashing, cracking, screens flashing, alarms calmly announcing that the *Cloud Catcher* was in "critical failure" and that "emergency touchdown" was inevitable. *"Prepare for crash landing,"* a voice had said. "How do I do that?" he'd roared, just before the ship had started to come apart.

But he didn't hear anything now. Everything seemed quiet and peaceful, besides a strange panting noise coming from somewhere close by. *If this is heaven,* thought Thing, *I want me money back.*

"Eh? Hey up there?" The voice barely touched the edges of Thing's hearing. Faintly he was aware that he was moving—cold air was flowing over his exposed nose and cheeks, and a gentle rocking motion made him think of a baby being put to sleep in a giant cradle. Then he tried to sit up.

The banging, throbbing agony in his head quickly put an end to that.

"Whoa, whoa!" Thing felt a juddering vibration, and the rocking motion came to a stop. A few seconds later he felt strong hands—*big* hands—on his shoulders and upper back.

"Hey. Boy! You awake? You all right?" Thing's eyes could barely focus. Above him all he could make out was a pair of half-hidden eyes and a lot of hair. No—*fur*, he corrected himself after a few seconds. *A fur hood.*

"What? Who're you?" His voice sounded like it belonged to someone else. He tried to clear his dried-up throat.

"Igimaq," said the stranger, and Thing saw him grinning. "And you?"

"M'name's Thing," he said. "'S a pleasure or whatever."

"Sit tight, then," said the man in the hood. "The wife's going to make me sleep in the outhouse if I bring another of you strange kids home, but I can hardly leave you here, eh? You've had quite the adventure." Thing's eyes started to close, and he was almost asleep again when he suddenly jerked awake, looking around in a panic.

"No!" he called. The man paused and glanced back at Thing's face with wide, concerned eyes. "No way! Lemme out o' these—whatever they are!" He tried to struggle, but it felt like his arms were lashed to his sides with iron ropes. "I gotta go, right now! She needs me!"

"Whoa now. Who needs you? You're not in any shape to go anywhere—"

"That's not important! Ems needs me, and I gotta get to her! Her *life's* in danger, and I—"

"Ems?" interrupted Igimaq. "Who's that?"

"Ems! Emmeline! Look, you don't know 'er," said Thing quickly, shaking his head and wincing. "I gotta find 'er. I gotta . . ." Thing's voice trailed off as the pain in his body started to wake up and kick him all over. He felt like he'd been wrapped in a carpet and beaten with sticks. Igimaq said nothing for a few moments. Thing thought he heard him chuckling, but told himself he had to be imagining it. What was funny about this situation?

"You're not going to believe this, eh," said the strange man eventually. "You an' me are looking for the same girl." Igimaq's gap-toothed smile was broad, and his eyes sparkled as he gazed down at Thing. "You're looking for Emmeline, right? Small, curly hair, know-it-all nose?" Thing's eyes flicked back and forth over Igimaq's face.

"What d'you want with her, eh? If you've hurt her, I'll—"

"Calm down, kid," said Igimaq, his good-natured grin growing wider. "I saved Emmeline once, and I let her get away, straight back into danger again. Now I—now *we*—have a chance to make it right."

"I don't understand," said Thing after a moment. "Who are you exac'ly?"

"Hardly matters," replied Igimaq. "I want to help your friend, you want to help your friend—that makes us friends, right?"

Thing studied Igimaq's face for several moments and finally barked out a laugh. "Well, what're we waitin' for, then? Tell these fellas to mush or whatever!" His head throbbed as he looked around, taking in the sled, the dogs, the flat white landscape, and the oddly greenish light in the sky. It looked like the underside of a river, he thought, swirling off toward the horizon, studded all through with bright, sharp stars. He searched for Emmeline's satchel and saw that Igimaq had carefully wrapped it in its own tiny fur and placed it securely beside him. Something about it made his heart lift again.

Igimaq watched all this with a grin. "Mush, eh? Maybe you want to drive?"

Within seconds he'd turned the sled around, and they were on their way.

Sasha's mind flickered painfully as she thought. *After all Madame's years of trying to scrape money together to fund the White Flower, all our attempts to infiltrate Bauer's gang, all the wasted time and effort searching for him in the wrong places ...* Despite her best efforts, a hot tear trailed down over her jaw. She glanced at Monsieur Pichon, but he wasn't looking at her, or at anything. His eyes were shut tight, his forehead was creased in a deep frown, and his cheeks were wet. *I never thought I'd be sharing this fate with you, Michel.*

"Comfortable back there?" called the pilot over her shoulder. Sasha kicked the back of her seat in reply, hoping to connect the toe of her boot with any part of her captor's body. The pilot laughed, leaning back to pull Sasha's gag free.

"Good!" she crowed. "I'm sure the beast likes a bit of sass in his breakfast."

"So it's true, then?" said Sasha, hoping her voice wouldn't crack. "You're taking us to the Kraken?"

"Now, now. I'm sure you don't need me to explain all that for you," replied the pilot, stretching to adjust one of her instruments.

"You're Xantha, aren't you?" said Sasha quietly, knowing she was right, even though it seemed impossible. "Xantha Strachan. Bauer's former partner."

"Good work, my dear," sneered the pilot.

Sasha tried to swallow with a suddenly dry throat. "You're really going to these lengths to get revenge on him? Or—no. Be honest. This is about the Kraken, isn't it? You want it for yourself."

"Siegfried Bauer stole *everything* from me." Xantha turned to face Sasha, and her voice was low. "We *worked* together, side by side, for years, and he rewarded me for my labors by stealing all my research. He took credit for everything we did! Every experiment. *All* my notes on the Kraken, on longevity, all gone, along with every drop of credibility I had." She turned again to face forward, raising her voice so Sasha could hear. "Nothing would be too much trouble to pay him back for that. And if I can steal his prize before he has a taste of it, all the better."

"We thought you'd died," said Sasha, wondering now how they could have been so gullible.

"Of course you did." Xantha's voice was light. "I

wanted it that way. It's remarkable how much planning you can get away with when nobody's on your tail." She turned around once again and stretched over to replace Sasha's gag, her fingers strong as a steel trap. Sasha whimpered and gave up struggling.

I've let everyone down so badly, she thought, her throat aching.

"Oh, look!" cried Xantha, like a child being given a new toy. She pointed out the front window of the skycraft at something that loomed in the distance like three dark fangs bursting through the surface of the ice, surrounded in a cloak of green light. "My learned colleague's facility isn't far away now. Don't you just *love* it when you can get someone to do all the heavy lifting for you?"

Despite herself, Sasha couldn't help but look.

Before them lay the vastness of the glacier.

Behind them lay the wreckage of the *Cloud Catcher.* Sasha felt something snap inside her heart as she thought about it.

And ahead—getting closer with every moment—lay Dr. Bauer's headquarters.

The place where I'm going to die, thought Sasha numbly.

Faster! Faster, horse! Please! Emmeline didn't have enough breath to say the words aloud, but the horse picked up its pace anyway, galloping so hard that Emmeline wouldn't have been surprised to see wings sprouting out of its back. Even if Emmeline hadn't known this horse was . . .

whatever the kobold had called it, she'd have figured out that it was special. No normal horse could run like this. The Northwitch's hollow laughter was far behind, and they'd passed several groups of men in large, clunky vehicles who'd fled for whatever cover they could find as the thunder of the horse's hooves drew close. Now all she could see was the glimmering green light of the aurora borealis, reflected in pools and from the broken ice—and straight ahead was something Emmeline hadn't quite figured out. She squinted up at it once more, but it was too much to take in all at once.

Three frames made of curved metal tubing were sticking out of the ice, standing so tall that their tops vanished into the sky. Each of them held something that looked like a shallow bowl tipped on its side, only on a much bigger scale. The aurora glowed brightest above and around them, its light reflecting back and forth off each of the bowls until it became one thick beam focused on the ice. Underfoot, Emmeline noticed cracks and gaps and wide crevasses in the surface of the glacier and the booming, straining sound of the moving ice made her throat ache with fear. *What if the horse misses a step? What if we fall? What if we get swallowed?* Emmeline tried to focus on the good stuff instead of the bad. She thought about what the Northwitch had said about Bauer melting the ice to raise the Kraken, and—stealing another glance at their destination— she felt her heart leap at the idea that this was where it was all going to happen. *It has to be here,* she told herself. *And if I'm right, then Mum and Dad ... they* have *to be here. Don't they?* Her mind bubbled with tentacles and teeth and deep, dark water where nobody should ever go, and her tiny spark of gladness sputtered out.

As the horse drew closer to the lights, Emmeline ran through her assets one more time. *One tin cup,* she thought breathlessly. *One silver spoon. One length of fishing line. One length of rope. One piece of greased paper.* Her mind stuttered. *Wasn't there something else?*

Shrinking against the horse's back, she tried as hard as she could to wish herself home, but no matter how hard she thought about it, it stubbornly refused to work.

Behind her the Northwitch was a nightmare in the dark, and she was coming.

43

Emmeline's horse eventually drew to a skidding, clopping stop, its breath a stream of vapor around its head. Emmeline slid down, landing heavily in the snow, her teeth chattering.

Before them lay a gigantic pool filled with auroral light, gushing, crashing water, and lumps of breaking ice as big as buildings. Thick streams of meltwater flowed out of it, carving channels in the ice as they went. The three bowl-like objects stood above the pool, tall as giants, and Emmeline leaned back to look at them more closely. Now she could see that they were mirrors, brightly polished and flawless, so clear that they seemed transparent. Emmeline felt sick as she watched the northern lights bouncing from one mirror to the other in an unbroken beam and being used somehow to penetrate the heart of the ice beneath her. She studied the metal gantries controlling the mirrors' direction and gazed at the low, sturdy buildings on the far side of the pool, their windows dark, and wondered who—if anyone—was in there.

Her heart trembled. If this was where the Kraken was going to rise, then she didn't have long to find her parents, if they were even here. She just had no idea where to start looking.

"I never gave you a name, did I?" she said, gazing into her horse's face. Its chest heaved as it caught its breath, and it shook with exertion all over. "But what am I saying? You probably *have* a name, right?" It whinnied, and Emmeline pressed herself against it, taking in a lungful of its scent, like sunshine and flowers. "The kobold said you were descended from someone called the Hoof-Thrower. That's a good name," she whispered, thinking of the stumbling fall the horse had taken across the ice when she'd first seen it. "But I'm going to call you Meadowmane, because of how nice you smell. If you don't mind." Gently Meadowmane began to nibble at the laces on Emmeline's boot, and she took that as permission. She wiped her nose and nodded. "Okay. Come on, then. Let's go find my mum and dad and get out of here."

Meadowmane allowed Emmeline to lean on him as, together, they started to walk toward the pool, hooves and feet sliding with every step.

A sudden gush of spearlike wind stabbed through the layers of Emmeline's clothing. She quickened her pace, keeping a fearful eye out for the Northwitch, but all she could see around her was swirling snow and gray, eternal gloom.

"Out," barked Xantha. "Now!" The craft carrying Sasha, Monsieur Pichon, and their captor had landed several minutes before, but Bauer's brightly lit site was still a mile or more away. Their gags had been removed, and Sasha worked the pain out of her jaw as she tried to moisten her mouth.

"But it's too far," she pointed out. "We can't walk that distance in this climate! I'm wounded, and Monsieur Pichon is—"

"I am fine," growled Monsieur Pichon suddenly, his face like a blade in the strange light. "Let's just get this charade over with, yes?"

"I'm sorry," Sasha began. "I thought you were—"

"Yes. Indeed. As you can see, I am perfectly well," he said, cutting over Sasha's words.

"Such touching concern for your scheming little friend," said Xantha, her voice mock-gentle as she attached a chain to Sasha's bound wrists. She slid across to grab hold of Monsieur Pichon, attaching his shackles to the chain with the snick of a lock. "Really, it's almost enough to make me weep. Get up, please. Daylight's not exactly burning, not at this latitude, but you know what I mean." She turned away, the movement dragging Sasha, and then Monsieur Pichon, out of their seats.

"*Courage*, child," came the warm, whispered words in Sasha's ear as she rose unsteadily to her feet. Monsieur Pichon stumbled against her, giving every impression of being a weak old man. "We will prevail."

As soon as they were outside, Xantha secured Sasha and Monsieur Pichon to the leg of the aircraft before bending to strap long skis onto her booted feet. Within seconds, the cold began to seep into Sasha's body. Her coat didn't come anywhere close to being warm enough. Monsieur Pichon said nothing, but Sasha was sure he felt the same.

She swallowed her pain, and her terror, and her heartbreak, as without a word Xantha unbolted the chain from the craft and fastened it to a belt around her waist. She turned and bared her teeth at Sasha before striking out on her skis, and that silent warning was enough to let Sasha know it would not go well for her if she tried anything. *I wouldn't have a hope anyway,* she thought. *Wounded, and weak, and we're barely able to walk as it is....*

Xantha set a fast pace. Sasha and Monsieur Pichon stumbled behind her through the ankle-deep snow, their eyes firmly fixed on their destination.

Igimaq looked out over the surface of the ice ahead, a worried frown creasing his brow.

"What's up now?" asked Thing. They'd already seen a red flare in the sky, which Igimaq had told him belonged to one of the other hunters from his village. They'd all set out together, going in different directions, with instructions to find Emmeline and fight whoever tried to get in their way. "That's probably Umiq," Igimaq had said as the red flare sputtered to its zenith. "Lily-livered fool." A red flare meant that one of the teams was returning home. A purple one, Thing now knew, meant that enemies had been kidnapped or neutralized or that a base had been destroyed. They hadn't seen any of those. Bright yellow meant that Emmeline had been found—they hadn't seen any of those, either.

But it wasn't flares, this time, that concerned Igimaq.

"The ice," he murmured. "It's—*wrong*." Thing glanced out at the landscape around them and went back to chewing on a strip of dried meat.

"Looks all right to me," he said, his words muffled. "White. Lots of it. What's wrong wi' that?"

"No, no," sighed Igimaq. "Too much water. More water than ice. More chances for—" His words were cut off as the sled suddenly lurched to one side. Thing felt Igimaq's strong hand on his shoulder before he'd even realized he was falling. From up front, the dogs started yelping as one of them, near the middle of the team, toppled right into a freezing pool. Faster than Thing could work out what was happening, Igimaq had launched himself from the sled.

"Stay calm, Miki!" he gasped, trying to get a grip on the dog's harness. "Quiet!" Dumbfounded, Thing watched as Igimaq wrestled with the terrified dog. His voice seemed to calm Miki down enough for Igimaq to help him out, but just as he managed this, a loud, bone-shattering crack, like a gunshot at close quarters, sounded all around them. Thing glanced from side to side, his senses jangling, but all he saw, in every direction, was desertion. On the horizon in front of them was that weird green glow, like a luminous tornado that stretched out across the sky.

"Ice is shifting," called Igimaq, turning back to Thing. "Got to get ready to move now!"

"*Move?* Move how?"

"Just help!" Igimaq hurried back to the sled and slung himself into it. "Hyup! Hey, boys! To the right now!" He whistled, leaning to the right to help the dogs as they struggled to get going, and the team instantly obeyed. As soon as they'd reached steadier ground, Igimaq brought the dogs to a halt. He jumped out and hurried to Miki's side.

"C'mon! Grab a fur. You gotta help me get him warm," he called over his shoulder. Thing shook off his confusion and hopped out of the sled, his feet splashing on the slushy ice. Within seconds he was beside Igimaq as they battled to undo Miki's harness straps and release him from the rest of the team. Between the two of them they wrapped up the shivering dog and wrestled him into the sled.

"Can you run alongside? Just for a while, till Miki warms up?" asked Igimaq, slipping back into his seat.

Thing hesitated. "Yeah, no problem. Lemme jus' grab this ol' bag, 'ere," he muttered, leaning in to pick up Emmeline's satchel and shaking it free of its fur. He was about to slip the strap over his head when Igimaq's strong hand grabbed his wrist.

"I'm not going to leave you behind," said Igimaq. "Okay?"

Thing felt suddenly dizzy. "Didn't think you were," he croaked, his heart leaping with relief.

"My mistake, then," said Igimaq with another warm grin. "Fling that back where it belongs, okay? We've wasted enough time."

"Right." Thing nodded, forcing himself to let go of the satchel. He settled it carefully as Igimaq whistled. With a jerk the sled pulled away. Thing wrapped his scarf up over his face, made sure his mittens were on tight, and took off after it as quickly as he could.

Unseen by Thing, who was concentrating on where to put his feet, or by Igimaq, concerned only for his dogs, the green glow on the horizon was getting stronger with every mile they traveled, almost like it knew they were coming.

Emmeline's breath was coming in fast, short plumes like pure white feathers. She felt as though she and Meadowmane stood out a mile on the open, deserted ice, and at every moment she expected to hear a voice calling her name or feel a hand clamping itself over her mouth.

A sudden loud rumbling reached her ears at the same time the ground beneath her feet started to shake. She heard a whinnying breath skittering out of Meadowmane's chest, and she shrank against him, his wide, warm flank feeling like a comfort blanket in the cold. Together they watched the giant mirrors calmly going about their work as though nothing were happening. *Is it coming now?* she thought. *Is the Kraken coming right now?*

As the tremors in the ice continued, Emmeline's eye was caught by a huge metal blade, like a giant knife, appearing out of the darkness at the far side of the pool. With a sinking feeling she realized that she recognized it— the ship that had brought her here, with its terrible wheels on either side, studded all over with the sharp points that had helped it grip the ice as it rolled out of the sea. . . . *Bauer!* She shook off a memory of being held captive and of having his disgusting, fleshy face up close. She watched the ship rock back and forth, settling itself securely on the ice. Several dark figures could just be seen moving as they disembarked.

She knew which one was Dr. Bauer, because as soon as she saw him, her stomach started to churn. It felt like he was standing right beside her, fixing her with his dark eyes and murmuring low words to her in a shadowy voice. Emmeline's eyes shut and she saw herself—like she was looking from outside—standing on the open ice, as clear as day. Bauer turned toward her and seemed to wave.

She felt her knees buckling, and she fell, face-first, onto the ice.

44

"**I've got t'stop—*whoop!* Sorry! Jus' for a min-**ute. Jus' to get m'breath." Gasping, Thing fell against the sled, wishing he could wrap himself up and go to sleep. Igimaq's face was a picture of worry, and his usually bright eyes were clouded.

"Time to get you in here, I reckon," he said, studying Thing's pinched face.

"I *hate* this," said Thing, surprised by the anger that flared up inside him. His father's voice roared in his ears again. "I'm *useless!* Stupid—*whoop*—lungs, stupid, stupid, stupid!" He wiped his running nose on the back of his sleeve and fought to stay on his feet.

"Stupid enough to find your way up here," mused Igimaq quietly. Thing struggled to hear him through the buzz in his mind. "Stupid enough to follow a friend, and to want to help, and to keep going when most other people would've given up. That sound stupid to you?"

"Yes," mumbled Thing.

"Not to me, it don't," said Igimaq. "Right, come on. Let's get you swapped for Miki." He shucked himself out of his seat. The dogs, tired and panting, but surrounded by a cloud of enthusiasm so thick you could smell it, stood to attention.

"But—*whoop*—come on. I can't carry on, can I? I'm—*whoop*—holding you back."

"Just quit your whining and help me," said Igimaq. Nimbly he made his way across the sled to his trussed-up dog, who was poking his head out of his furs inquisitively, sniffing the air. "That's right, Miki boy," he whispered. "Soon have you goin' again." Ignoring Thing, he started to undo the dog's furs, smiling as the animal tried to lick every exposed piece of skin he could find. Thing just stood and stared, his father's voice falling into whispers, eventually fading completely.

"Quit yer whinin'? That's it? That's all you're goin' to say?"

"What else would you like?" asked Igimaq, flashing a quick smile. "Now come on. We're nearly there. Emmeline needs us, right? So hurry up."

Thing shrugged as he hurried around the sled to help, and before long they had Miki reharnessed and were on their way once more.

Ahead of them the green funnel in the sky glowed brighter and brighter. Thing saw it and said nothing, and Igimaq did just the same.

Sasha could hear Monsieur Pichon struggling to breathe. He stumbled more often than not as they trailed behind Xantha like a pair of disobedient puppies. If he fell, Sasha wondered whether he'd just be cut loose and left there to freeze.

"Please!" she called, knowing the answer she'd receive. "Please, let him rest!" Xantha's only reply was to lean forward, jerking the chain cruelly. Sasha hissed as a bolt of pain seared her wounded side. "He'll *die*! What's the point of all this if you're just going to kill him here?"

"Die here, die there, it's all the same to me," shouted Xantha. "I only need one of you, anyway."

"But that's in*human*!" called Sasha, frustrated tears jumping to her eyes. Xantha said nothing. She just kept scanning the ice ahead of them, looking for cracks that were too wide to cross.

"Do not . . . waste . . . your breath, my dear," rasped Monsieur Pichon. Sasha turned to him and saw the old man trying his best to smile. His eyes had sunk back into his head, and his skin was dull. "You may as well . . . beg a cloud . . . not to rain."

"Come on," she said, her voice low. She drew as close to Monsieur Pichon as she could. "Lean on me, Michel."

"You need your strength to carry yourself, Natasha," he replied. His smile became a grimace as another bout of coughing rattled him from head to foot.

"Slowly," said Sasha, soothing. She leaned close and hooked her shoulder beneath Monsieur Pichon's armpit.

Her boots slid sideways as he leaned on her, and she could tell he was doing his best not to. "Please, Michel. I have no intention of letting us die out here. You've got to keep going, right? Just until we get to the compound."

"Whatever your master plan is, my girl, I am . . . all for it," gasped Monsieur Pichon, his breath hot on Sasha's cheek.

"As soon as I think of it, I'll let you know," she murmured. After a few seconds she realized the rattling, smacking sound she was hearing was Monsieur Pichon trying not to laugh out loud.

"If she throws me to the beast, I shall give him indigestion," declared Monsieur Pichon. "The worst he has ever had."

"Now, that sounds like a master plan," said Sasha, leaning her head on Monsieur Pichon's, just for a second. She closed her eyes as images flashed through her mind—images of what the future might hold if Xantha or Bauer succeeded in raising the Kraken and using its power. A world frozen into stillness, dead and white and cold. Or drowned cities, destroyed buildings. Bodies floating in the streets. And if the part about its blood granting eternal life was true . . . She shuddered. As bad as things had become, there was plenty of room for them to get much worse—and Sasha knew that was only the things *she* could imagine. Who could tell what Bauer would do once he had the Kraken at his command?

"Enough of that!" snapped Xantha, yanking the chain hard. With a yelp Sasha stumbled; as soon as she moved away, Monsieur Pichon fell to his knees.

"Michel!" she cried, desperately trying to stop and help him up, but Xantha strode forward, her skis barely slowing. Eventually Monsieur Pichon regained his feet, but Sasha could see how every step he took was a struggle, and she knew he would only get weaker.

He caught her eye, just once, and gave a brief smile, but Sasha didn't have the heart to return it. All she could do was blink to clear her eyes and focus on her own steps. They were within a quarter of a mile of the compound now, and Xantha started to pick up the pace even more.

Fear blocked out everything else in Sasha's mind, even the cold and discomfort and sorrow and loss. She took in the scale of the massive mirrors, and her eyes searched the gigantic slush pool, into which the thick, bright beam of auroral light was vanishing, and tried to work out how long they had before the Kraken came.

Judging by the water and the lumps of floating ice, and the creaking and groaning of the ice field, it would be far too soon for comfort.

Meadowmane gripped Emmeline's coat in his teeth and pulled. Slowly, gradually, her cold, pinched face emerged from the freezing water that covered the ice like a film. With a flick of his head, he flipped her onto her back, shaking his mane over her. He whinnied straight into her ear, pawing at the sludgy ground.

Then, with a sudden, lung-ripping gasp, Emmeline sucked in a breath. Her eyes popped open.

"Meadowmane!" she spluttered, coughing. She scrambled to her feet, taking deep breaths. A chattering shiver rolled up and over her, and she stood still until it passed. "We're in the right place, boy," she whispered into the horse's flank. "If *he's* here, then so are my parents." A spark of anger roared into a fire inside her. *So, what are you waiting for?*

Bauer's men were moving now, making their way toward some of the low, dark outbuildings beneath the mirrors. Emmeline saw Bauer turn to shout instructions at someone she couldn't see, and—without her even having to ask—Meadowmane nudged her up onto his back.

Before she knew it, they were clip-clopping to a halt right beside Dr. Bauer's ship, but Bauer himself was nowhere to be seen. Emmeline's anger flickered out, sucked away into the depths of the icy gloom all around them, and was replaced by a sudden flood of terror.

Then a loud, mechanical whir burst through the air, and one of the mirrors overhead started to move. The light it was reflecting changed as its angle did, becoming brighter and stronger and more focused, and Emmeline saw the water in the pool begin to boil. Huge, rolling bubbles formed slowly at first and then with frightening speed—but, strangely, there was no steam and no heat. The air all around was as cold as ever. She slid down from Meadowmane's back, her heart thudding in her ears, and wondered what to do next.

The hum of a mechanism kicking into life, its whine higher-pitched than the mirror's, drew her eyes upward.

It was a cage being slowly lowered. Inside it were two

figures wearing tight leather suits and strange masks over their faces. On their backs were two small silver tanks, and the people were holding hands like their lives depended on it. The shorter of the two had long, dark, curly hair that burst out of the helmet attempting to contain it and rippled down its owner's back in a way so familiar to Emmeline that her heart cracked open.

Before she could think, Emmeline raced to the edge of the pool. She skidded to a halt, barely stopping herself from falling headlong into the water.

"*Mum!*" she screamed, her voice bouncing between the mirrors like a bell being struck. "Dad!"

The figures in the cage jerked like they'd been slapped. Emmeline watched as they searched for her, and eventually—the cage still dropping—they found her.

Mrs. Widget pulled her breathing apparatus from her mouth.

"Emmeline!" she screamed. "*Run!* Run now, darling! Get away from here!" She didn't have time to say anything else before a horrible shriek rang out from behind Emmeline. She turned to see a dark lasso flip into place around Meadowmane's neck. One of Bauer's men held the other end of it, leaning hard against the horse's attempts to escape. Spots of bright red blood began to appear beneath the lasso, which, Emmeline saw, was studded with something sharp—metal or shards of broken glass. With every movement Meadowmane made, the barbs cut deeper and deeper into his flesh. He cried louder, and Emmeline stood, immobile, for a second too long before lunging toward him.

But she never made it that far.

"Now, now, my dear." Bauer's spine-shivering voice twisted its way into Emmeline's ear. She felt his strong arms wrap around her body and lift her clean off her feet. "Not so fast, eh? Let's say hello to your mama and papa first, shall we?"

"Let me go!" shouted Emmeline, lashing out with her boots, desperate to find something to kick. "Let me go this second, and stop hurting Meadowmane!"

"*Meadowmane*, is it?" Dr. Bauer murmured, right into her ear. "Well, I never. Who heard of an Æsirsmount allowing itself to be named by a *mortal*? Aren't you a singular little creature, after all, my Emmeline." The sound of these words made Emmeline's stomach turn.

"I'm not *your* anything! Let me go!"

"Oh, I think not," he replied smoothly, turning to face the pool once again, with Emmeline clamped in his arms. Directly above the pool's freezing, bubbling surface, the cage stopped with a sudden jerk, making Emmeline's parents stumble against its bars. Bauer moved toward the pool, and for a dizzying second Emmeline wondered if he was going to pitch her into it, straight down into darkness, but he stopped right at the edge.

The cage swung gently on its chain. Emmeline's parents hung helpless inside it, the aurora reflecting off their breathing equipment.

"Eloise!" called Dr. Bauer, and Emmeline saw her mother let go of her father's hand and grip the bars of their cage, her eyes glued to Emmeline's face. Slowly she began to sink to the floor, her hands sliding down the bars as she went. "And, Martin! Hello there!" Emmeline's father, white-faced with fury, stood as still as a statue. "Look who I found! Why, it's your precious child, little Emmeline. What on earth would have brought her up here, I wonder?" Emmeline felt her teeth rattling as she listened. She focused on her parents as Bauer continued, his voice like a growl. "I think we all know what will happen if you refuse to carry out my wishes. One word is all I need to say, and your daughter will be lost to you forever."

"Leave her *alone!*" Emmeline's father's voice was rough and raw and booming. "She has nothing to do with any of this!"

"Oh, I beg to differ," said Dr. Bauer. "In fact, she is instrumental."

"Don't hurt her!" shouted Emmeline's mother. "We'll do whatever you want, just please! Leave our daughter alone!" Emmeline saw her father drop to a crouch and wrap her mother up in a hug. Their gazes never left her face.

"What wonderful news," called Dr. Bauer. "I'm glad you've seen sense." With that, he gave a sharp nod to someone Emmeline couldn't see. The mechanical whir started up again, and the cage continued its downward journey at a much faster pace.

"No! Wait! *Dad!*" Emmeline yelled. "Mum!" They sprang to their feet, but the floor of the cage had already touched the water's surface. Too quickly for them to reply, the cage was swallowed by the rolling blueness, and Emmeline's parents disappeared from view. Her heart sank with them.

"Now let's start again, shall we?" said Dr. Bauer, turning away from the pool and striding into the darkness, with Emmeline still clutched to his chest. "I was so very sorry to have our little chat disturbed last time."

She aimed a bite at his fingers, but fast as a snake, he gripped her across the forehead, pinning her so tightly that she couldn't move.

"Don't get any big ideas," he snarled.

45

"Gotta be quiet now, boys," whispered Igimaq, leaning forward in the sled. They slid across the snow like ghosts. Wrapped in furs, Thing gazed up at the structure that loomed above them. It had been visible for miles, and he'd known it was going to be big, but this? This was beyond anything he could have imagined. The green glow—was it being *sucked* down out of the sky?—was swirling slowly and coming to a point as it entered the first of the three massive mirrors. He held his breath as he followed the path of the light with his eyes, watching it bounce back and forth between the mirrors, getting stronger and brighter as it went, until eventually it beamed straight into the pool of bubbling water beneath them.

Well—*pool* wasn't really a good word. It looked more like a lake, Thing thought.

"What the . . . ," breathed Igimaq, staring around at the scene. The light from the sky was reflected in his dark eyes.

"What is it?" whispered Thing.

"No idea," replied Igimaq. "Something not too good, I reckon."

"I reckon too," said Thing with a shiver. They drove on, Igimaq never taking his eyes off the mirrors for a second. Then Thing felt him tensing up, like a fist being clenched.

"This is it. This is where it's going to *rise*," said Igimaq, sitting up straight. "He's really going to do it." Thing saw his hands shake. Igimaq swallowed, and it sounded loud in the silence.

"Do what? What's risin'?"

Igimaq didn't answer for a long, dark moment. "Have you ever heard of the Kraken?" he asked eventually, still not looking at Thing. "Monster-squid thing, lots of arms, huge snappin' beak that can break bones without even thinking about it, gigantic round eyes—"

"Yeah!" said Thing a little too loudly. Igimaq put a finger to his lips. "Yeah," Thing repeated in a quieter voice. "Yeah, I know what you're talkin' about. The eye of the north! The eye with all the wigglin' legs. I saw it on a map once." He remembered the moment he first saw the strange symbol on Sasha's map, back when all of this had seemed like such a grand adventure, and sighed at his own stupidity.

"Right," said Igimaq, frowning slightly. "Well, it's been sleeping, many years, deep inside this ice, where it should've stayed for the rest of forever. But this guy—the guy that has Emmeline—well, he's been trying to wake it up for a long time now. We thought he was a bit of a madman, really, a southlander who'd soon get sick and tired of the cold and the ice and go home to his fireplace and his cocoa." Igimaq grinned a little sadly. "Guess we underestimated him."

"But why would anyone want to wake it up?" asked Thing, confused. "Sounds like the kind of thing as should be left alone, if you ask me." He gazed back up at the mirrors again, hearing the distant moan of their motors as they changed direction. The beam into the water didn't falter.

"Well, yeah. *We* don't want it woken. The last time that happened, well . . ." Igimaq grimaced. "It's ancient, you know? Probably won't be too happy at having spent the last whatever hundred years frozen stiff." Igimaq paused, taking a thoughtful breath. "The legends I was raised on have *plenty* to say about it, not much of it good. My grandfather liked to keep me awake at night by telling me stories about how it's bigger than ten whales put together and unstoppable once it gets going. It can destroy anything it likes with those massive tentacles it's got, and it has a bellow that can shatter solid rock. Its blood is supposed to be the elixir of eternal life or something— because it's immortal, some say. If you drink it, there's no killing you. It has eyes that can see straight to the bones of anyone foolish enough to stand against it, and its gaze can turn anything to ice. Yeah." Igimaq shivered. "It's not the kind of thing you want to see knocking about again. You know the Ice Age? This guy was behind all that."

Thing listened, cold air streaming in and out of his lungs, his nose running like a tap, and wondered what he'd been thinking by coming up here in the first place. If his brain had had a boot, it would've been using it to kick him.

"You said it got woken up before?" he said eventually. "It must've been stopped then, since someone put it back in its box. Any ideas 'ow they did it?"

"Nobody remembers," said Igimaq.

"Brilliant."

"Yeah," said Igimaq before whistling quietly. Without so much as a whimper, the dogs picked up the pace.

"What does he want Ems for, then? I mean, what was the point of goin' to the trouble of kidnappin' some random kid?"

"He'll want to use her as his sacrifice, I reckon," said Igimaq distractedly, still gazing up at the structure. Thing grabbed Igimaq's arm and stared into his face, hoping he'd misheard.

"*What?* What are you *talking* about now?"

Igimaq blinked at Thing. "Well—ah. It's like this. The legends claim that when the Kraken is awoken, the first person to offer it a living sacrifice can, so they say, control it—make it do whatever its master wants, destroy whoever they're not overfond of, knock mountains over like they were twigs, freeze whole oceans solid, all that sort of stuff. Anyway. So the stories go. I reckon this lunatic wants to be the one to offer the sacrifice. I'd be willing to bet Ems is it, too." Thing quivered, and his heart hopped so fast that it felt ready to pop.

"But—that's *crazy!*"

287

"Men that go about stirring up ancient monsters aren't famed for their levelheadedness, I s'pose," said Igimaq mildly, guiding the dogs around a pool on the ice.

"We can't let him do this," said Thing, his hands clenching into fists.

"We'd better be quick, then," said Igimaq. "He's got a bit of a head start."

"Magnificent," breathed Xantha, gazing up at the mirrors. As she spoke, the one nearest them moved slightly, just barely changing the angle of its reflection. The beam of auroral light going into the water thickened by several feet as a result, and a fresh explosion of bubbles danced across the surface of the semifrozen lake. "Whatever else I might want to say about Siegfried Bauer, he's certainly good at what he does. Working out that only the light of the aurora could pierce the ancient ice of the Kraken's cavern? Genius."

"He's insane," spat Sasha. "But then, so are you."

"Now, now, my dear," said Xantha, turning to face Sasha, the light of the aurora reflecting in her eyes. "Watch your mouth, like a good girl." At these words Sasha growled and lashed out with her right foot, smashing it into Xantha's shin as hard as she could. Just as she was drawing back for a second attempt, Xantha grabbed her boot and sent her sprawling to the ground.

"Excellent. That makes one decision a little easier," said Xantha, smiling maddeningly down at her. She slid her fingers into a pouch at her belt and drew out a pair of handcuffs, which settled in her grip with a soft clink.

"What decision?" Sasha struggled to her feet, her bound hands and aching side making it very hard to keep her balance. Monsieur Pichon lay in a huddled heap on the ground, gazing up at the structure overhead with watery eyes. He barely had the strength to breathe.

"Well, I was going to get you to fight one another for the privilege of being my sacrifice, but this is much easier," she sneered. "You can have the best seat in the house while your colleague goes to greet the beast." Sasha's mind reeled as she listened. *So it's really happening. They're really going through with a sacrifice, like the old legends say, and if it actually works as it's supposed to* ... She felt a stab of despair. *And Michel has no chance of fighting them. But you do! You could have saved him from that fate, but instead you had to mess it all up....*

"No! Please take me. Take me! Leave Michel here. Honestly, he's old—what use is he?" Sasha felt a painful swelling in her throat as she spoke. "Come on!"

"He will go down the hatch just as easily as you would." Xantha smiled,. fastening an ice-cold cuff around Sasha's right wrist. Not far from them stood a support strut for one of the mirrors. Xantha dragged Sasha toward it, the iron around Sasha's wrist biting into her skin.

"You can't do this," said Sasha. "You can't throw an innocent old man to his death!"

"You'd rather I threw an innocent young woman to hers?" asked Xantha, forcing Sasha's hands on either side of a bar of the metal strut and fastening the free cuff around her other wrist. Hopelessly Sasha pulled at the bar, but it didn't give an inch. "I am not a total monster, whatever reports about me would have you believe."

"I hope the Kraken crushes you," Sasha growled. "I hope it leaves you for dust."

"Oh, there's no fear of that," said Xantha. "No fear whatsoever. You know, it'll be wonderful, not only to have the Kraken under my control, but also to swoop in at the last second and steal victory from Siegfried. Particularly when he's gone to all this trouble." Xantha looked around, taking in the entire structure with a glance. She leaned in close to Sasha and placed a hand over one of hers. "Let me thank you, right here, for helping me bring my dream to fruition."

Before Sasha had a chance to aim another kick, Xantha danced away from her, laughing over her shoulder as she went. She grabbed Monsieur Pichon under the arm and pulled him to his feet, and Sasha watched as they vanished into the distance. It made her heart hurt to watch Monsieur Pichon being dragged through the snow to certain death, and the pain of not getting a chance to say goodbye made her head throb.

"It—can't—happen—like—*this!*" she groaned, clanging her handcuffs against the bar with every word. She gritted her teeth and pulled as hard as she could, but it was no use. She sank to her knees, her head whirling, and tried not to hear Xantha's cruel laughter being carried back to her on the breeze.

"Madam? Are you—are you all right?"

The sudden voice, silvery and barely audible, made Sasha jump. Her cuffs rattled as she rose to her feet.

"Who—who's there?" she said, scanning the darkness all around her.

"It's just me," replied the voice. Sasha blinked, trying to work out where it was coming from, but it seemed like it was coming from nowhere and everywhere all at once. Then a swirl of snow, and there he was—a tiny boy, barely five years old, dressed in an old-fashioned frock coat and a jaunty red scarf. He stood in front of her, smiling broadly. His cheeks, deeply dimpled, were rosy, and his small hands were bare, but his eyes were a dark navy blue from lid to lid.

"What on *earth*? Where did you come from?"

"Oh, from somewhere close by," said the boy, his voice like tinkling icicles.

"Where's your mummy?" Sasha's heart thundered in her chest. *Keep him away from Xantha!* flashed across her mind.

"Oh, she's around here somewhere," said the child vaguely. "You know, I can set you free. Do you believe me?" Sasha tried to smile, but her tears rolled down her cheeks as she did. *Why not play along?* she told herself. *There'll be nothing left of us soon.*

"I'm sure a clever boy like you can do anything," she said. The child laughed, his tiny teeth shining in the gloom, and stepped toward her until he was close enough to touch her skin.

The next thing Sasha knew, she was at the heart of a whirling wind, with spikes of ice flinging themselves at her from all angles. A shattering pain surrounded her heart, and her chest filled with cold. She tried to scream, but the ice just flew into her throat, choking her. She buried her face in the crook of her elbow, feeling the sting of the ice shards digging into her flesh, and squeezed her eyes shut against the howling gale that lifted her up into the air. The handcuffs shattered and fell to the ground, a vivid weal on Sasha's skin rising where the freezing metal had touched her.

"One sacrifice is much the same as another," came a voice, huge and roaring, like waves crashing onto a rocky shore, and Sasha was swallowed by the icy storm.

46

One of the things Emmeline disliked most about
herself was her fear of heights. She was constantly trying
to force herself to be brave, and if not that, then noncha-
lant, and failing even that, to be careful—in which case, of
course, there was no need to be afraid.

If only things had been slightly different, then this
would have been the perfect training exercise.

The thick leather strap from which she was suspended
was cutting into her hands, and the wind was blowing
right up her dress, prodding at her with its icy, needly
fingers. She swayed slightly, rocking to and fro in the air
three hundred feet above the gaping lake below—the lake
from which she expected the Kraken to appear any second
and, more importantly, into which her parents had disappeared. She squeezed her eyes shut and gripped the strap

around her wrists as if it could give her even a small bit of comfort, but it was attached to a chain that vanished into the metalwork above her, and so clutching it did nothing at all to help. She couldn't even reach her pockets—mournfully she realized her tools were useless to her now.

A voice boomed close by, making her jump.

"Your parents—bless them!—clever little things that they are, will nearly be finished by now. Thank goodness for their unparalleled knowledge. Do you know, experts in ultralarge, *unique* creatures are rare as hens' teeth these days? Thank goodness for OSCAR and their specialists." Emmeline swung herself, spluttering, to face Dr. Bauer. He was standing on a platform suspended between two of the mirrors, a few feet from where she hung. She didn't want to look at him, but at least it meant she didn't have to look down. "Anyway, my apologies if this is painful, my dear. Rest assured you won't be here very long."

"What's going to happen to my mum and dad?" shouted Emmeline.

"Well," replied Dr. Bauer, raising his eyebrows as if he were giving the question some serious thought. "Let's see. Assuming they have enough oxygen left to reach the surface, and the cold doesn't kill them—which is unlikely, naturally—they'll probably be destroyed by the Kraken when it raises itself out of its prison. It won't be taking care where it puts its tentacles, if you know what I mean. But at least it won't *eat* them; the beast dines only on the living, of course." His words made Emmeline's insides turn to water.

"You can't do this!" She kicked out, aiming at Dr. Bauer. All that did was make her swing, sickeningly, in midair.

"Now, now, my dear," he said. "We don't want you feeding yourself to the beast before it's ready for you! Stay still now, won't you?" Emmeline's anger started to trickle away, only to be replaced by fear and sickness as she felt herself swinging to and fro, to and fro, like a pendulum.

"So if you're quite all right there, Miss Widget, I'm just going to pop off now. Important to get to safety before the beast rises—I'm sure you understand." Emmeline could hear the sneer in Dr. Bauer's voice, and her whole body boiled with hatred. She swung herself to face him again.

"I won't *let* you do this!" she shouted. Dr. Bauer just waved and turned his back before carefully picking his way down a set of metal stairs and vanishing into the shadows. As soon as he was gone, Emmeline cast her gaze around, trying as hard as she could to find some way out of her predicament. *Could I climb up the chain? Get across to the side? Maybe I can swing myself over to that platform!* It was hard to see, but she felt pretty sure Dr. Bauer hadn't left her enough slack to do that.

She swung gently, her lungs burning, and thought hard.

"I might not have much choice about being here," she muttered, "but that does *not* mean I'm going to hang about like an hors d'oeuvre. And don't you even *think* about screaming, Emmeline Mary."

So, squeezing her eyes tight against the drop, she started to do the only thing she could.

"Hey, hey, look," said Igimaq suddenly, his body tensed and ready to spring. He removed a hand from the sled and pointed straight up, right at the narrowest point between the mirrors. Thing and Igimaq had pulled into a patch of shadow beneath one of the struts a few moments before. As the dogs had lain, panting happily, on the cold ground, they'd been trying to keep an eye on everything all at once.

"Where are you lookin', mate?" Thing asked, squinting into the sky. The brightness of the light beam was making his eyes water. "I couldn't see a roast dinner with all the trimmin's at that distance."

"Hanging in the middle of the gap between the mirrors," said Igimaq. "It looks like—yep. I think it's Emmeline."

Thing felt like someone had slapped him. "What? She all right?"

"Looks to be," said Igimaq, shading his eyes with one hand. "Hard to know."

"What on earth's she doin' up there?"

"Bauer has her ready, like a stunned seal." Igimaq dropped his hand, his face crumpling. "I've really let her down now. We should've hurried. I should've come straight here. I should've—"

"But if you'd come straight here, you wouldn't've saved me," Thing pointed out. He licked his lips, thinking fast, never removing his eyes from the flailing dot that was Emmeline, high above.

"True enough," said Igimaq, trying to smile.

"And if you hadn't saved me, we'd have no chance of saving Ems."

"What's that, now?" Igimaq's eyes flew open and he stared at Thing.

"Do you have a knife or a blade I could borrow for a while?"

Igimaq raised an eyebrow and grinned as he pulled a small knapsack toward himself. He flipped it open and reached inside.

"Wouldn't be much of a hunter without one," he said. The blade of the knife he gave to Thing was wrapped in leather, and its handle was made of something that looked like bone, carved to fit snugly in a palm.

"Perfect," said Thing, sticking it into his belt. "Wish me luck, then."

"Luck," said Igimaq.

"Right." Thing sized up the structure. *Shouldn't be a problem. Bigger than anythin' you've done before, but come on—it's Ems up there. Get to it!*

Then, quietly as a shadow at midnight, Thing launched himself out of the sled. Barely touching the snow, he ran toward the nearest strut, landing on it with the grace of a cat. He looked up, calculating his route. He was fairly sure he could see a clear path almost the whole way up, nearly all of it hidden behind the shadow of the nearest mirror, and he told himself that the bits he couldn't see from here he'd manage when he got closer. Swinging himself for extra momentum when he needed to, landing silently and steadily each time, he flew. Every move was nimble, every handhold strong, every foothold secure, and very soon he was twenty, then thirty, then forty feet in the air, and climbing.

"Well, isn't that something," whispered Igimaq far below. "You looking, boys?" Miki's ears pricked up and Balto's tongue lolled out of his mouth as, jaws hanging, they watched Thing's progress.

"Careful," muttered Thing. The last few handholds he'd managed to grab hadn't been all that satisfactory, and he'd had to stop for a minute to get his head together. The higher he went, the slippier the crossbars and struts were becoming, and the colder the air was too. His breath tore in and out of his chest like a saw, but—so far—the whooping had stayed away. He took stock of his surroundings as he got his breath back. From where he was, he could clearly see Emmeline hanging, like meat in a butcher's window, from a long, thick chain attached to a metal bar, and he wondered how much longer he had before she'd be Kraken food. He couldn't help but smile, just a little, as he watched her swing herself back and forth, grunting as she went, curling her legs up a little higher every time. He just hoped the creaking of the chain wasn't a sign that it was about to give way.

He thought about shouting her name but then decided against it. The last thing he wanted was to draw anyone's attention. Not until he was ready for it, at least.

"Right. Get to it," he muttered, carefully picking his way forward. His toes, through his thin soles, gripped the strut nearly as well as his fingers did in his thick mittens, and he made slow but steady progress. *Don't look down,* he kept repeating to himself. *Focus on the goal.*

Something inside his ears shivered into life then—something sharp. His body went limp, against his will.

Don't look down! How often 'ave I to tell you? Don't look down! Focus on the goal!

Thing's nostrils flared as he struggled to breathe, and fear gripped him.

… Useless thing! …
… Can't even do a simple tumble right …

Thing gritted his teeth and steadied himself. He reached for the next handhold, forcing his terror down, away into a corner of his mind. His lungs felt like they were filling with glue.

… Stupidest thing I ever saw! You are the stupidest thing that's ever lived!

"I am not!" Thing growled. "I am *not!*"

Yeah, that's right. You really think you're fit to perform, do ya? Well, I've got news for you, kid. …

Thing grabbed hold of a bar and made sure his grip was steady. He swung himself out over yawning nothingness before landing securely. He fought to breathe, feeling the roots of his fear begin to lift out of his lungs. *I can do this*, he told himself. *I can!*

... News for you, kid ...

The voice faded, lost beneath the rasping of Thing's quick breaths, until eventually it was hardly there at all. Thing paused for a rest, his heart thunking calmly and steadily, and listened closely.

And the voice said nothing at all.

Three more moves and he'd made it. He couldn't climb any farther.

Panting, he clung to a crossbar, his mind boggling at how high up he was. The wind whistled through him as though he weren't there. He was afraid that if he sat still too long, he'd freeze solid. He spent a few minutes waiting for his lungs to close over like they usually did, but they stayed clear. It felt like something had been unbuckled inside him and he had space, at last, to breathe deeply.

But that wasn't helping him help Emmeline.

"Nothing for it. Come too far to give up now," he whispered. He wriggled his fingers around inside his mittens, keeping the blood flowing through them, and slid his hand forward along the bar Emmeline was hanging from. It vibrated slightly as she swung, on and on, and he finally worked out what she was trying to do. As he watched, she raised her legs as high as she could, doing her best to grab the chain between her knees. She slipped, but that didn't stop her from trying again, and again.

Good girl, Ems, he thought, smiling. *Jus' what I'd do too.* He refocused his gaze on his own task, making sure he had his balance. When he was certain of his grip, he slid the other hand along, bringing his body with him. Carefully, hand over hand, Thing edged his way out.

Ten feet below him, Emmeline was oblivious. Thing could hear her gasping for breath and watched as she finally managed to get her legs right up, displaying a pair of ruffled, long-legged knickers covered in yellow ducks wearing blue bow ties. Her dress and coat hung free, floating in the breeze, and on she swung. *Shouldn't have bothered comin' up 'ere at all,* Thing thought. *Five more minutes an' she'd've cracked it.*

"Hey down there! Nice bloomers!"

Emmeline lost her grip on the chain, and her legs dropped with a jerk. As the chain juddered and shook beneath him, Thing couldn't help but laugh at her small, sweaty face as she peered up at him like she couldn't believe what she was seeing.

47

A few minutes later Emmeline was astride the bar, right side up. She sat in stunned silence, getting her balance, quivering with a mixture of shock and cold.

"Hold still so's I can cut you out of this contraption," laughed Thing, sliding Igimaq's knife carefully under the tight, twisted leather strap. Emmeline's hands were bleeding and raw, but she didn't seem to care.

"What—I mean, *how*—I mean—what are you *doing* here?" she finally managed to gasp.

"Nobody kidnaps my friends and gets away wi' it," he replied, rubbing her stone-cold fingers between his own mitten-warmed ones.

Without warning, Emmeline threw herself forward and grabbed Thing up into a huge hug, almost knocking them both off their precarious perch. Through her coat Thing could feel her body trembling.

"It's all right," he said. "Come on, now."

"He's got my parents," Emmeline whispered. "They're—they're in the water. I think he forced them to wake the Kraken. He told them he'd kill me if they didn't. I have to get them back, Thing. I *have* to."

"Of course y'do," said Thing in the way that only a person without parents can. He cleared his throat. "We'd better get down, then, before he sees you're gone. We've dawdled too long as it is, don't you reckon?"

"D-down?" Emmeline released Thing from her grip and risked a look.

"It's okay, right? I got up here. I can get us down."

"No—no! What I mean is, we don't have time. The Kraken—it's literally coming any minute now. We'll be too late if we go back down." A light popped on behind Emmeline's eyes, and she raised them to stare at Thing. "At least, we'll be too late if we go back down the way you came up."

"What on *earth* are you babblin' about?" Thing's mind burst with images of falling hundreds of feet into a freezing pool of water, just in time to be snapped in half by a giant sea monster—or, worse, falling hard onto the cold ground and ending up as little more than a splat. He wobbled a bit on the bar.

"Just—come on. Trust me. Can you trust me?" Emmeline's smile was a bit manic.

"Um—"

"Come on! Please. Just scoot back the way you came. Go on!" Reluctantly Thing started easing his way back, and Emmeline hopped her way forward, until soon they were hidden in the shadow of the mirror, clinging in relative safety to the bars all around them. The low whir of the machinery controlling the mirrors set Thing's teeth on edge, and the light, passing just feet from them, was bright and dizzying.

"Right. Now what?" Thing's heart was beginning to thunk.

"Give me your hand. No, your other hand. Brilliant." Emmeline rummaged in her pocket and drew out her length of rope, which she tied in a knot around Thing's wrist. Then she tied the other end securely around her own, using her teeth to pull it tight. As she did this, her eyes fell on the shining surface of the mirror, and she watched it carefully, counting under her breath as it moved forward, then back. Forward, then back ... She shuffled herself around so that she was facing its concave face.

Its concave face, which reached nearly all the way to the ground.

"No," said Thing, his mind suddenly running into a brick wall. "You're not—"

"What? Are you afraid?"

"Afraid? Don't be daft!"

"Well, come on, then. If a *girl* can do it . . ."

"Oh, for the love of . . . Right. Go on, then."

"You ready?"

"As I'm goin' to get."

"Okay. One, two—"

Before she'd reached three—and before she had time to think things like *What if I've timed it wrong? What if we hit the mirror too hard? What if we get smashed to bits?*—Emmeline gave Thing a shove between the shoulder blades. He had no time to suck in a lungful of air before they were free-falling. A thick green-blue beam of auroral light enveloped them as they fell, and in it Thing heard overlapping voices, hissing like the whispers of giants.

... Betrayed we are betrayed she has betrayed us all ... The Creature must remain at rest ... None shall disturb it ... Betrayed betrayed ... no loyalty ... we no longer serve she who calls herself the Northwitch ...

Then the bowl of the mirror, polished smoother than any piece of glass Thing had ever seen, caught them. Within seconds they were flung off at the other end. They fell about six feet through empty air and came to rest just beside the edge of the huge, bubbling lake.

Dimly Thing thought he heard Emmeline yelling, a mix of triumph and relief in her voice. He just moaned, wiping the snow off his face and wondering how you could tell whether you'd broken a bone if your body was too numb to feel anything.

"Did you—did you *hear* 'em?" he asked, cracking open an eye and gazing up at the light overhead. Explosions of color sparkled inside it, and strange-looking shapes, almost like beings with long, stretched-out limbs, moved within the beam.

Or at least he *thought* so.

"Hear what?" said Emmeline, already up on her knees. She brushed the snow off her front as she spoke.

"The voices. The voices in the light," muttered Thing, his eyes drifting closed again.

"Thing? Come on!" His face burned with sudden cold, and he sat up quickly as a trickle of freezing water snaked down his neck. "Wakey, wakey!"

"Oi!" He spluttered. The handful of snow Emmeline had smacked against his cheek slithered off as he moved. "What's the hurry, eh?"

"Just come on. We've got to find the controls for the cage," said Emmeline. "Which means we've got to get to Bauer. And we've got to rescue Meadowmane."

"Who's Meadowmane?" Thing got to his feet and loosened the knot at his wrist. Emmeline wound the rope up and put it back into her pocket.

"Never mind. I'll explain later," she said, waving a hand in the air. "Let's worry about first things first. Any ideas on saving my folks yet?"

"Nope. But I know a guy we can ask. Come on!"

"You *know* someone? Up here?" But Thing didn't take the time to answer. He turned and started running, leaving Emmeline to shrug, gather her long coat in her wounded hands, and race after him as fast as she could.

She followed Thing toward the nearest strut and saw him stop short. The confusion was clear on his face as he looked all around the structure, not believing his own eyes.

"But . . . ," said Thing, turning around to stare at her. "They should be here."

"There's tracks," Emmeline pointed out, nodding toward the ground. "Pretty messy, but we could follow them, maybe."

As Emmeline spoke, a tiny pop of purple, like a distant star, flared into life over to their right, followed quickly by another. Emmeline frowned at them as Thing took a couple of running steps in their direction, letting loose a yell of triumph, the words to explain what the lights meant already on his lips: *Purple flares mean we're winnin'!*

But before he had a chance to speak, a light exploded across the surface of the ice, bright enough to make them both wince, and yellow enough to drown out the green beam bouncing between the mirrors behind them.

"What's *that*?" called Emmeline, squinting into it and trying to shade her eyes with her hand.

"How'm I s'posed to know?"

Silently Emmeline and Thing drew closer to one another. The light increased with every second, and above the gentle thrumming of what they took to be an engine, they could hear faint hallooing and the sharp *yip-yip* of dogs. Thing squinted into the murk and saw the smudged shapes of several dogsleds peeling off to the left and right, vanishing into the darkness around the lake. Another purplish flare exploded in the sky, and Thing couldn't help but grin.

"Siegfried Bauer!" A huge voice boomed through the air. Thing yelped in surprise, quickly turning it into a cough. "Face us, and account for your crimes!"

Emmeline took off running toward the light, Thing hot on her heels, as an airship hovered into view, floating with a sort of grace above the glacier. Slung beneath the balloon was a large-windowed cabin surrounded by a balcony. As Thing watched, a rope ladder was thrown over the side of it, unrolling faster and faster until it slapped down on the ice.

On the prow, bright and proud, was a hastily completed painting of a white flower.

"You lot took your sweet time gettin' here," called Thing as Edgar landed heavily on the sludgy ground.

He laughed, taking them in with a relieved gaze. "Well, you know. We wanted to take the scenic route." Thing snorted, shaking his head slowly.

Emmeline grinned as she flung herself at Edgar. "It's great to see you," she whispered. Edgar hugged her with his good arm, smiling down at her messy hair. "Where's Sasha?" She looked up into his face in time to see a dark frown cross it.

"I was about to ask you the same thing," said Edgar to Thing.

"Listen, she's hurt—" Thing began, but he was cut off by an unearthly howl. It rippled through the air, coming from behind them like a storm-force wind. Emmeline was almost knocked off her feet as it passed over the dirigible, rocking it from side to side on its moorings. Distantly she heard yelling and raised voices as the people yet to disembark were thrown around inside the cabin. Thing grabbed her arm to steady her as the gust died down, but she didn't have a chance to ask what had happened before a second bloodcurdling yell was heard from beyond the airship.

"Get off! Come on!" roared Edgar, running back toward the dirigible's moorings. "Now!" Emmeline saw panicked faces around the cabin railing, and a clamoring queue for the rope ladder. "Make way for Madame, please! Let Madame Blancheflour off this ship!" A scuffling at the top of the ladder drew Emmeline's eye, and to her utter amazement, she saw a tiny, elegant old lady being led toward the ladder by a large, stiff-collared gentleman—a gentleman whose familiar face was the most welcome thing she'd seen for days.

"*Watt!*" she cried, tears springing to her eyes as the butler she'd known all her life searched for her, finally locking on to her gaze. "How are you even *here*?" Watt carefully handed Madame Blancheflour onto the ladder before straightening up and saluting Emmeline.

"Miss Widget! A joy to see you so well," he called. He was still wearing his crisp black-and-white uniform, and every thread of it made Emmeline think of home.

"Get off the ship! That thing—whatever it is—it's coming back!"

"Not while there are ladies aboard, lass," he replied. "I'll be with you presently!"

"Don't be ridiculous, Watt!" shouted Emmeline. "Come on! There's no time—" But her words were swallowed by a third terrifying shriek, and the wind rose again. This time it felt like it was full of blades. Emmeline yelped, her eyes watering. She tried to huddle into her coat, but she might as well have been standing on the ice dressed only in her underwear, for all the good it did.

The nightmarish sound passed over their heads again, whipping around the dirigible so hard it almost knocked it out of the air entirely. Emmeline forced her eyes open, hoping to see Watt safe and alive, but instead her gaze was dragged to something floating in the air high above her head.

Something that sparkled like freshly fallen frost. Something hard and sharp and beautiful. Something cold as a distant star. It was looking down at Emmeline, and at all the people below it, with an expression of pure hatred on its strange, familiar face. Its eyes, too large to be human, were a dark, slushy blue.

"Sasha?" gasped Emmeline. *"No!"*

"Sasha!" shouted Edgar, his voice like a twig underfoot. "What on earth?"

"It's not Sasha!" Emmeline shouted, her heart throbbing. "It's—I think I know what it is!"

"What's happened to her?" Edgar's eyes were filling with tears in the freezing air, and he blinked them away, never dropping his gaze from the glittering figure above.

"It's the Northwitch. She's taken her," said Emmeline.

"What?" shouted Edgar, his eyes wild.

But the creature wearing Sasha's body didn't give Emmeline time to answer. It swooped through the air toward them, bringing a freezing wind with it. The snow was kicked up all around Emmeline, Thing, and Edgar, and even as they watched, the dirigible was ripped right off its moorings. Madame Blancheflour slid down the last few feet of the rope ladder, rolling herself away across the ice once she landed.

The Northwitch swooped once, twice, around the stricken airship before making her move. Like an arrow, she flew straight for the balloon, putting her—putting *Sasha's*—arms out in front, pointed perfectly, as though she were a diver about to enter the water, and burst right through it like a needle jabbing through a piece of cloth. With a huge *whumpf* the balloon exploded, and Emmeline felt Edgar's arm go around her as he pulled her to the ground.

48

"This is *unbelievable!*" shouted Thing over the roar of the flames. Overhead the balloon kept exploding, *boom-boom-boom*, until eventually the whole thing was one ball of fire. It began to sink to earth, prompting the last few remaining passengers to fling themselves off in an attempt to roll clear of the debris.

"Just stay down!" called Edgar. "Don't look at it!" But it was impossible not to. Emmeline felt a small hand wiggle its way into her armpit as someone tried to drag her farther away from the fire. She turned to see the face of the tiny old lady Watt had helped to disembark.

"Wh-where's Watt? Where is he?" Emmeline asked, even as she was pulled backward.

"Do not fret, *ma chérie*," murmured the old lady. "All

is well." Just then a huge *crump* sounded out as the ship finally crashed to the ice.

"No, it's not! Don't lie!" shouted Emmeline. The lady frowned down at her.

"Perhaps not right at this moment," she conceded. Emmeline was barely able to listen. Her head was thumping as hundreds of thoughts jostled for position inside it. *Save Mum and Dad, save Sasha, see if Watt's all right, what's happened to Thing, where's Meadowmane, get away from the Kraken....* She didn't know which one to listen to first.

"What?" she said rather rudely, realizing that Madame Blancheflour had asked her a question.

"Your parents, *poupette.* Where are they?"

"In the—in the water. They're waking the Kraken. He forced them! Honest! He—"

"Hush." Madame Blancheflour stroked Emmeline's cheek. *"Je comprends."*

"She all right?" came a voice to her left. Thing, skidding to his knees, landed on the ground beside her. "Ems?"

"I'm fine. I'm fine!" She sat up, shaking off hands and concerned looks. "Come on! We haven't time to sit about!" She struggled upright, wobbling a bit.

"Yeah, all right, keep your wig on," said Thing, rolling back up onto his feet. "What's first, then?"

"Hey," said Edgar suddenly from a few feet away. "Do you hear that?" Over the dull roaring of the flames, and the thumping of her own heart, Emmeline realized she *did* hear something out of place—a tiny, shrill voice, screaming as loud as it could. This wasn't the howling of the Northwitch or the noise of the burning dirigible all around them, but something different.

"Help me!" the voice shouted. *"Please!"*

Emmeline turned to face the structure again. In midair, between the mirrors and right above the frothing pool, keeping well clear of the light beam, was something that looked like a flock of crystal birds. Swooping back and forth, forming and reforming, the sparkling shards seemed almost playful, but the terrified cry for help came from inside it again as Emmeline stared.

"It's Sasha," said Edgar, moving to stand beside her. "I'd know her voice anywhere. *Sasha* Sasha, I mean, not that . . . thing. Whatever it was." A look of pained confusion flickered over his face.

"But where . . . ," Emmeline began, and then it all became clear. Through a gap in the flickering black cloud, she saw Sasha. She was suspended as if something had a hold of her arms. Her head swept from side to side as she followed the path of the dark, whirling ice crystals billowing around her.

"Sasha!" roared Edgar. "Hold on!" Her eyes flicked toward the ground, searching, but it was clear to Emmeline that she couldn't see him.

"Edgar!" she cried. "Please!"

"I think there's a staircase somewhere—" Emmeline started to say, but she was interrupted by another shout, this time one that came from high above them, somewhere in the structure itself.

"If you think you're going to take this from me, you're

tragically mistaken!" Emmeline didn't recognize the voice, but Thing did.

"It's *her*! The nutter who chased me at Monsieur Pichon's place! It *can't* be!" Thing stared up at the mirrors, squinting.

"Who?" said Emmeline.

"Not a blimmin' clue," Thing answered. "All's I know is, she came after me, and then she—or one of 'er crew, at least—shot at the *Cloud Catcher*. She must've followed me in that big black flyin' thingie. I s'pose she took Sasha here too. And—look! She's got Monsieur Pichon!"

"*Who?*" said Emmeline again.

Edgar's face had darkened. He looked back at the structure.

"Michel," he breathed, his lips in a grim line. "So our mystery guest has a sacrifice to make too. This Kraken is a popular fellow."

"*Sacrifice?*" said Emmeline. "What?"

"First fella to sacrifice a livin' thing to Mr. Kraken gets to control 'im," said Thing. "Splish, splash, aaaargh! Y'know, all that." Edgar stared at Thing like he'd suddenly started to tap-dance, and Emmeline's jaw dropped as she listened.

"Who told you—" Edgar began to ask.

"No time—we've got to get Sasha down from there," said Thing. "Come on!"

"But how?" asked Emmeline as she hurried behind Edgar and Thing toward the nearest strut.

Then a loud *clang-clang-clannnnng* noise kicked off, high above, echoing and reverberating in everyone's head.

Emmeline gritted her teeth as it rattled through her skull. The roaring, howling noise they'd heard before started up again with a vengeance.

Clang! Clang! Clang!

"How do you like that, you infernal thing!" shouted Xantha, sounding triumphant. Emmeline looked up and saw her beating a length of metal piping against a crossbar of the structure. The noise was unbearable.

However little Emmeline liked the sound, though, the Northwitch liked it even less. She shrieked like a demon, and—over all the clamor—Emmeline heard Sasha screaming again. Emmeline watched as the Northwitch's movements came to a sudden, stuttering halt. *It's not the noise,* Emmeline realized. *It's the vibration!* The ice crystals making up the Northwitch's body weren't sure what to do—some of them dived on Xantha in an attempt to attack, and others zoomed around in rings, tighter and tighter, until they fell out of the sky altogether. Sasha seemed to be slipping out of the Northwitch's grip—as she tried to keep herself together, she was losing her hold on her prisoner. The ice shards, confused and rattling, flew without direction or control.

Emmeline didn't know why her hand slid to her coat pocket, or why her shivering fingers closed around the handle of the heavy silver spoon she'd taken from Dr. Bauer's boat. She kept her eyes on the Northwitch the whole time, watching as she solidified into her woman shape every few seconds, then broke up again into thousands of screaming shards.

In some dark corner of her brain, Emmeline saw an opportunity.

Wait for it, she told herself. *Careful* ... The ice fragments were swirling, looping erratically, but Emmeline knew it was only a matter of time before they rearranged themselves once more.

Then, quick as a blink, the Northwitch's body reappeared, grasping Sasha firmly by the upper arms, and Emmeline flung the spoon as hard as she could, right at the center of the Northwitch's forehead. Like a tiny silver pinwheel, it flew through the air and smacked, bowl-first, against the Northwitch's face, making a satisfying crash.

With a yell that raised the hair on Emmeline's head, every single crystal in the body of the Northwitch shattered into randomly sized, sharp-edged pieces of dark ice, very different from the fine, sparkling powder that Emmeline had seen before. They began to plop into the Kraken's pool like hailstones.

Lots of things happened at the same time then.

With one final scream Sasha dropped out of the sky, and before Emmeline could draw breath to call her name, she had disappeared beneath the surface of the water.

An explosion on the far side of the pool punctured the night as Dr. Bauer's knife-prowed boat suddenly burst into flames; a hoarse cheer went up, along with another purple flare.

The bright flash of a gun flickered once, twice, in the darkness of the structure, high up, and bullets pinged off the metal beside Xantha. She turned, horrified, and dropped her pipe, fumbling at her belt instead. Monsieur Pichon took his chance, aiming a punch that knocked her off balance. As they wrestled for the gun she was attempting to pull from its holster at her hip, a third shot rang out from above—and Monsieur Pichon's face collapsed in pain. Using the last of his strength, he wrapped his arms around Xantha's body and fell from the balcony, dropping like a stone to the hard ground far below.

"Siegfried!" Xantha shouted, and then they were gone.

Emmeline ripped off her fur coat and ran to the water's edge. She dived straight in.

Edgar roared and drew his pistol out of its holster. He fired into the shadows but knew he hadn't a hope of finding his target. It must have been Bauer who'd shot Michel, he realized, but Bauer was nowhere in sight. *Coward!* thought Edgar, desperately scanning the structure, his gun trained on anything that moved.

Thing stood, struck numb, wondering where Igimaq had gone and wishing he knew what to do.

"Emmeline!" he shouted, falling to his knees by the side of the pool. *"Ems!"* He couldn't see anything in the dark water. The green beam hissed overhead.

"Where is she? Where's Sasha?" shouted Edgar. His gun wobbled a bit as he swung it, but there was still no movement in the structure above them.

"I dunno!" said Thing. "We've got to *do* somethin'!" His eye caught Emmeline's discarded coat, lying like a wounded animal on the ice. *Her rope!* he thought desperately. *Get the rope!* He slithered over to the coat and started to rummage in its pockets. He touched the cold metal of

Emmeline's tin cup and then something indescribably soft and warm. Confused, he grabbed at it and pulled it out.

He held it up in front of his eyes, barely daring to breathe.

It was as if he had a star trapped in his fingers. The fur—if that's what it was—glowed with a pure brightness, and something in it made Thing's breathing slow and his heart stop thundering. Without really knowing why, he opened his fingers and let the shining strands of hair float away on the breeze like dandelion seeds, disappearing into the gloom.

"What are you doing?" shouted Edgar, reholstering his gun. But before he could shrug out of his coat, the soft darkness all around them came to life. Huge silver-gray animals—*They're like bears,* Thing thought, *except not really at all*—came lumbering out of the silent shadows toward them. A sound like distant whispering filled the air, rich with half-formed words that seemed strangely familiar. Each creature had a pelt made of the same shining stuff as the fur Thing had just pulled out of Emmeline's pocket. The creatures loped straight past him and Edgar and dived headfirst into the pool, disappearing beneath the surface without causing so much as a ripple.

"What—*what?*" Edgar's breath caught in his throat. "What were they?"

"You're askin' me?" said Thing, his head spinning. For a few breathless seconds they stood by the side of the pool. Behind them Watt and Madame Blancheflour watched, their eyes full of despairing hope.

And then—with a burst of water and gasping that

made Edgar and Thing recoil from the pool's edge—one of the creatures slid itself onto the icy shore with Sasha wrapped in its arms. Less than a second later another creature followed, this one carrying Emmeline, limp and unconscious. And, finally, three more emerged a few feet away, carrying between them a finely wrought cage with two slumped people at the bottom of it. Thing knew without needing to be told that these were Emmeline's parents, and the pain in his chest grew too heavy to bear, because it seemed clear to him that they were—that they *had* to be—dead.

49

The next few moments passed in a blur for Thing.
He felt hands helping him to drag Emmeline clear of the
water and get her wrapped up in her fur coat, and he was
firmly shoved to one side while someone—Thing didn't
know who—breathed into Emmeline's mouth and made
her cough up all the dark water she'd swallowed. He saw
Edgar take Sasha in his arms and run with her toward the
wreckage of the downed dirigible, the only source of heat
anywhere on the ice. He was aware of some of the others
going to free Emmeline's parents from the cage. Somewhere there were shouts and shrill noises, and the distant
rattle of gunfire, but he didn't have space in his head to
care about any of it.

Once the strange gray creatures had ensured everyone was out of the water, they began to climb toward the

mirrors, swinging up through the struts like a destructive wind. A loud crack overhead, followed by a sputtering of the intense green light, let Thing know that they were destroying Bauer's structure, bit by bit. There was movement everywhere—people running, people shouting, orders being given.

But all he cared about was Emmeline's bone-white face.

He dropped to his knees beside her once again, and someone lifted her into his arms.

"Come on, Ems," he said, the cold water from her hair trickling over his skin. "Come on." She didn't move. Her eyes were sealed tightly shut. Thing stroked some stray strands off her forehead and shook her gently, hoping she'd slap him or something. A shout came from behind him, and he turned to look.

"We've got to *move*! Everyone, now!" Edgar's voice was huge, even from thirty feet away. "Get away from the water!" For a second Thing wondered why. Then he felt hands grabbing him all over and lifting Emmeline off his lap. In the next moment he was running, and all around him the ice was breaking, smashing into shards right beneath his feet.

A noise bigger than anything he'd ever imagined pushed him forward in a seismic wave. It wasn't a roar, or a shout, or a bellow—it was all three, and more. Deep within it was a sound like every window on earth shattering at once, and the screaming wail of metal being bent to its snapping point.

Thing skidded to a halt in the shadow of the wrecked

White Flower dirigible, which was still faintly burning. He felt a strong, familiar hand on his shoulder and looked up to see Edgar there, his eyes keenly trained on the pool.

The pool, which was more like a fountain now.

Sudden as a scream, the murky water exploded upward like a terrible geyser. Thing watched, his mouth hanging open, as a pointed head, its color somewhere between black and blood, began to rise from the water—and kept coming. Eventually an eye bigger than a Ferris wheel came into view, huge and round and threaded with red. The sight of it made Thing's breath taste like metal. The Kraken's baleful pupil glared at them all, moving from face to face as if searching for something. Then the Creature turned, water sluicing off its skin, and its massive, shining beak filled Thing's mind. It was as dark as a nightmare and big enough to swallow a four-story house with room to spare. The most blood-chilling cry he'd ever heard was coming from it.

A single tentacle, as thick as a railway car, burst its way up through the ice then, swooping through the air toward them. Every inch of it was covered with sharp suckers, like giant, cruel mouths full of snapping teeth.

"Get back!" called Edgar. Thing scrabbled across the ice to where Emmeline was lying. She was still pale, her skin cold to the touch. He grabbed her, trying to drag her away, as another tentacle ripped itself free of the ice and reached toward them. Thing watched as a third broke through, and then a fourth. Very soon the Kraken would pull itself up out of the pool, and when that happened, there would be nothing anyone could do.

An unexpected noise made him turn back to Emmeline. To his astonishment, he saw a huge horse—white-coated, red-maned, its chest and front legs spattered in what looked to be blood from a nasty gash to its neck. The horse was bent over Emmeline, whinnying softly. It nudged her face, huffing out a hot breath, and shook its mane, and as it did, Thing's mind immediately filled with butterflies and sunshine, peaceful summer days and birdsong. He felt warm to his toes.

"Meadowmane," he breathed, reaching out a hand to stroke the horse's neck, being careful of the wound. "This *has* to be you." Emmeline's hand, which he'd been holding tightly in his own, flexed slightly, and he looked down. Her eyes moved around behind her lids, and her lips parted just a little. Meadowmane whickered again, and she stirred further.

All around them people were screaming. Sasha was conscious, but she wasn't strong enough to move. Edgar had her wrapped tightly in his arms, and they were weeping together, his face in her hair. Madame Blancheflour was crying too, a single tear rolling down her soft old cheek. Before them the Kraken roared, its might turning all their bones to jelly. Thing looked from face to face, the despair in his heart flaring into rage. *We have to do somethin'!* he shouted inside his head. *We can't jus' sit 'ere, like a picnic!* He opened his mouth and drew a deep breath, ready to yell.

Then he felt something hard strike him across the back of the head. Sharp, sudden pain exploded behind his eyes, and he fell to the ground.

"It's not too late," he heard a voice mutter as he fought to stay conscious. Meadowmane shrieked, rearing onto his back legs to aim a kick, his wound ripping open once more.

"It's not too late!" Thing heard again, the words hissed and scratching. *What's not too late?* he thought, dazed. He tried to sit up. Through blurred eyes he saw a bent, huddled shape making off with a bundle, wrapped in a coat. A fur coat—*Emmeline's* coat!

"Hey! *Oi!*" he shouted, wincing. "Help! It's Bauer! He's got Ems!" Madame Blancheflour jerked and spun on the spot, her eyes searching. Her small body tensed like a hunting hound, and she pointed into the darkness.

"There he is! *Vite!*"

Thing scrambled up off the ground. Vaguely he was aware of people peeling away and following Bauer across the ice, but nobody seemed to know exactly which way he'd gone. The shadows had swallowed him.

Thing tried to take a step but staggered. He pressed his fingers against the back of his aching head, and when he brought his hand away, it was bloody.

"Help!" came a faint cry. "*Thing!*" He shoved himself up and turned, following Emmeline's voice. He blinked and there was Bauer, Emmeline in his arms like a gift—or, Thing realized with a sickening roll, an *offering*. Bauer was running toward the Kraken like a man with the law on his tail, and Thing struck out after him, his head throbbing with every step. He tried not to think about the huge tentacles all around, ready to pick him up and drop him into that terrible beaked maw like a plump grape or a piece of cheese.

"Thing! Wait!" Edgar's voice carried, but Thing didn't stop. His feet slid in the snow, but he kept going. He was gaining slowly.

"*Put! Her! Down!*" he shouted. He was reaching top speed, his muscles singing, when he realized something strange—his strength was growing with every step. *I still ain't whoopin'*, he thought as his legs pounded. *I can breathe!* All he could hear, despite his fear for Emmeline, were his own thoughts. Of his father, there was no trace. He let out a whoop, this time of triumph, and picked up his heels.

Bauer and Emmeline were almost back at the pool. The ice around it heaved and strained as the Kraken shifted, another tentacle just about to wrench itself free. *If it touches her . . .* Bauer's crazed laughter reached Thing, and he growled, running faster still, ready to kick, to punch, to *kill*, if it meant saving Emmeline from the Kraken's jaws.

"*Hey!* Hyup! Hup!" A sudden jingling shattered the air between them. Bauer's step faltered as he looked to his right, a confused frown on his face.

"What the—" he had time to say, just before a leather strap weighted at both ends with heavy rocks came flinging through the air. The strap wrapped itself round his legs, bringing him to the ground with a crunch, and Emmeline flew from his grip, landing on the ice like a sack of laundry. Bauer lay in a heap, howling, while Thing—a wild, buoyant feeling in his chest—turned to see Balto, his tongue hanging out, come galloping toward him.

"That's enough out of you, you warbling walrus," Igimaq shouted at the roaring Bauer, pulling his sled alongside Emmeline's crumpled form. He gently lifted her in and nestled her beside him as carefully as he could.

"Igimaq!" gasped Thing as he drew near. "Am I glad to see you!"

"Didn't think I'd gotten bored and gone home, did you?" He grinned. "Hurry—hop on." Thing jumped up on a sled runner and they raced back to the others, leaving Bauer far behind. Meadowmane made straight for Emmeline as soon as Igimaq pulled up, and Thing watched his friend's eyes grow round as saucers as the horse nudged and whickered at her, warming her with his breath.

"An _Æsirsmount?_ What sort of girl is our Emmeline, hey?" Igimaq sounded half-strangled.

"A what-a-what?" said Thing.

"Æsirsmount. A horse of the old gods. My grandad used to tell us stories about these guys too. This one's great-great-great-something ancestor would've been ridden by Odin, or someone like that, way back." Igimaq, hardly daring, reached out a hand to stroke Meadowmane's side. "I never thought I'd see one of these guys in the flesh, but I sure am glad our Emmeline found one. He probably didn't want to see the Kraken woken either, poor fella, no more than any of the creatures on the ice did, but at least he kept her safe as long as he could."

Before Thing had a chance to ask who Odin was, a boom rang out and everyone looked at the Kraken again. Most of its body was now out of the water. There was no sign of Bauer—the Kraken's gleaming belly was rolling its way heavily across the place where he'd last been seen, coming fast and crushing everything in its wake. Thing counted six flailing tentacles, each of them monstrous in its own right. He shrank against the side of the sled, wishing it had wings so that they could all clamber into it and get away. *But where'd we go?* he wondered despairingly. *There ain't goin' to be any place on earth safe from this thing.* He blinked, watching Igimaq as he turned too. Emmeline stirred in the sled, taking in the scene before her.

"Oh, no," she moaned, a tear escaping. "We're too late." She wiped at her face, her skin red with cold. Her other hand fell on a familiar object—her long-lost satchel, half-buried amid the furs in Igimaq's sled. Like it was the face of an old friend, she ran her fingers over it.

"Ain't you goin' to open it?" asked Thing, hope flaring in his chest. "Maybe there's somethin' in there that'll help." Emmeline turned to him, smiling sadly.

"Nothing that'll help against a Kraken," she said, and his face fell as he realized she was right.

"Who made the sacrifice?" said Igimaq suddenly. Everyone looked at him, eyes wide. Madame Blancheflour slithered across the ice and gripped the edge of his sled.

"What do you mean?" she asked. "Nobody has sacrificed to the beast."

"Somebody must have," said Igimaq. "He'd have long made us into fish food by now if he weren't waiting for his command." Madame Blancheflour looked stunned. She sought out Edgar and Sasha, who stared at her with huge eyes. Edgar shrugged, one-shouldered.

"Anyone?" shouted Madame. "Does anyone know who sacrificed to the beast? Are they still living?" Madame's eyes roamed through the crowd: what was left of the members of her beloved Order of the White Flower, pinched and shivering; Watt, her great friend, who had guarded Emmeline so faithfully and well; and, wrapped in whatever clothes could be found, near the back, Emmeline's parents, lying still and cold. Nobody spoke.

Behind them the Kraken thrashed, waiting. It let out another roar that blew the hair back on everyone's heads. The ice around the pool cracked and smashed, the pattern radiating out under their feet, as the beast lifted itself farther out of its prison. A tentacle landed heavily, too close to their dirigible for comfort.

"It's not going to wait forever," said Igimaq pleasantly.

50

Even though it was hopeless, and they knew it, those who could run, ran. Those who couldn't did their best to walk, or hobble, or shuffle, supported by anyone who had an arm to lend. Igimaq piled Madame Blanche-flour and Emmeline's parents into his sled, much to the dogs' dissatisfaction, and off they went. Thing jogged beside them, casting worried glances up at Emmeline every few paces. She was mounted on Meadowmane, her face creased with pain. Behind her, stark and horrifying against the starlight, was the Kraken.

Yowling like ten thousand hellcats, the creature finally pulled its last tentacle free. Raised straight up into the air, it went so high that Thing couldn't see its tip. Had the mirrors still been standing, the Kraken would have dwarfed them.

Meadowmane was having a hard time keeping his footing. The ice was splintering so fast that Emmeline knew, in the pit of her heart, that before too long they'd all be swallowed by the glacier. She started to imagine how it would feel to fall into a never-ending crevasse, and she shuddered.

From behind her came a shriek so angry, so otherworldly, that it made her want to curl up into a ball and hide, and she felt the vibration, the thunderous shaking underfoot, that let her know the beast was coming fast. Meadowmane cried out, stumbling with every step.

Who made the sacrifice? Emmeline fought for breath as she remembered Igimaq's words.

It didn't eat my parents, she thought, throwing a pained glance toward Igimaq's sled, where their silent forms lay, wrapped in furs. Her heart was too full to think about them, and she hoped there'd be a chance to see them properly one last time, before the end. *It didn't eat me, or Sasha. Monsieur Pichon and Xantha died in the fall—so it didn't eat them.* She swallowed. *And surely Dr. Bauer was squished as the Kraken hauled itself out of the pool. He was right in its way, and it's not like he was able to run.* She racked her brain. *And everyone else is here.* She shook her head, leaning into Meadowmane's neck. His familiar warmth, and his scent, filled her mind. *Come on! Think!*

With a start Emmeline realized it had begun to snow. Tiny, crystalline flakes were tumbling out of the pitch-black sky, gentle and delicate as lace. Emmeline held out her hand, bloodied and bruised, and a miniature snowflake fell on her raw skin. It sparkled, just for a second, before it melted away.

Something at the base of her brain gave a kick, and she blinked as she tried to keep hold of the thread of thought.

Sparkling.

Ice.

The Northwitch.

The Northwitch! She went into the lake, and she didn't come out! Emmeline caught her breath, her heart clanging like a handbell. *Does she count? It needs a living sacrifice . . .*

"But who put her there?" She scrunched her eyes shut and tried to think. Xantha had bashed the pipe against the structure, and the noise had paralyzed the Northwitch, but was that it? Was *Xantha* the one who had made the sacrifice? In that case, there was no hope—she was dead now too.

But was that it? Wasn't there something else?

Then, suddenly, Emmeline remembered, like a dream, how it had felt to pull the heavy stolen spoon out of her pocket. How she'd balanced it in her fingers. How she'd flung it, and how it had swooped through the air and smashed straight into the Northwitch's face—shattering her into a million pieces.

All of which had fallen into the Kraken's pool.

She blinked once and made her decision.

"I've got to go back, boy," she murmured, leaning forward to grip Meadowmane's neck, her every muscle tight and urgent. "Will you help me?" Meadowmane whinnied, and the sound of it made Thing turn, almost tripping over an opening in the ice. The look in Emmeline's eyes scared him.

"I'll see you later!" she called, raising her hand.

"Oi! No you bleedin' don't! Where you off to now?"

Emmeline just shook her head and pulled Meadowmane around.

"*Emmeline!*" yelled Thing. She didn't stop. "Blast it!" he muttered.

The snow fell on Thing as he ran, flickering into his eyes and getting stuck in his mouth. Meadowmane's tail stood out like a burst of flame. Then Thing realized he could see, out of the corner of his eye, *other* flecks of reddish orange, like a load of distant campfires—but all of them were moving. The air was full of thumping hooves and whinnies.

Exhausted and confused, Thing ran on.

The Kraken roared into view like a giant tidal wave, slick and oily and horrifying. Its beak was wide open, and its huge eyes—big as planets, big as Thing's imagination could go—were fixed on the horses, and the girl, running toward it. Its tentacles seemed miles long. Somewhere he heard the cry of an animal in pain as a barbed sucker lashed out among the red-maned horses. Still, Thing kept running. Emmeline was somewhere ahead of him, but in the sea of white and red he was finding it hard to keep up, and almost impossible to keep track of her.

Then he heard her voice, a clear note amid the tumult.

"Go back!" she was shouting. "Go back into the ice! I *command* you!" He saw Meadowmane rearing up and smashing his front hooves down on the ice. A huge crack opened between the horse and the Kraken, a shivering yawn in the ice. Soon all the horses were following suit, rearing and stamping in unison, their hooves sparking off the ice and causing a multitude of wide, weeping cracks to open up, as though a giant knife had slashed at the glacier's face. Over and over they did it, making the ground in front of the Kraken begin to collapse into itself like a sinkhole into darkness. They burned, blinding white and fire red, and Thing felt awed by their power. Watching them, it was easy to believe they'd galloped straight out of a legend.

They're trying to make a new hole for it, Thing realized. *A new prison!* The Kraken seemed to realize it too, and it roared again, lashing out at the horses with renewed energy. Thing ducked as a tentacle whipped over his head, dripping and glistening and muscular and vicious, and he stayed down for a long time after that, trying to catch his breath. *I hope those ol' stories were right,* he thought, his eyes on Emmeline's tiny frame.

"Go! Leave us in peace! I made the sacrifice to you, and I am telling you to return to the ice and never bother us again! Those are the *rules!*" Emmeline's voice sounded so insignificant amid the roaring of the beast and the whinnying and stamping from all around. Thing rolled himself to his feet and watched as, leaning on Meadowmane's patient neck, Emmeline stood up as high as she could.

"Didn't you hear me, you giant piece of fish bait?" screamed Emmeline, shaking her fist at the Kraken. "I told you to *go back into the ice!*"

At that the Kraken released a bellow so gigantic it left Thing's knees knocking. A stinking, wet wind filled with rage sprayed all around. All Thing wanted was to throw himself on the ice and beg for mercy, but Emmeline wasn't having any of it.

"I'm not going to tell you again!" she shouted.

As she spoke, the Kraken whip-cracked a tentacle in Emmeline and Meadowmane's direction. It was tipped with sharp hooks that looked like bone, each of them longer than a man's body. With a bloodcurdling shriek the beast swept Meadowmane off his feet. Thing blinked wildly as both the horse and Emmeline disappeared from sight and the Kraken itself tipped sideways like a giant tree being felled.

Finally Emmeline's command had been heard. The Kraken started to slither slowly back into the ice, seeming none too happy about it.

Not that Thing cared much, right then, about anything but Emmeline.

He flung himself forward, crossing in three huge leaps the distance between where he stood and where Emmeline had fallen. He slid to his knees just in time to stop himself from spilling headlong into the crevasse, within which he could see the Kraken struggling to gain purchase on any bit of ice it could reach. Its tentacles were flailing, and one giant eye rolled to face him. It saw Thing and bellowed.

"Get out! Go on!" he yelled at it. Creeping to the edge of the cracking, growing crevasse, he forced himself to look down.

He couldn't see any trace of Meadowmane or Emmeline,

just a few drops of what appeared to be blood on a jagged lump of ice about ten feet from the lip of the crevasse. His heart punched against his rib cage.

Then a tiny noise—barely more than a whimper—drew his eyes to a ledge a few feet to his left, where a small figure lay curled up. He couldn't see Emmeline's face, but he knew it was her, all right.

"Ems! Hang on, mate! I'm comin'!" Thing slithered to his feet and raced toward the spot, then flung himself down into the crevasse. The ice was shifting and moving all around them, creaking and cracking and booming as it went, and Thing had a terrible feeling this ledge wouldn't be a ledge for much longer. He spared a second to look around for Meadowmane again, but there was no sign of him, and Thing hoped he'd somehow scrambled to safety. *He wouldn't leave Ems, though, would he?* "Come on, Ems," he said, slapping her face lightly. "Come on! You've got to wake up. Please, mate! We've gotta move!" Thing watched her eyes flickering, and a tiny frown appeared on her forehead.

"Maybe you'd like me to dance a jig," she said, her voice cracked and hoarse. Her mouth curled up into a tiny hint of a smile.

"Nah. Not a jig," said Thing, grinning through his tears. "A Highland fling, maybe."

"Not a chance," she said, wrapping her arms around his neck.

Thing had just managed to climb out of the fissure, Emmeline clinging to his back, when the ledge they'd been on collapsed into the chasm. With one final roar the

336

Kraken slid down, deep into the huge crack in the glacier, and the Æsirsmounts watched it go, standing around the hole like a troop of fiery sentinels. Emmeline clambered down from Thing's back, looking around, as the horses began to disperse.

"Meadowmane," whispered Emmeline, turning back to face her friend. "Did you see him?" Thing just shook his head, and Emmeline crumpled as she stared down into the darkness that had swallowed the Kraken—and, presumably, the gentle horse who had given his life to save hers.

She grabbed Thing's hand, and he gripped her fingers tightly.

Thing shoveled another grilled kipper into his mouth, grinning happily—if a little greasily.

"I could get used to this, y'know," he informed the table. "Just sayin'." Mr. Widget lowered his newspaper and twinkled across at him.

"It's nice to have some life about the old place, right enough," he said, glancing at his wife. Mrs. Widget, her broken arm still strapped to her side, chuckled as she spooned up another mouthful of porridge. It sat grayly on her spoon, quivering slightly.

"This really isn't the same without Mrs. Mitchell," she sighed. "The new cook just doesn't have her knack."

"Well. She's not a traitorous tattletale, either," Mr. Widget pointed out, folding his newspaper and putting it to one side. Emmeline still couldn't quite believe Mrs. Mitchell, the permanently floury cook, had been the one intercepting telegrams and passing details to Bauer, but looking back, she saw it made a sort of sense. Few other people were trusted enough to have access to the Widget family. It had simply been a happy accident that Mrs. Mitchell had also been extremely good at the job the Widgets had been paying her to do. Mrs. Widget looked at her husband and grimaced before digging into her porridge with fresh enthusiasm.

"Come on, darling," said Mr. Widget, turning to Emmeline. "You know the rules now. No working at the table." She whuffed out an impatient breath and placed her pencil between the pages of her notebook, marking her place.

"We're going to carry on later, though, aren't we?" She closed the notebook carefully. A label on the front of it said THE OSCAR FILES in Emmeline's handwriting. "We're just getting to the good bit on that last case."

"The one with the unicorn?" said Mrs. Widget thickly, swallowing her porridge. "Or the one with the griffin? I can't remember where we'd got to."

"The unicorn, Mum," Emmeline reminded her. "You were telling me about how you found it, up on that mountain in Peru."

"Ah, yes. We missed your fifth birthday because of that expedition," she replied, blinking slowly as she gazed at her husband.

"Doesn't matter. I don't remember it anyway," said

Emmeline, not quite truthfully, reaching for a nearby plate piled high with toast.

"That's not going to happen again," said Mr. Widget, covering Emmeline's free hand with his own. "No more missing birthdays. No more lying—or not telling the truth, at least. No more trying to keep you safe by keeping you afraid."

"It's all right, Dad," she said quietly. "Really."

"It's not," he said. "But we're going to change all that now."

Emmeline smiled and took a huge, buttery mouthful as she met Thing's eye. He grinned at her.

"And what about the name question, young man?" said Mrs. Widget, turning to him. "We can't very well tell people our new family member is simply called Thing, can we?"

"Nothin' wrong with it," retorted Thing. "Done me well so far, it has."

"That's true," agreed Mrs. Widget. "But still. I'd prefer you to have a public name, if you know what I mean. A name for your passport for when we visit Igimaq and Qila, and Madame, and Sasha and Edgar."

"Like the Queen an' her two birthdays," said Thing happily, before burping. "'Scuse me," he added quietly.

"Exactly." Mr. Widget smiled.

"And you're sure you don't want us to make any more inquiries into the whereabouts of your family—I mean, your birth family? It's up to you, of course—"

"Nope. Plus, I'm happy right 'ere." He sliced a glance

across the table at Emmeline. "Ain't you happy to have me 'ere?"

"Don't ask ridiculous questions," sighed Emmeline, returning to her toast.

"That's settled it, then," said Mrs. Widget, looking at her husband. "Perhaps we should have Watt bring in the paperwork, darling. What do you think?"

"I have it ready, madam, in the drawing room. It is laid out on your writing table, as neatly as I could manage." Watt leaned over to Emmeline and ruffled her hair, causing her to shoot him a look of exasperation.

"Thank you, Watt," said Mr. Widget. "Excellent work, as always."

"A pleasure, sir."

"Hey—you know this name thing?" said Emmeline, wiping butter off her face with the back of her hand. "Well, how would you feel about Michel?"

"Michel," said Thing, feeling a sudden need to blink. "Not sure I'm big enough to fill out a name like that, t'be honest." He cleared his throat quietly.

"I think it's extremely fitting, young sir," said Watt. "If I may say."

"Michel," repeated Thing, considering. "Michel T. Widget. Sounds sort of important, yeah?"

"You'll grow into it, you know." Emmeline shoved in another mouthful of toast. "Give it time," she muttered crumbily.

Thing looked at her and grinned. "Yeah," he said, settling himself more comfortably in his chair. "Michel. I like it."

"The Order of the White Flower needs a Michel anyway," said Emmeline, reaching for more toast. "Wouldn't be right otherwise."

"What's this?" said her father. "There *is* no more Order of the White Flower business. At least, not for you, young lady."

"Next time you need a Kraken dealt with, then, who's going to do it?" Emmeline sighed, taking a bite.

"She saves the day once and thinks she's an expert," said Mrs. Widget, glancing at her daughter with a twinkle in her eye.

Emmeline swallowed quickly. "But, Mum—you *will* be going on expeditions again, won't you? OSCAR's not been disbanded, has it?"

"You're still too young, Emmeline," said Mr. Widget. "We've discussed this. Let's not go over it all again."

"But—"

"Darling. You heard your father. Now let's just finish breakfast and get on with having a lovely day, all right? One without mortal peril, if nobody minds," said Mrs. Widget, going in for another spoonful of porridge.

Emmeline slumped in her chair and was moodily pulling her toast to crumbs when a sharp kick to the sole of her boot made her jump. Her mother was engrossed in her breakfast, and her father was absorbed in his paper, and Thing—*Michel,* she corrected herself—was staring at her across the table. He grinned and nodded up at Watt. Emmeline glanced at the butler, who threw her a wink, and Emmeline smiled.

"Michel and I are going to—going to *play,*" she said,

grabbing her notebook and sliding down from her chair. "All right?" Her mother waved distractedly, and her father whuffed his mustache, his eyes on the news, and in the next blink the room was empty but for the two of them and the lingering smell of Michel's kippers.

"How long d'you reckon we have before she stows away in our luggage or something?" Mrs. Widget muttered to her husband. He met her eye and smiled.

"We started as teens," he reminded her. "Not so much older than she is."

"Still," she murmured. "When it's your own child . . ."

"Something tells me she'll be just fine," said Mr. Widget. "And if not, that young Michel has a head on his shoulders. Don't worry, dear."

Watt quietly reentered the room. "The children are in the library, sir, madam," he said. "Not at *all* engaged in searching for case notes from previous OSCAR expeditions."

"Just keep them away from the most dangerous stuff, Watt, particularly the dragons," sighed Mrs. Widget. "For as long as possible, at least."

"Very good, madam," he said, using all his butler training to keep the grin from his face, for that, of course, had been the first file Emmeline had asked him to fetch. "Very good, indeed."

ACKNOWLEDGMENTS

Every writer's first book is their dream come true, but not every first book is the book of its author's heart. This book, for me, is both.

Thanks are due to so many people:

To my parents, who indulged and encouraged my love for reading and turned a blind eye to the fact that I had books stuffed into my bedroom drawers, where they'd probably have preferred me to have socks, or makeup, or magazines, or love letters. . . . Thank you, Mam and Dad. LYTTMAB. I owe everything to you.

To Graham, the single finest human being I have known. Even if you weren't my brother, you can bet your U2 belt buckle that you'd be my best friend. I love you, but I can't promise I'll never call you Hugo again. Thanks for all the stories we share.

To two Alans, one Garner and one Fletcher, for being, in their various ways, my greatest teachers. Alan Garner's novel *Elidor* has shaped my life like a potter shapes clay, and Professor Alan Fletcher helped me to believe in myself when I most needed to. I owe a huge debt to them both.

To my friends, who are many. I am lucky, and I know it. Love you guys. To my extended family, thank you for always being proud of me, and helping me to celebrate the good and the bad with equal aplomb.

To my agents, Polly Nolan and Sarah Davies of Greenhouse Literary Agency, whose poise and skill made a rocky road less challenging, and who have fought for me and my book against all odds. Thanks especially to Polly for her incisive and brilliant editing, and to Sarah for her superlative deal-making, and to them both for keeping me between the ditches. I hope I've made your hard work worthwhile.

To Melanie Cecka Nolan, whose interest in this story is the reason we're all here. Thanks for taking it on, and for editing it so expertly, and for loving it so much. Thanks to Erica Stahler, whose meticulous copyediting saved me from breaking the laws of physics once too often, and to Alison Kolani, director of copyediting at Random House, as well as proofreader Amy Schroeder. A special nod of gratitude has to go to Dr. Tine Defour, Sandra Hessels, Caro Clarke, Julia Yeates, Louie Stowell, and Olivia Hope for their help with my French and Dutch; you spared my blushes, ladies. *Merci. Bedankt.* Thanks especially to Jeff Nentrup, whose artwork on the book jacket brought Emmeline and Thing to such glorious life.

To a tiny girl who didn't exist when this book was written, or when it was sold, and who will be almost two by the time it publishes: thank you for being the piece I didn't know was missing until I found it. Of everything that has ever been, or will ever be, I love you the best.

To my husband, Fergal, go thanks for the sacrifices you've made to help me get here, for the space and time to write, and for always quietly assuming I'd be capable. Bucket. This one's for you, and for our little star.

And to you, the reader who has welcomed Thing and Emmeline into your heart and imagination, making them as much yours as they are mine—thank you for being the best part of this journey.